A Song of Grief and a Song of Creation

Book Three of the Chronicles of the Lawbreaker

Larry Z. Daily

A Song of Grief and a Song of Creation / Larry Z. Daily – 1st ed.
ISBN: 979-8-9913879-5-8 (eBook)
ISBN: 979-8-9913879-4-1 (paperback)

Praise for The Minstrel and the Prophet

Stellar traditional fantasy bursting with magic, adventure, and prophecy. - BookLife

This is a masterful blend of vivid world-building, character-driven story-telling, and thematic depth. A must-read for lovers of epic fantasy. – The Prairies Book Review

A tense, character-driven epic fantasy that is impossible to put down. – BookView Review

Praise for The Ring and the Sword

The Ring and the Sword ... is a captivating fantasy incorporating themes like resilience, sacrifice, destiny, self-discovery, and unyielding hope. Daily masterfully balances action-packed scenes, suspenseful events, and touching moments to create a narrative that is both rich in character development and grand in scope. - Ibrahim Aslan for Readers' Favorite

This one is for Stephanie. You were there when I really needed a friend, and you said this one was your favorite.

And in memory of my Mom, Ruth Daily, whose bequest eased getting the books into publication. I'd rather that you had been here to see them.

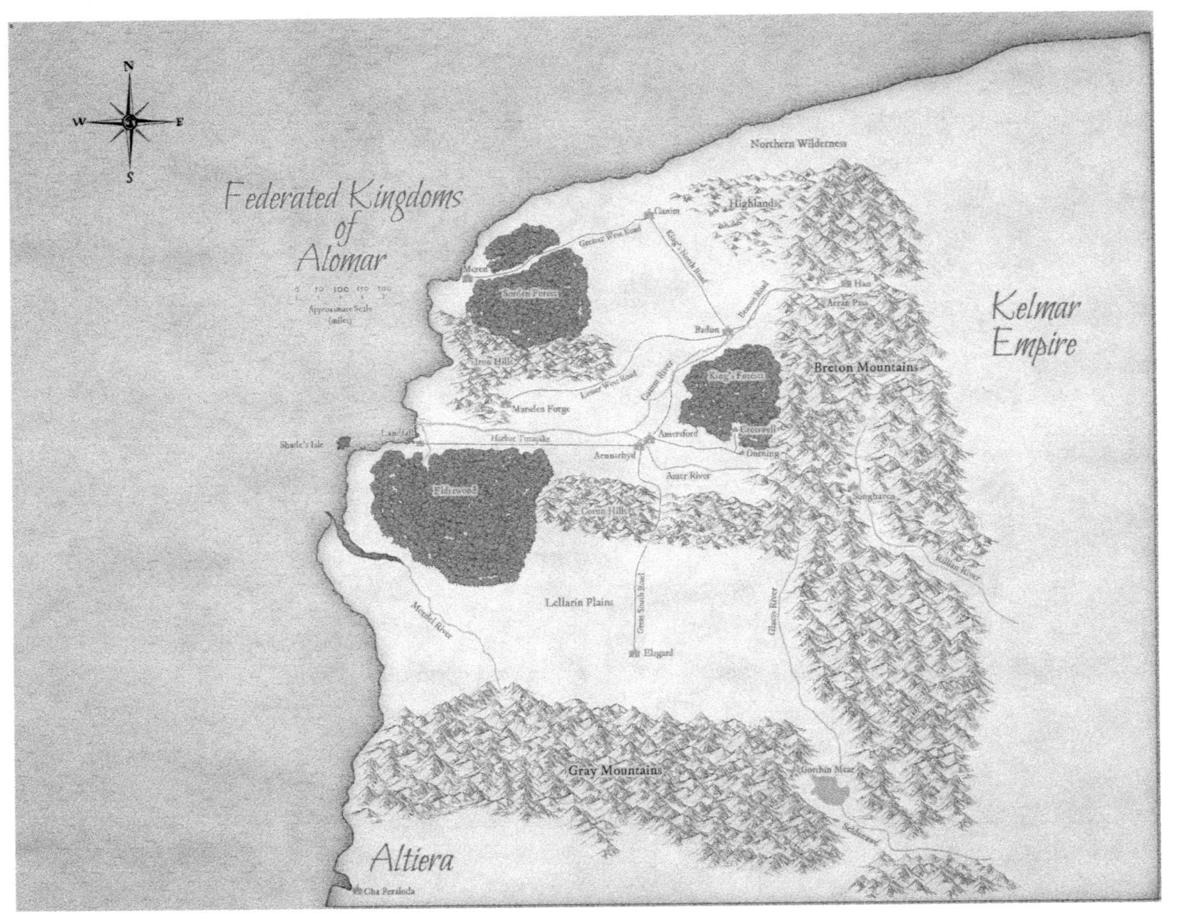

Federated Kingdoms
of
Alomar
0 10 100 150 200
Approximate Scale
(miles)
N
S
E
W
Kelmar
Empire
Altiera
Northern Wilderness
Highlands
Meren
Sorden Forest
Greater West Road
Ganim
King's North Road
Beacon Road
Hau
Aerin Pass
Budon
Breton Mountains
Iron Hills
Lesser West Road
Comm River
King's Forest
Marsden Forge
Crosswell
Amersford
Onrunng
Harbor Turnpike
Landfall
Shade's Isle
Aennorhyd
Amer River
Songhaven
Eldrwood
Gorin Hills
Lillian River
Lellarin Plains
Great South Road
Glaen River
Mendel River
Elagard
Gray Mountains
Gorthin Mear
Cha Peralota

Part Four

A Song of Grief

After the battle
Back in the saddle
Into the sunset heroes will ride
Tho' they won
Look what they've done
To humankind

- from Pass It On
- Bill Danoff

CHAPTER ONE

I *leaned back in my chair and regarded the young minstrel across the table from me. As patrons, we were both somewhat out of place; the inn catered to the working people of the town: sailors and fishermen, shipbuilders, and potters. Our role here would ordinarily be to perform. The midday crowd had come and gone hours before and now the inn's common room was filling again for the evening meal. As they entered, I saw people notice the bright blue sashes that marked us as minstrels. They looked a bit surprised and happy to see us and then disappointed when they noticed that we didn't have our instruments with us.*

"I thought dragons were a myth," my companion said, drawing my attention back from the crowd. "And now you say that you actually saw one? That you talked to it?"

I ignored the disbelief in her tone and answered her questions with one of my own.

"How did you find me?"

"Mother told me how much you enjoy cassaca in the winter," she answered. "I figured that I'd find you wherever the best cassaca was served."

At that moment, the server arrived with two large bowls of the spicy stew that the Altierans called cassaca. We ate in silence for several minutes. As we did, I studied the woman across the table from me. She was digging into her food with the same earnest enthusiasm she had brought to questioning me. She reminded me so much of...

I shook my head. That pain and loss were long in the past, though the wounds had never truly healed. I turned back to my food. My companion was correct; though it catered to working people, the inn was known throughout both Altiera and the Federated Kingdoms of the Alomar for having the best cassaca *to be had. I had taken only a few more bites of mine when my companion raised her head and laid aside her spoon.*

"You were telling me about the dragon," she said.

I had ridden out of *Evendim* with the Elven army–the *Eldarin* army–in the middle of the third moon of *Tymnahunoch*. Three days later, a fierce snowstorm struck and blinded by the gale-driven snow, I was separated from the rest of the army. A falling branch swept me from my mount and left me on foot in the midst of the blizzard. In seeking shelter, I found a cave. It was in the cave that I found the dragon.

It was curled up like a cat when I entered and was watching me out of yellow eyes. It was red except for a row of black scales standing upright down its back.

"*Vorath, Endollin,*" it said. The voice sounded vaguely feminine to me.

"You know me," I replied, unsure whether I was making a statement or asking a question.

"Indeed. I have been waiting for you."

"Waiting for me?"

The dragon didn't answer but raised her head and looked at a passageway leading to another, more brightly lit chamber.

"You should go in now," she told me.

I crossed the dragon's chamber and entered a short passageway that led to a large cave. That cave was larger than the dragon's and was lined with a thick layer of ice, lit from within by an eldritch blue-white light. Directly across from me was a large block of ice, shaped like an altar. The place could have been a chapel dedicated to some ancient spirit of winter. Standing upright in the altar was the sword *Endolsar*.

I almost turned away. I was a minstrel–I am a minstrel–and I had no right, no desire, to bear a sword. I almost turned away, but then I saw the consequences: my mind was filled with images of the world blighted the way the land around Cammlin had been, crops black and rotting on the ground, trees barren and broken, livestock bloated and dying. I saw all the world's people living lives of fear and misery and desperation.

"You can stop it," the dragon whispered in my mind. "You can stop it all. You are the only one who can."

I turned back to the sword and took the hilt in my left hand. As I wrapped my fingers around the grip, all the light in the chamber narrowed into a single beam that was like an extension of the blade of *Endolsar* piercing deep into the ice, down to the very heart of the world. The great dark stone in the pommel woke, glittering violet with sparks of red and blue, twin to the stone in my ring. I gave a gentle tug, and as the sword came free of the altar all the light vanished.

I followed the gentler glow from the other chamber back to the dragon. As I entered, it used a forelimb to push something toward me.

"The king thought you would need these," she said.

It was a leather belt and scabbard, both worked with a variation of the loops and swirls that the *Eldarin* carved into their doors to confound evil and prevent it from entering their buildings. The ring had the same design on it. His visions of me had given Lorrestian hope, but it seemed that he was taking no chances that I might be possessed of an evil spirit. I smiled as I fastened the belt around my waist and slid the sword into the scabbard.

"How am I going to find my way back to the army?" I wondered aloud.

"I was able to reach the mind of your *aynekahrn* and keep it from fleeing," the dragon answered. "It is waiting just inside the mouth of the cave."

"My thanks to you," I replied.

"My time here is limited," she said. "I was bound in this place by my oath to ward the sword. That oath is now fulfilled, and another binding now compels me. There are things that I must tell you before I am drawn away."

"Drawn away?" I asked. "How will you get out? You're larger than the tunnel."

"Size is of no concern. I am but a thought..."

It looked to me as if the dragon was fading, her edges beginning to blur.

"Han has fallen," she told me. "The Kelmar have driven the Alomar out of the pass."

The dragon was definitely fading away. I could see through her to the rock wall behind her.

"This is happening more quickly than I'd hoped." The dragon's voice was faint but sounded even more feminine. "Ware, *Endollin*. The world is at stake and..." I thought she said something about Mar, but she was gone. The light was gone as well, leaving me alone in the dark.

I'd been facing the dragon before she disappeared, so I knew that the exit was to my left. I took several slow, careful paces forward, my arms extended in front of me until my hands met the wall. Then I carefully felt my way along the wall until I reached the exit. I squeezed through the narrow part and was soon back in the mouth of the cave where *Yrtenstal*, my *aynekahrn*, was indeed waiting patiently, his head held low to avoid the ceiling. He nearly filled the space inside the cave mouth, but I managed to squeeze alongside him so that I could check him over. It took only a few moments, and I spotted no obvious hurts. Then, my mount cared for, I dug into my saddlebags for the travel bread and dried fruit that I had packed in case I was separated from the rest of the army. I hadn't eaten since we broke our fast that morning. As I ate, I turned my attention to the world outside the cave.

The worst of the storm was over and only a few scattered flakes of snow still fell. I stepped just outside the cave. The sky overhead was still full of gray clouds, but as I looked beyond the nearby trees, I thought I could make out patches of blue in the distance.

I pondered what I should do next. I needed to find my way back to the *Eldarin* army, but I wasn't sure how to go about that; I had no idea where I was. I also wasn't sure how late in the day it was. The ground was covered in several inches of snow, and it was still quite cold so I didn't want to have camp in the open with no tent and no blankets. I had the means to make a fire and I considered staying in the cave for the night. If I could locate some firewood, I could be reasonably comfortable.

I turned to go back into the cave to pack away what remained of my food when *Yrtenstal* stepped out, raised his head and neighed. Down below, I heard several answering neighs.

"Lauren," a familiar voice called. "Lauren, are you here?"

"Up here, Pyrett," I called back.

A few moments later, Pyrett, Ryan, and a soldier I did not know came riding up the hill. I saw Pyrett and Ryan notice the cave at the same moment and then their gaze shifted to me. Their eyes lighted on the sword. Pyrett smiled, but Ryan looked troubled.

"You found it," Pyrett said.

"I found it," I confirmed.

"Are you well?" she asked. "Can you travel?"

"Yes. I'm well. How far do we have to go?"

"Only a few miles. We're setting up camp near the Glaess while scouts look for a place to ford the river."

I turned and tried to mount *Yrtenstal,* forgetting the sword strapped to my right hip. As I lifted my right leg to swing it over the *aynekahrn,* it caught the scabbard and unbalanced me. I lost my grip and ended up flat on my back in the snow. Someone–I thought it was the soldier–stifled a laugh. As I rose, Pyrett said, "You may want to strap that across your back."

I wasn't going to do that. At that moment, my guitar was safely stowed on a wagon, but I usually carried it across my back. I wasn't going to let a sword take its place. Instead, I removed the sword, re-buckled the belt, and looped it over the saddle horn while I mounted. Then I strapped the sword back on.

As we rode, Pyrett told me that I was only one of nearly two dozen who got separated from the main part of the army in the storm. When the weather finally cleared and our absence was noted, King Alain made the decision to halt on the banks of the Glaess River and send out search parties to locate the missing people while others searched for a ford. It was chance that had led Pyrett and Ryan to me.

Ryan was uncharacteristically quiet as we rode, but several times I caught him watching me, a thoughtful and somber expression on his face. I urged *Yrtenstal* in Ryan's direction but before the *aynekahrn* had taken two steps Ryan caught my eye and shook his head slightly. Puzzled and a little hurt, I fell in behind Pyrett.

The *Cadwynir* captain led us up over a ridge into a hollow on the north side of the mountain the cave was in. We turned west to follow the stream at the bottom of the hollow, picking our way carefully down a path that wound its way among moss-covered boulders. A short time later we were challenged by sentries warding the approaches to the camp, but they quickly recognized Pyrett and allowed us through. Then the sides of the hollow fell away, and we exited the mouth of the hollow onto a broad, grassy meadow that sloped gently down to the eastern bank of the Glaess. Row upon row of dull green tents had been erected on the meadow and everywhere *Eldarin* soldiers were engaged in caring for their *aynekahrn* or preparing food. Others were sitting in groups, singing or swapping stories and maintaining their weapons or gear. Another pair of sentries stopped us momentarily as we reached the first line of tents. After a brief conversation, we worked our way through the neatly organized camp toward the tent we shared with King Alain.

As we passed through the camp, soldiers and *Cadwynir* paused in their tasks to glance our way. As they realized who we were, I could hear their conversations fall silent and then resume in excited tones. "He found it!" I heard one man call to his companions. "The *Endollin* has the sword!" another shouted. The calls outpaced us so that when we drew rein in front of our tent, the king was already outside waiting for us.

As we dismounted, Konne, Rolugh, and Iseabail converged on us from different directions. The soldier who had accompanied Pyrett and Ryan gathered up the reins to our mounts and led them off to be cared for.

"*Endollin*, you found the sword," the king said.

"As your father intended," I replied, bowing slightly.

"I would hear the manner of that finding. Please walk with me. You others," he said, gesturing to Konne, Rolugh, Pyrett, Iseabail, and Ryan, "I would like you with us as well." He turned to two nearby soldiers. "We are going to the pavilion. Please have someone bring us a hot meal but see that we are not otherwise disturbed."

The two men hustled off to arrange for the food. Alain turned back to us.

"I have had a pavilion set up just downstream from camp," he told us. "We can speak as privately there as we can under the circumstances."

We followed him out past the downstream edge of camp to where the pavilion had been erected. It was simply a tent without walls sheltering a dozen folding camp chairs.

"This is hardly the most formal environment for a meeting," Alain said, glancing around with a wry smile on his face. "Still, it is the closest thing to privacy that we are likely to get. Before we begin, Pyrett, you were away when the scouts returned. They found a crossing perhaps six miles upstream from here." He then turned to me. "Lauren, may I see the sword?"

As my hand closed on the hilt, the pommel stone woke, glittering violet tinged with red. I slid the sword out of its scabbard and then extended it, hilt first, to Alain. As I released the sword to him, the stone went dark.

"*Endolsar*," he said quietly, reverently. He held it point up and examined it with a rapt expression.

"Moonstone," he said, lightly touching the stones that graced the quillons. He looked at me. "To the *Eldarin*, moonstone symbolizes love, compassion, and new beginnings. An odd choice to adorn a weapon."

Alain tried a couple of easy swings and then returned the sword to me, a question written in his furrowed brows and pursed mouth.

"It is exquisitely balanced," he said. "Do you know what virtue it has? Have you sensed any latent power?"

I shook my head as I sheathed the sword.

"No," I replied. "Perhaps it will wake only when I face Mar and the Keepers."

"Do we know when that will be?" Konne asked.

"No," I said again. "At least I do not."

I looked around at the others, but they were all shaking their heads.

"Let us sit," the king suggested. "Then I would like to hear how you found the sword."

All of us took a seat except Rolugh and Iseabail, who busied themselves building a small fire in the center of the circle of seats. They all turned to face me.

"Hold a moment, Lauren," Ryan said quietly. "The food is here."

Several soldiers entered carrying plates of hot food that was steaming in the cool air. Each plate contained chicken, a thick piece of bread liberally spread with butter, and a mixture of boiled vegetables. The men also gave each of us an empty mug and set several pots of tea near the fire to keep them warm. They bowed as we thanked them and then left to return to the camp.

For a time, none of us spoke as we dug into the food, anxious to enjoy it before it grew cold. The bread was the last of what we'd brought with us from *Evendim*. It was already a bit stale but had been held close to a fire until the surface browned. I finished it off quickly and then started on the chicken. We all finished our meals at about the same time. Ryan and I rose from our seats and filled everyone's mugs with hot tea. Then they all turned to me again.

I sat and wrapped my hands around my mug for warmth.

"I'm not sure when I got separated from the army," I started. "I thought I was following the person in front of me, but I really couldn't see through the wind and the snow. Then a falling branch caught me in the chest and knocked me off *Yrtenstal*. I began looking for shelter and found a cave. I thought I saw a light in the back of the cave, so I went back to investigate. There was indeed a light back there, a glow emanating from nowhere in particular. In that chamber I found a dragon. She sent me to another chamber that was lined in ice. I found *Endolsar* there, standing upright in an altar of ice."

There was wonder on the faces of most of them, but Iseabail looked skeptical.

"I thought dragons were myths," she said. "I thought that they were creatures which only existed as a heraldic device."

"Until a few hours ago, I would have agreed with you," I replied. "But then, a few moons ago, I thought that all the Elves had been killed in the Great War and that unicorns were a myth."

They were all silent a moment.

"So, now we discern the answer to the riddle," Alain said, changing the direction of the conversation. "The sword was in an altar of ice and was warded by dragon fire."

"Lorrestian never wrote anything about a dragon," Ryan noted. He glanced at Iseabail and then said, "I thought all of us believed that dragons were not real."

Alain looked thoughtful.

"Tales of dragons exist in the lore of the *Eldar*, the Alomar, the Kelmar, and the Altierans," he said after a moment. "That in itself should have suggested that there might be some truth behind the stories. Perhaps father's Sight guided him to one of them."

"There's more," I said. "When I returned from the inner chamber with the sword, the dragon spoke to me again. She said that she had been bound to the cave by her oath to ward the sword, but that another binding was pulling her elsewhere. Just before she disappeared, she told me that Han has fallen and that the Kelmar have forced the Alomar out of the pass. She warned me that the world is at stake. I thought she said something about Mar, but she was fading so fast that I couldn't make out what she was saying."

"Why do you refer to the creature as she?" Pyrett asked.

"Something about her voice sounded feminine," I answered.

"You say Han has fallen?" Konne asked.

"That's what she told me," I replied.

"Then we were correct," the general responded. "The Kelmar are trying to trap the Alomar in a huge pincer move. We must get to *Aennsrhyd* before the Kelmar."

"I agree," Alain said, rising from his seat. "Get the word out to the commanders. I want everyone up and camp broken down so that we can be underway as soon as we have enough light to see."

The rest of us rose and I was preparing to follow everyone back to camp when Ryan said, "Lauren, walk with me."

The others looked at us as they filed by, slight frowns of curiosity on their faces, but no one questioned us. I followed Ryan in the opposite direction. We walked in silence until the tents and the pavilion were out of sight. There we found a flat-topped boulder overlooking the river. I sat beside Ryan and for a time we simply watched a pair of mallard ducks searching the bank for a nesting site.

"Lauren, I think that it is time that we have a conversation that I have been putting off since we first met," Ryan started, his voice hesitant.

I didn't respond and he finally looked my way. I simply nodded my assent.

"You clearly have power," he said.

I hung my head, my heart full of grief and guilt and shame.

"And I killed eight men with it," I said, my voice choked with shame.

"Those eight men were trying to kill you," he countered. "But, for the sake of argument, I'll grant that your power killed eight men."

I looked up and turned to him, not sure where he was going.

"But, in turn, you must grant that your power has saved your life," he said. "Not just then, but back when we first met, when a falling tree would have killed you. That same power led you to Lorrestian's workshop, to the sword, and to me."

He paused for a moment.

"Your power also saved the *Eldarin* from the darkness infecting our hearts–from Mar, if that was indeed her."

We watched the ducks for a few more moments, but then they gave up their search and flew away downstream.

"Your power also joined the *Eldar* to the Song of the Seasons in a way that none of us had ever experienced before."

"The Song of the Seasons?"

"Lauren," Ryan reminded me, "I've spoken with you before about the Song of the Seasons. What I did not tell you then was that the Song runs deep in *Eldarin* belief and experience. Each of us experiences it differently and that experience is deeply personal. Parents will discuss it with their children when the children are old enough to understand, and married couples will discuss their experience with one another. That is all. Only rarely would one of the *Eldar* discuss the Song with anyone other than a spouse or a child and it would be rarer still to even mention it to someone who was not one of the *Eldar*."

I'd had no idea.

"*Se an manana hint sel dolgin hyda tiom,*" I said softly. "I am honored that you shared with me. Why are you bringing this up now?" I asked.

"You have experienced the Song," Ryan answered. "The first time was when we first met, the first time we celebrated the turn of the seasons together. Not only did you experience the Song, but you made me feel it too, more strongly than ever before. You did it again–twice–for all of the *Eldar*. No one has ever done that before."

"Ryan, I feel like you're trying to tell me something, but I'm not sure that I understand."

He finally turned to look directly at me.

"Lauren, I told you when we spoke of the Song before that only to humans and the *Eldar* is it given to choose their note in the Song. You seem to focus only on the fact that your power killed eight men. You neglect the fact that it did so to protect you. You're concluding that whatever is inside you is evil and to be feared. When you do so, you're forgetting the most basic lesson of the Song. Good and evil are a choice, a choice that you get to make. A knife is just a tool. Used one way, it can help craft a flute like the one I've seen you with. Used another way, it can take the life of an innocent. The knife is neither good nor evil. It is the choice of the knife wielder that is good or evil. Your power is like the knife."

He paused a moment to let me consider his words.

"Hear me. You now have both the ring and the sword. I am certain that the time is rapidly approaching when you will have to choose your note in the Song. I feel deep in my heart that what the dragon said was true: the world is at stake and its fate will be decided by what you choose to do. You must make that choice, and you will probably feel as if you stand alone in the choosing. Remember this, though, Lauren: You must choose your note, but there are other singers. You are not alone."

The lower edge of the setting sun had just kissed the horizon.

"We should get back to camp," Ryan said.

We stood. Ryan started to step away from the stone, but I held out an arm and barred his path.

"Ryan," I said. "Rhion. My thanks to you for your guidance. You are still my Master."

He just nodded. As I started to step away, he said, "Lauren, remember this as well. Whatever else you may be, you are still a human. You may make mistakes. A single mistake does not make you an evil person."

This time, I just nodded and then together we returned to the camp.

Overnight, the weather changed. Shortly after we settled in to sleep, the wind picked up again, this time from the south. Outside our tent, the star banner flapped and snapped as the wind gusted and that, coupled with the rustling of the tent itself, kept us all from deep sleep. Before morning, quite a few tents had blown down, much to the annoyance of their occupants. Well before dawn everyone was awake and beginning to pack.

The temperature had warmed considerably, and the snow from the previous day was gone. We packed our heavy cloaks away along with the tents. The cooks had already stowed their gear, so we scrounged whatever cold food we could find to break our fast. As soon as we had enough light to distinguish the river from the land, we set out for the ford.

For the most part, our path kept us near the river, often right at the water's edge. Sometimes, though, we nearly lost sight of the river as we skirted shallow marshes. Several miles upstream the land began to climb. To our left, the course of the river was littered with boulders, some almost completely submerged and others standing high above the churning white rush of the water. The muted thunder of the river as it crashed through the rapids rattled my bones and sent a fine mist into the air, bringing back some of the chill of the previous day. Two miles or so past the rapids, we reached the ford.

The river was wide and shallow at that point, and I watched as a company of *Cadwynir* crossed. Their mounts picked their way carefully, watchful for holes or depressions hidden under the water. Once on the other side, they spread out to ward against potential threats. As soon as they were securely on the other side, another company began the crossing. The second group crossed a little more quickly, as if their *aynekahrn* were surer of their footing. I became aware that all our mounts were intently watching those who crossed, as if they were learning where it was safe to step. Soon, the *aynekahrn* were trotting across the ford and by midmorning, all of us were gathered in the meadow on the west side of the river.

Alain almost immediately sent a company of the *Cadwynir* ahead to scout the route we would take to the Great South Road. He sent another two companies south with orders to shadow the Kelmar army and to keep him apprised of their movements. We spent an hour inspecting our mounts and ensuring that our supplies were secured and then we mounted and set out for the Great South Road.

All the rest of that day we rode. The *aynekahrn* kept up a pace that would have killed a horse and the miles flew away behind us. The daylight faded and still we rode. The moon was just past full and provided enough light that we could ride until well after sunset. When we finally stopped, we simply slept on the ground; the weather was warm enough that we could sleep without the tents and the king didn't want to spend the time setting up and breaking down camp each day. The next two days were the same: we were up before dawn and rode until long after sunset, stopping only when the *aynekahrn* finally needed to rest and then just long enough for our mounts to recover and for us to eat a quick meal. On the third day after we crossed the Glaess, we rose early again, but in the late afternoon we reached the Great South Road at the point where it began its climb into the pass through the Corun Hills. We stopped there for the night.

The Corun Hills were often seen as an outflung arm of the Breton Mountains, but scholars pointed out that the rocky bones of the two ranges were of different types. The hills ran from the foothills of the Bretons in the west into the very heart of Elderwood in the east. The hills were not nearly so tall as the Bretons; the highest peaks were in the west where the hills mingled with the foothills of the mountains, and they dwindled to true hills in the east. The Great South Road had once passed through the Hills at the Blafaen Pass on a direct route from *Aennsrhyd* to *Elsgard*. Around the time of the Great War, though, the hills above the road and many of those supporting it gave way, blocking the pass. The road was rerouted fifty miles to the east through the Echi Pass, the only other easy route through the hills.

Though we stopped before dark, we didn't set up the tents, concerned that we might damage the grasslands enough to betray our passage to the Kelmar. We did, though, have our first hot meal in days. The next morning, we broke our fast and mounted just as the sun rose above the eastern horizon. We had a long day ahead of us; the King–concerned about leaving traces of our passage that could alert the Kelmar to our presence–wanted to get through the narrow defile at the summit before we stopped for the night.

The Great South Road was a little over 25 feet wide and was paved with tightly packed gravel. Despite nearly a thousand rounds with no maintenance, the roadway was still in excellent condition, no doubt due to the workings of the *Eldar* who constructed it. The road wound its way up into the hills, twisting and turning to maintain the easiest grade. Most of the way, bushes and trees crowded up against the edges of the roadway, predominantly sycamore, ash, red maple, black walnut, and yellow poplar. In some places, however, the land widened out into grassy, sunlit meadows. As we approached the summit of the pass, the ground on either side of the roadway rose until we were riding through a deep defile that was several miles long. The slate walls towered over us, and the clopping of the *aynekahrns'* hooves was magnified and echoed back at us in a confusing cacophony of sound. It was getting late in the afternoon and the sunlight no longer reached the floor of the defile. We rode in semidarkness until the ground sloped back down. At its north end, the pass opened onto a large grassy meadow. The sun was nearing the western horizon as we exited the defile and we spread out into the field, no longer concerned about leaving traces of our passage. While the cooks set about preparing an evening meal, the rest of us began scouring the surrounding forest for fallen trees and large branches, which we hauled back into the defile. The plan was to build as large a pile of wood as we possibly could to close off the north end of the pass. By itself, the pile would not long halt the Kelmar, but the *Cadwynir* were going to be concealed in the thick forests that covered the heights above the defile with the bulk of our supply of arrows. They would light the pile and, while the Kelmar endeavored to dowse it and clear the roadway, the archers would pick off as many as possible. They wouldn't be able to stop the Kelmar, but they could slow them down and, perhaps, do a little to even the odds when we finally met them head on.

When it became too dark to see, we all began to settle in for the night. I selected a spot where it seemed a thick layer of grass would provide some cushioning, wrapped myself in my blanket, and laid down. After what felt like hours, I was still wide awake and staring up at the stars. I was tired–the long day's ride followed by hauling wood for several hours had worn me out–and my spot was comfortable, but I simply could not sleep. I finally gave it up, strapped on my sword, and slipped off to the edge of camp.

When I was far enough away from everyone that I thought the glow from the pommel stone would not draw attention, I drew the sword and began a series of practice exercises. I was focused on *Endolsar*, trying to sense something in it that would give me a clue about what it could do, how it would help me defeat Mar and the Keepers. I'd been at it long enough to work up a sweat when a quiet voice behind me said, *"Endollin?"*

Quiet though it was, I was startled, and I spun around, snapping *Endolsar* into a guarding position.

"Peace, *Endollin*," came Pyrett's voice. "I mean no harm."

"Pyrett," I replied and lowered my sword. "You startled me."

"My apologies. I noticed an odd flickering light on the edge of camp and thought it merited my attention." She paused a moment. "While I appreciate your putting what I taught you to use, this seems an odd time to practice."

I smiled as I sheathed my sword and stepped closer to her.

"I couldn't sleep," I answered. "I thought I would try to discover what the sword can do. My apologies for disturbing you."

"You did not disturb my sleep. I am on watch." She gestured toward the sword, though I could barely see the motion. "What have you learned?"

"That it gets heavy very quickly when you start swinging it around."

She gave a short, sharp bark of a laugh and then said, "With luck, you won't have to swing it enough that that will be an issue."

I spent the rest of the night walking Pyrett's rounds with her. The next morning, we were in the saddle by the time the sky began to lighten. Alain left Iseabail in command of all but two companies of the *Cadwynir*. They were to build the barricade at the end of the pass as large as they could before the Kelmar arrived and then do as much damage as they could without directly engaging in battle. Then they were to join us in *Aennsrhyd*. Evening found us in the rolling grasslands between the Corun Hills and the Amer River. The day after that, in the late afternoon, we drew rein just out of sight of *Aennsrhyd*.

Konne, Rolugh, Pyrett, Ryan, and I gathered around the king.

"Rhion, you have more experience with the Alomar than the rest of us. How likely is it that they're watching to the south?" Alain asked.

"That's hard to say," Ryan answered. "If Marc is with the High King, he will have left Jaret in charge. Jaret is both bright and cautious and it would not be unlike him to keep watch on all approaches to the city. On the other hand, we don't know what's going on to the north. If Han has fallen, Jaret may have pulled in all his troops to safeguard Amersford."

The king nodded and looked around the group.

"Suggestions?" he asked.

"Let me ride up to the gate," Ryan said. "I'm known in Amersford. If anyone is there, I shouldn't have a problem when they challenge me. If no one stops me, I'll take a quick look around and get back here as quickly as I can."

As he spoke, Ryan was removing the leather ties that were holding back his hair which he then pulled forward to cover his ears.

"Very well," Alain agreed. "We will wait here."

Ryan turned his mount to ride toward the city.

"Ryan, wait," I said.

He turned toward me, a puzzled look on his face.

"You they will know," I said. "But they'll be extremely surprised to see you ride up on a unicorn."

Everyone in the group smiled, and Rolugh slipped off her *aynekahrn* to undo the straps holding the steel horn on the forehead of Ryan's mount. At her nod, Ryan set off up the road, leaving the rest of us waiting safely out of sight of the city.

"We may as well get something to eat," Alain said as he dismounted.

Ryan returned just as we were finishing a cold meal.

"I hope you saved me something," he said as he swung down from the saddle.

Alain sent a soldier off to fetch some food and turned back to Ryan.

"What did you find?" he asked.

"There was no one manning the towers or the gates," Ryan answered. "I scouted the immediate area of the gates and saw no evidence of recent activity."

"My thanks to you, Rhion," the king said. He turned to Pyrett.

"Captain, please take your *Cadwynir* into the city. We need to know whether anyone is in there. If you come across any of the Alomar, do not make contact."

Pyrett nodded.

"I understand, your Majesty. Assuming there are no problems, it shouldn't take us more than an hour or so to clear the city."

True to her word, Pyrett was back in a little over an hour. She reined in her mount and began speaking even as she slipped out of the saddle.

"*Aennsrhyd* is deserted," she reported. "We fanned out through all sections of the city and found no one, though it does appear that several of the buildings near the north gate have been occupied recently."

"Marc maintained a garrison there," I informed them.

"We did not show ourselves outside the north gate," the *Cadwynir* captain continued. "But we did explore outside the east and west walls of the city. It appears that many heavily laden wagons crossed the bridge and passed to the west of the city. We cannot imagine who it was or why they did not follow the paved road through the city."

Ryan smiled.

"Many of the Alomar believe that *Aennsrhyd* is haunted," he said. "They tend to avoid it when they can."

"Haunted?" Pyrett asked in disbelief. Then she shook her head and continued her report. "I've set watch in the towers at the south gate. My people are also clearing out buildings near the south gate to house us. Several of them are also working on cleaning up the park in the center of the city. I believe it might serve as a meeting place with the Alomar." She paused and then added, "The standing stone there is an unchancy thing."

"I wouldn't touch it," Ryan said, glancing my way.

"We didn't plan to," the captain answered.

"Very well," the king said. "Shall we take *Aennsrhyd*?"

We all nodded.

"Mount up," the king ordered.

A short time later, we pulled up before the gates of *Aennsrhyd*. They had been forged of iron by Phelan, the greatest of the smiths of the Alomar. The hinges had been so cunningly wrought that, despite their massive weight, each gate could be closed by a pair of men.

"A thousand rounds with no maintenance and no signs of rust," Konne observed.

"Are we sure that Phelan wasn't one of us?" Rolugh asked. "The craft inherent in these gates surpasses anything we have ever done." She turned to me. "Are all Alomar cities warded by such doors?"

"No," I replied. "Only Amersford. Every other city gate that I've ever seen or heard of was wood."

"Much of value has been lost on both sides since the Great War," Alain said.

We sat in silence for a moment and then the king spurred his mount into the city. A heartbeat later, the rest of us followed. Once inside the gates we dismounted, and soldiers led our mounts off. Pyrett suggested that the one-time inn that Ambrose, Ryan, and I had stayed in before might be the best choice for a headquarters. Pyrett, Konne, Rolugh, Ryan, and I joined the king in the center of the floor.

"We need to make contact with the Alomar," Alain said. "Now that we are here, however, I am at a loss as to how to accomplish that without risking bloodshed."

"Let me cross over to Amersford," Ryan offered. "As I said, I am known there. I can approach Jaret and assess how willing he will be to work with us."

The king nodded and turned to Konne and Rolugh.

"Set up a watch in the south gate towers and station archers on the south wall. Close the south gates. Have the other walls patrolled but tell the guards to be inconspicuous. If any of the Alomar cross the river, I want them to clearly see that we are preparing to hold the city against a siege from the south, not against them."

"It will be done," Konne said, and he and Rolugh left to carry out the king's orders.

"I'm going over to Amersford now," Ryan said. "I hope to be back with news in the morning."

The king, Pyrett, and I walked out with Ryan and watched him head off to where our *aynekahrn* had been stabled. It was growing dark and for the moment, there was nothing for us to do.

"We may as well try to get some sleep," the king said. "Tomorrow promises to be interesting."

I stood alone in utter darkness. I could not see where I was or what it was that I stood on. The dark was so complete that I could not see my hands when I waved them in front of my face. For an instant I thought that I could see a flicker from *Elinaur*, the ring that marked me as the *Endollin*, but if it was there, it was quickly quenched. Then I heard it: the *Arimë Daelyr*, but twisted and perverted, the aching loveliness turned to a vast ravenous hunger. In the darkness, tendrils of chill malevolence brushed me, wrapped around me, began constricting and robbing me of breath. As I fought to breathe, I could make out a faint whispering, just at the edge of hearing. I strained to take a breath and to make out the hissing words. Then they became clear. Still a whisper, a harsh, grating, genderless whisper, but clear. "Worship me," the voice said.

And I woke in a panic, gasping for breath.

I rose as quietly as I could and stepped out of the building into the monochrome light that comes before dawn. A few soldiers hurried from one place to another, no doubt engaged in some tasks to make the city more defensible. I stood for a moment, trying to decide what to do and then heard a quiet rustle of clothing behind me.

"I heard you call out in your sleep," Alain said. "Are you well?"

"Just a nightmare," I replied as he stepped forward to stand alongside me. Together we stared out across the square watching color slowly return as the morning light grew stronger.

"Are dreams ever just dreams?" Alain asked. "Do they not speak to us of our lives, the problems we face, and our concerns and fears?

"Perhaps," I admitted. "I dreamed that I was trapped by Mar."

"You fear that you are going to fail," Alain said. It sounded almost like a question.

I turned to face him directly.

"How could I not fear that? Alain, I'm just a man. I have a sword that I barely know how to use and if it does anything other than stab people, I don't know how to make it do so. I don't know whether stabbing Mar would be enough or if I could even manage that. Is it possible to kill a goddess? I seem to have some power inside me, but I can't seem to use that either. Supposedly I can save the world, but I'm afraid that I will destroy it simply because I do not know what I'm doing."

I hadn't meant to say any of that to anyone, especially the king, but it came pouring out of me as if I couldn't even control my own mouth.

"My apologies," I said. "I did not mean to burden you with all of that."

He didn't answer me for a moment, but held my gaze with his own, his sea-gray eyes dark in the wan light, his face unreadable.

"Perhaps," he said finally, "all of it will come to you as the ring and the sword came to you: in their own way in their own time."

Before I could answer, one of the *Cadwynir* rode up from the north and slipped from the saddle almost before his *aynekahrn* had halted.

"Your Majesty, I come from those assigned to keep watch on the north wall. Two riders are crossing the bridge. One of them appears to be Rhion."

The king considered for a brief moment and then responded.

"Meet them at the gate. If it is indeed Rhion, have him bring whomever it is that accompanies him here."

"Yes, your Majesty."

"As you return to the gate, have anyone along the direct path from the gate to here pull back. And unbind your hair as Rhion does. I do not want whoever is with Rhion to see us until they are here."

"Understood, sire."

The man returned to his saddle and set off at a trot toward the north gate.

"I should find the cooks," the king said. "It appears that we are having guests for the morning meal."

A little over half an hour later, I was standing alone in the square outside the former inn as Ryan rode up with another man. As they drew near, I recognized Jaret, Chamberlain of Amersford. The chamberlain saw me, shot a glance at Ryan, then turned his attention back to me. I couldn't read his expression. They halted some ten feet from me. Jaret's gaze never left me, and he did not speak.

The silence dragged on long enough to become uncomfortable. I was just taking a breath to speak when Jaret cut me off.

"Lauren, son of Dalach and Minstrel of Alomar. Ryan told me that you would be here."

I didn't respond. The chamberlain's hands were nervously twisting the reins of his horse.

"There is quite a handsome reward being offered for you."

Involuntarily, I took a step back as fear ran cold through my veins.

"I do not, however, intend to collect on it. I remember the last time you were here. You saved Marc. I have not forgotten that."

He and Ryan dismounted and walked toward me, each holding the reins to his mount.

"It is good to see you, Lauren," Jaret said.

"And good to see you, Jaret. Are you well?"

"As well as can be," the chamberlain answered. "The Federation has been unsettled in the past round of the seasons. First, word came out that you had murdered the High King and Ambrose. People were searching for you everywhere. Then we got the news about the attack on Songhaven. The fact that one of the Keepers was involved in that changed a great many hearts. And then came the invasion of Han and, again, the Keepers were involved. People who had been howling for your blood suddenly began questioning whether the Keepers truly have our welfare at heart. There are still some very devout people who believe that the Keepers' actions are justified retribution for the sins of the Alomar, but most of the population is growing angry at the injustice of their actions. Many are beginning to ask if it was not the Keepers themselves who killed the High King.

"You should be able to travel openly in the Federated Kingdoms now, though you should probably exercise some caution. It will be good to have you back."

The chamberlain paused and looked around the square.

"I am puzzled, though," he said. "Ryan told me that there were allies in the city, but I have seen only one guard at the north gate, and he kept his distance. Have you brought an army of ghosts?"

"It may seem that I have," I replied. I gestured to the door of the inn and Alain stepped out. He had changed out of his traveling clothes into formal raiment, a deep blue tunic and trousers trimmed with gold piping. On his head he wore his silver coronet, set with a thumb-sized piece of the opalescent Elf stone. His hair was bound back, revealing his pointed ears. He was conspicuously unarmed.

"Jaret," I said, "This is Alain, son of Lorrestian, King of the *Eldar*." I turned to Alain. "Your Majesty, I present to you Jaret, son of Mahun, Duke of Kerith and Chamberlain of Amersford."

Jaret's thin face went pale, his green eyes wide. His hands, almost always in constant, compulsive motion, dropped to his sides and were still. He didn't move as Alain approached, but his face displayed ever increasing terror.

"Duke Jaret," Alain said. "I mean you no harm. Indeed, I have come to offer our assistance against the Kelmar. In addition, I have information that you and the Federated Kings require."

Jaret finally moved. He looked from Alain to me and then back.

"He's..." he started, then his voice choked off. He swallowed. "He's an Elf."

"My people call ourselves the *Eldar*," Alain said quietly.

"Jaret, the *Eldar* are good people," I said. "They took me in after Songhaven was attacked. They cared for me. They are truly here to help."

Jaret had finally recovered his wits.

"I am beyond surprised," he said. "Like most of the Alomar, I believed that the Elves were gone."

"We were in hiding," Alain said. "But there will be time for history later. There is a force of some four thousand Kelmar marching across the Lellarin Plains. We believe that their intent is to take the Bridge and trap your army on the north side of the river."

That news seemed to settle Jaret as the need to plan overrode his fear.

"I do not have the men to stop them," he said. "Marc took nearly all of our forces with him to try and stop the Kelmar coming through the Aeran Pass."

"I have two thousand with me," Alain informed him. "We arranged an ambush in the Echi Pass to delay them and give us time to get here and fortify the city. We also hope the ambush will reduce their numbers somewhat. We will prevent them from taking the bridge."

"Were there Keepers with them?" Jaret asked.

"We believe so," Alain answered.

"Then you will not be able to stop them," Jaret said. "Now I have news for you. You already seem to know that Han has fallen. Since then, Badon and Canim have also been taken. The Alomar army is heading here, pursued by the Kelmar."

The king and I exchanged glances.

"Taken?" I asked. "We understood that the Alomar forces were all concentrated in the north. How could Badon have fallen already?"

Jaret's expression was a mixture of anger and defeat.

"The Kelmar outnumber us more than two to one and they have several of the Keepers with them. The story has been the same in all three cities: the Keepers use their power to blast down the gates and the Kelmar soldiers flood into the city. They overwhelm and kill any soldiers they capture and then they sweep the city searching door-to-door. Any home where they find a weapon, they confiscate the weapon and kill everyone in the home. Any leaders–civic or military–that they capture, they kill. They found

Larsen in a cell in Badon and killed him. They hung his body from the wall over the south gate of the city. We have heard from people who escaped from Badon that they are actively seeking Anders, his family, and the petty kings."

"This is it, then," Alain said quietly. "This is Mar's final attempt to subjugate the Alomar."

"It appears to be," Jaret said. "But we cannot stand against them. They are too many and they have the Keepers on their side. We know that Amersford will fall. I have been moving food and weapons out of the city."

"That would be why we saw evidence of large numbers of heavily laden wagons moving past *Aennsrhyd*," Alain observed.

"Yes. I have been communicating with the High King and War Duke Dalach. We need to do something to limit the numerical advantage of the Kelmar. Our plan is to retreat westward toward Landfall."

Alain smiled.

"You plan to make a stand at the Dergun Fens."

"We do," Jaret confirmed. "The only way across the fens is via the causeway. It will limit how many of them can come against us at one time."

The chamberlain paused at that point and the color drained from his face again.

"Have I just betrayed my people?" he asked, chagrin straining his voice.

"You have not," the king responded. "The *Eldar* are here to support the *Endollin* and the people of the Federated Kingdoms."

"The *Endollin*? What is that?"

"He is," the king answered, gesturing toward me.

"Lauren? He is a minstrel. Marc has also referred to him as the Lawbreaker. Is *Endollin* the Elvish word for Lawbreaker."

"*Endollin* is not an *Eldarin* word. It is a word in the Language of Making. It can mean lawbreaker, but it can also mean lawgiver. In either case, we mean no harm to the Alomar."

"Why should I believe you? How do I know that you did not do something to me?"

"Consider the history, Duke Jaret," the king said. "My people have little reason to love the Keepers. What they are doing to you now, they did to us a thousand rounds ago."

Jaret looked unconvinced.

"Jaret," the king continued. "What do you believe that I could do to you? I have no magic. That gift belongs only to humans. I have no way to compel you to speak."

Jaret still didn't respond.

"I have a wife, Jaret. We have a daughter. She is of an age with Lauren. I could have stayed hidden with them. I left them to come to your aid. If we fail to stop the Keepers and their Kelmar, they will find my wife and daughter and they will kill them. Do you think I would allow that to happen?"

The king's fear was evident in the pleading tone of his voice. Jaret's look softened.

"I, too, have a daughter," he said and then paused for a moment, obviously wrestling with a decision. Then he said, "Let us hope that together we can keep them safe. If we are to do so, we have much to do."

"We were about to break our fast," Alain said. "Would you care to join us?"

The next quarter moon passed quickly. Jaret shuttled back and forth between Amersford and *Aennsrhyd* coordinating the efforts of the Alomar and the *Eldar*. A few humans came to *Aennsrhyd*, wagon drivers bringing food and other supplies. For the most part, they were wary, but not hostile. Some were curious and wanted to meet the recurring villains of the Repentants' stories. None of the *Eldar* crossed to Amersford; Alain and Jaret thought it best to limit contact until the humans grew accustomed to the fact that the *Eldar* were back.

Jaret was in daily contact with Marc and the high king. Messengers were flowing up and down the King's Post Road several times a day and slowly a plan was taking shape. It was clear that we would not be able to stand at Amersford. Attempting to do so would simply result in a repeat of the defeats at Han and Badon with the loss of many more men. Instead, the high king was pushing the Alomar army to retreat as quickly as possible. They would flee across the Amersford Bridge and then head down the Harbor Turnpike toward Landfall. As they passed *Aennsrhyd*, they would be joined by the *Eldar*. Archers would be left on the walls of the Twin Cities to delay the Kelmar as long as possible; they would flee to ships docked at the wharves when the gates were breached. The combined army would turn and stand on the west side of the Dergun Fens. The high king had sent a messenger to Altiera requesting aid when Han fell. The hope was that the Alomar could hold out at the Fens until the Altieran reinforcements arrived.

I had little to do. I worked on my swordplay each day with Pyrett. Ryan and I found time each day to make music for off-duty soldiers. Other times I went to work in the stables helping to tend the *aynekahrn* or I lent my hands to whatever other work needed to be done. As a result, evenings found me exhausted, but I did not sleep well. My dreams were troubled by the perverted version of the *Arimë Daelyr*. Even if my dreams didn't wake me, I still woke unrested with the discordant song echoing in my head. I began to dread sleep.

Near midday on the eighth day after our arrival, Pyrett had me sparring with one of the *Cadwynir* in the square inside the gates when one of the men on watch called out that riders were approaching from the south. We immediately set aside our training weapons and Pyrett sent my sparring partner to alert the king and Jaret. Together, we climbed the stairs to the top of the wall. Even at a distance we could see that there were only three riders. In minutes, it was clear that the two in the lead were *Cadwynir*. We quickly returned to ground level and the king ordered the gates opened just enough to admit the riders single file.

I recognized the first of the *Cadwynir* to enter. His name was Jorith, and he was one of the *Cadwynir* who accompanied me and Élan to *Elsgard*. I did not know the other *Cadwynir*, but he held the lead to the mount of the third rider. As he entered, there were mutterings of surprise from the people in the square.

The third rider was a Kelmar scout.

CHAPTER TWO

Both *Cadwynir* dismounted and while Jorith strode toward King Alain, the other ranger went to their captive. The Kelmar scout's hands were bound to the horn of his saddle. He looked to be about my age but appeared to be somewhat smaller than me. He was thin, almost emaciated in appearance, but the ropey muscles visible in his arms suggested a wiry strength. His black hair was cut short. His face was browned from the sun and the lower half was covered by a neatly trimmed beard and mustache. He wore trousers and a short-sleeved tunic of some mean cloth, both dyed a shade of green that seemed almost brown. He also wore a brown felt vest with red piping at the lower edge.

"Your Majesty, Captain," Jorith said, and bowed. He flicked a quick glance at Jaret.

"Jorith," replied the king. "You are acquainted with the *Endollin*. This is Jaret, Duke of Kerith and Chamberlain of Amersford. You have news?"

Jorith turned to where his colleague was helping the Kelmar dismount.

"News and more, Your Majesty."

"I can see that. Please report."

"As you wish, Your Majesty. As ordered, we rode south with all possible speed and located the Kelmar army. We shadowed them for several days and gained a sense of their speed and direction. According to our estimates, they would have reached the Great South Road just outside of *Elsgard* five days ago. Their pace should pick up on the road; we guess that unhindered they should reach here in a little over a quarter moon."

"But they will not be unhindered," Jaret said, making it sound somewhere between a statement and a question. He looked back and forth between the *Cadwynir* and the king.

"Indeed, they will be hindered," Jorith replied. "As we approached the summit of the pass, our fellow *Cadwynir* pulled us aside and guided us around the defile. They have not been idle since you left them, Your Majesty. The barricade is now quite substantial. We should have at least ten days before they arrive."

"Excellent," the king said.

"And what about your travelling companion?" Pyrett asked.

"We believe that he is a scout," Jorith replied. "We stumbled upon him quite by accident. We came out of tall grass into a shallow gulley with a small stream at the bottom. Our friend seems to have laid down to drink from the stream and then fallen asleep."

Our little group smiled at that and then the *Cadwynir* continued.

"He was quite surprised when he woke to find himself surrounded. He began to cry out but stopped when we shook our heads and drew our swords. Since then, he has said nothing to us, though I hear him muttering prayers at night."

"He's very thin," Jaret observed.

"He is," Jorith agreed. "I do not believe that the Kelmar army is well fed. Our friend here hasn't said much, but he eats as if he's never seen food before. He's actually filled in a little since we found him."

He paused for a moment.

"We disarmed him, of course, as soon as we captured him. He carried only a sword and a short dagger. Neither of them was well made. I've seen an apprentice smith's first attempt at a sword that was better made than the weapon this man carried."

"I see," the king said. "Is there anything else?"

"No, Your Majesty."

"Well, then, have him brought over here."

Jorith gestured to his companion who led the unresisting Kelmar to us.

The scout was, indeed, half a head shorter than me and exceedingly thin. Up close, he appeared even younger, with perhaps only seventeen or eighteen rounds of the seasons. His brown eyes were wide and under the tan his skin was pale. He was clearly trying to stop himself from trembling.

"I am Alain, son of Lorrestian and King of the *Eldar*," the king said in the Alomar tongue. "So long as you do not attempt to harm anyone, you will not be harmed. Do you understand?"

The scout nodded but did not speak.

"What is your name?" the king asked.

The scout did not respond. At that moment, however, a young man wearing the red sash of a warrior rode into the square and dismounted. I knew him. His name was Keilin, and he had volunteered to carry messages to and from Jaret when he was in *Aennsrhyd*.

"Your Majesty, my lord Duke" he said. "My apologies for the interruption. I have a message for Chamberlain Jaret."

"What is it, Keilin?"

"My lord Duke, the wizards are becoming perturbed. They say that they are still waiting to hear whether they are to be evacuated along with the army. They want to know if you have an answer for them."

I was watching the Kelmar warrior. When he heard the word "wizard" his eyes grew wide, and he went even paler.

"Keilin, I've told them that they will be evacuated," Jaret said. "How many times to I have to repeat myself?"

"Their concern, my lord, is for their books."

"Excuse me, Your Majesty," Jaret said to the king. He turned and walked toward the messenger. "We do not have the wagons to transport their library and even if we did, we do not have the time nor the men to load them."

Alain turned to Pyrett.

"Captain, take this young man inside and get him some food. We'll be in to talk to him momentarily."

As Pyrett led the Kelmar scout into the headquarters building, Jaret returned.

"My apologies, Your Majesty."

"No need to apologize, Jaret," Alain said. "You have much to do. I very much dislike adding to your burdens, but I am afraid that I have one more thing for you to deal with."

"And what would that be?" Jaret asked, a puzzled frown wrinkling his face.

"I am remanding the Kelmar scout into your custody," Alain replied.

"But your people captured him."

"They did, but we came here to render aid," Alain explained. "We did not come here to take over. You are in command. You should oversee the interrogation and whatever information you can get from that young man is yours to use however you see fit."

I saw something shift in Jaret then, some last lingering doubt about the intentions of the *Eldar* was resolved. The chamberlain looked as if he were about to speak, but then he just nodded.

"We should go talk to him then," he said finally.

"Duke Jaret," I said, "I have a thought about that."

They both turned to me.

"He has obviously been ordered not to speak if captured. Now he has been captured. And if the Kelmar church teaches their people the same things that the Repentant teach to the Alomar, he believes that he's been captured by supernatural beings who will cause him to be cast into the outer darkness if he cooperates with them. So far, he's been treated with relative kindness and compassion, but he's most likely seeing that as a trick to get him to do something that will damn him in Mar's sight. He's terrified and clinging to the order not to speak because it's the only thing that makes sense to him now."

Alain and Jaret both nodded their agreement with my reading of the situation.

"What do you propose?" Jaret asked.

"Let me take his food to him. He looks as if he is about my age and we're both human. I might be able to create some sense of normalcy. Maybe that will be enough to get him to open up."

"Very well," Jaret said. "It is worth trying."

"One thing, though," I added. "I'm not going to give him my real name. There is a good chance that all of the Kelmar know that Mar is seeking a minstrel named Lauren. If you come in, call me Arlow."

"Arlow?" Jaret asked.

"That's the name I used when I was hiding from the high king's men. I'm used to answering to it."

One of the soldiers was approaching with a plate of food for the Kelmar. I took it from him and stepped inside the building. I nodded to Pyrett and then glanced at the door. She got my unspoken message and stepped out. The scout watched me as I approached.

"You can call me Arlow," I said. "I have some food for you."

He took the plate from me and began eating without saying anything. He kept his eyes on his food. I let him eat for a while and then said, "You are very resolute and very devout. You remind me of Jorlith of Landfall."

He stopped eating and slowly raised his eyes to mine.

"You know the stories," he said quietly. The words were clear, but his accent and pronunciation of some of the words were strange to me.

"For he who seeks knowledge, what could be sweeter than knowledge of Mar," I answered, quoting from the *Torun Mar*.

"You know the scriptures."

"You seem surprised," I observed. "I may be Alomar, but we do know the teachings of Mar."

"But you turn your backs on Mar."

"Not all of the Alomar do," I said gently.

He set the plate down and focused on me.

"What did you call yourself?"

"Arlow."

"I am Malash."

I nodded.

"Malash," I echoed him, but then said nothing further. He took another couple of bites of the food, then looked at me.

"You have no questions for me?"

"Would you answer them if I asked?"

"If I do not answer, will you kill me?" he countered.

I shook my head.

"No. We will not kill you."

"But if I answer, you will use what I tell you to kill Kelmar."

"They are trying to kill us," I pointed out.

"Then I will not speak."

"I understand. Malash, I am a minstrel. I would like to learn more about your people. And, yes, the Alomar leaders would like to know why you've attacked the Federation. I thought we could do that just by talking."

He frowned at that.

"You want to know why we invade? Not how many of us there are and where we are going?"

"Malash, we have our own scouts," I told him. "We already know that there are four thousand of you and that your army is heading for Amersford. Why would we need to ask you that? We would like to understand why."

He just glared at me, anger narrowing his eyes and twisting his lips.

"You want to know why we attack? I have eaten more since I have been taken than in the entire moon before that. My people have next to nothing. Barely enough food to keep us alive. What little money we have goes to buy food."

He waved his hand up and down, pointing at my clothing.

"Even our most exalted leaders are not dressed as finely as you are. We live lives of misery because almost everything that does not go to the church goes to the military. We must be strong to hold back your aggression. We attack you in desperation to stop your relentless attacks on us."

I had no idea what to say. I sat down, hardly noticing that I did so. Malash was still glaring at me, but tears glittered in his eyes. We sat staring at each other for several moments, then he broke eye contact and resumed eating.

"Malash," I said finally, "Why do you think the Alomar invade the empire?"

"Every Kelmar knows it," he replied.

"Have you ever witnessed an Alomar attack?"

"No."

"Have you ever known anyone who witnessed an Alomar attack?"

"No. Our leaders tell us of the raids. They tell us of farms burned, men and women and children slain."

His vehement hostility was almost palpable. I decided to change tack slightly.

"Do you know what this means?" I asked, tugging on my sash.

"It means that you are a minstrel," he answered.

"Do you know what minstrels do?"

"You sing songs."

"That is not all," I prompted.

He didn't answer for a moment, but then said, "You study."

"We do," I confirmed. "I have studied the history, and I can tell you that no Alomar army has set foot on Kelmar soil since before the Great War. No Alomar soldiers raid Kelmar towns or villages."

"Why should I believe you?" he demanded. "Why would our leaders lie to us?" His expression became guarded. "How many children do your parents have?"

Puzzled, I answered, "Just me. Why?"

"Were they punished?"

"Why would they be punished?"

"Your people have as many children as they possibly can, correct?"

"Only if they want to. Some have none, some only one or two. It is up to each couple. Malash, what is it that you really want to know?"

He'd been watching me intently.

"You are not lying to me," he said softly. "The Alomar do not have as many children as possible so that you can grow your army?"

"No," I confirmed, shaking my head.

"The Kelmar do. The priests order us to have as many children as possible. When the boys are old enough, most are conscripted into the army.

Few are left to grow food and most of what is grown is taken to feed the soldiers or for the church."

He looked at me, his gaze intense.

"You do not live that way?"

"No," I answered. A sudden thought occurred to me. "Would you like to see how we live?"

Without waiting for an answer, I went back outside. As I exited, Pyrett stepped back in. Alain and Jaret noticed me and joined me just outside the headquarters.

"Well?" Jaret asked.

"His name is Malash," I replied. "He hasn't said much else, but I think I'm making progress. I believe I can get him to talk, but I need to do something a little out of the ordinary to make that happen. Jaret, do you have any people here in *Aennsrhyd*?"

"I do," he replied. "I have a small escort inside the north gate. Why?"

"According to Malash, living conditions inside the empire are difficult. I've told him a little about how different it is here, but he doesn't believe me. He wants to but he doesn't. I think if we give him a tour of Amersford–under guard of course–and he sees how we really live, he might be convinced to speak with us."

Jaret looked at me, a speculative expression on his face. Then he glanced at Alain, who simply shrugged.

"We will try it," Jaret said. "But I will accompany you."

Together we went back into the headquarters. Malash was finishing the last of the food on the plate.

"Malash," I said. "This is Duke Jaret of Kerith and Chamberlain of Amersford. You are in his custody, and he has agreed to allow you to see Amersford. Do you wish to see how the Alomar live?"

"I do," he replied.

"We will accompany you," Jaret said. "We will be joined by some of my soldiers. Though we do not intend you harm, your safety is not assured if you attempt to escape. Do you understand?"

"I do."

"Then let us go."

A short time later, the three of us were riding into Amersford. Malash was riding between Jaret and me, and a soldier rode in front of us holding the lead to Malash's horse. We were accompanied by three other soldiers, one on either side and one behind. All were clad in the white and blue of Amersford.

As on my previous trips to Amersford, the streets were filled with people. This time, however, there were many wagons mixed in with the crowds of people. Each of them was loaded with what looked like everything a family owned and all of them were heading toward the north gate of the city.

"Many of our citizens are fleeing the city," Jaret said when I asked. "They're heading for the outlying towns and villages with everything they can carry."

"Why?" Malash asked.

For a moment, Jaret just looked at the Kelmar scout with an expression of stunned surprise.

"Because an army of your people is approaching from the north," Jaret said mildly, but he was obviously straining against snapping at Malash. "In the cities they have already taken, they've tended to kill civic leaders. These people fear for their lives."

Jaret was silent for a heartbeat.

"If I am still here when they arrive, they will kill me as they did my counterpart in Badon," he said, so quietly I could barely hear him.

A leaned forward so that I could look past Malash at Jaret.

"Ashlin is gone?" I asked.

Jaret simply nodded in response. Malash was looking back and forth between us. It was clear that he was unsure whether to believe us or not. After a moment, Jaret asked, "What did you wish to see, Kelmar?"

Malash didn't respond. He was looking around him, trying to take in everything.

"These people cannot all be nobility," he said.

"They aren't," I responded. "Why would you think they are?"

"They look so well-fed and so well-dressed," he answered. "Only the nobility and the religious and military leaders look like that."

That brought a quick look from Jaret.

"And the women..." Malash began but never finished the thought.

"What about the women?" I asked, looking around us. I saw nothing out of the ordinary.

"Your women show their faces. They wear clothing that shows the shape of their bodies. They are immodest."

"What do Kelmar women wear," Jaret asked, stunned out of his silence.

"Men should desire only Mar," Malash said in answer. "A woman must not try to take for herself what belongs only to Mar. She must not try to attract a man's desire, so a woman wears only a long dress of sackcloth. Such a dress is fitted with the *teant* to hide her shape."

"I do not know that word," I said. "What is a *teant*?"

Malash frowned at me as if he was puzzled that I did not understand.

"It is a wicker frame, an oval, that rests on a woman's shoulders under her dress. It holds the fabric away from her body to conceal its shape. When a woman goes out in public, she wears a sackcloth hood over her face. Thus, women honor Mar by not attempting to compete with her. Do no Alomar women dress so?"

"I have never seen such a thing," I told him.

"Nor have I," said Jaret.

"You said that some Alomar do not turn their backs on Mar," Malash said accusingly.

"Some do not," I replied. "But, Malash, there is nothing in the *Torun Mar* that calls for women to dress in such a way."

"The *teant* was not handed down in the scriptures. The requirement came from the priests, who received it directly from Mar herself."

Jaret called for us to stop in front of the king's estate.

"Malash," he said. "We are in the center of the city. What do you wish to see?"

The scout swiveled in his saddle, trying to see all around him.

"Where do the people live? People like me. Where do they live?"

"Let's go to North Quarter," Jaret instructed the soldiers accompanying us.

The western side of Amersford was the residential side of the city and the northern part of that was where the crafters, tradespeople, and soldiers tended to live. For the most part, the homes there were small and wooden, but solidly built. They were built up against one another and most were fairly narrow, with only a small sitting room and kitchen on the first floor and bedrooms on the second. The people of Amersford were proud and the homes were all kept freshly painted and most had a small flower garden between the front of the house and the street.

"Soldiers live here?" Malash asked, his eyes wide.

"They do," Jaret confirmed.

Malash fell silent and hung his head. From the way he shook, he may have been crying. After a moment, Jaret directed the soldiers to take us back to the headquarters in *Aennsrhyd*. During the ride back, Malash didn't speak, and he kept his eyes down, trusting the soldier holding his mount's lead to keep him from harm. As we drew rein in front of the abandoned inn, Malash finally raised his head. Tear tracks streaked the grime on his face.

"I was told that your people had nothing and that you raided us for our wealth, to take the little that we have because you had less. Now I have seen. We have nothing that you need. I was told that if I was captured that I would be starved and beaten. Instead, I have been well fed and treated with kindness. I no longer know who to believe or what to believe, but my parents raised me to tell the truth. Ask me your questions and I will answer them as best I can."

A short time later, Jaret, Alain, Malash, and I were sitting in camp chairs in the inn. Malash had been staring at Alain since we sat down.

"Your Majesty," he said when he finally dared to speak. "You said earlier that you were a king, but you do not look like the other Alomar."

"That is because I am not Alomar," the king replied. "I am of the *Eldar*. You would know us as Elves."

The scout's eyes widened in surprise.

"But all the stories say that the Elves are small and ugly," he exclaimed.

"The stories were meant to denigrate us," Alain explained.

"Is everything I was taught a lie?" Malash cried.

"No," I said gently. "You were taught not to lie and that truly is a virtue. You were taught to love your family, to work hard, and to be loyal. Those are all good things."

Malash stared at me, a forlorn expression on his face.

"They are coming to take it all away," he said, his voice shaking. "They want to make your Federation part of the Empire. Mar wants you back. The wealth of these lands will go to the church and your children will be soldiers whether they will it or not."

"Malash, if the Kelmar conquer the Federation, why would such a large army still be needed?" Jaret asked.

"Because there are other people to be brought under Mar's dominion. The Altierans do not worship her. According to the priests, she plans to make them worship her."

"We do not wish to see that happen," Jaret said.

"I am not sure that I do, either," Malash said. "Not anymore."

We sat in silence for a moment, and then Alain asked, "What can you tell us, Malash? How much of the strategy do you know? How well equipped are your people?"

"I am just a scout," he replied. "I do not know much. I do know that we were ordered to take the Amersford Bridge and to hold it. We were not to let anyone across. We were also ordered to search the banks of the river and to destroy any boats we found. No one was to escape.

"Most of us carried weapons like the ones I had. They are not very good. Our officers had better ones. Some of us also had bows but a limited number of arrows. One of my tasks was going to be to collect arrows fired at us after each attack."

He paused for just a second.

"Our strength was that two of the Most Holy Keepers were with us."

"Malash, I know that telling us that must have been difficult," Alain said. "What you have given us will be very helpful."

"There is one more thing," Malash said. "Just before we marched, we were told to watch for a certain man. A minstrel named Lauren."

I fought to control my expression.

"If we found him, he was to be captured and taken to the nearest of the Keepers. We were never told why." He glanced at me. "Do you know him?" he asked me.

"I do," I said quietly.

He frowned at that and then a look of resignation washed over his face.

"It is you, is it not?" he said. "You are Lauren."

He looked from one to another of us, his expression strained.

"A quarter moon ago, I was just a soldier. I knew that I was probably going to die in the service of my goddess when we reached the Federation. We had been marching for almost two moons, and I was exhausted. I laid down to drink from a stream and fell asleep. The next thing I knew, I was captured. Now I am talking to Elves, who are not ugly and evil as I was taught they were, and a man who is wanted by my goddess and who also does not seem to be evil. What has happened to me?"

His last words faded into a sob.

Alain gestured that we should leave the scout alone. He and Jaret and I gathered just outside the door.

"What do you think?" the king asked us.

"In terms of what their army is doing, he hasn't really told us anything that we didn't already know or hadn't surmised," Jaret replied.

"True," Alain agreed. "But what he has told us is true. As a low-ranking scout, he probably would not know much more than he has told us. Given what he said about the state of their weapons, we could easily defeat them if they were not accompanied by the Keepers."

"Is there any way that we can counter them?" Jaret asked.

Alain turned to me.

"I've not determined yet what the sword does," I answered his unasked question. "I don't know how to call up whatever power I might have."

"Perhaps the wizards could help," Jaret suggested. "I could ask for someone to come and meet with you."

"That might be helpful," I said, "as long as they aren't going to accuse me of practicing Dark Magic and try to lock me up."

Malash stepped out of the inn, squinting against the bright sunlight.

"May I join you?" he asked.

"Please do," Jaret said.

"Thank you, my lord Duke. May I ask what you plan to do with me?"

Jaret glanced at Alain, who gave a small shrug.

"We have made no plans concerning you," Jaret answered. "I can say that we are not going to hold you as a prisoner indefinitely."

"We cannot simply let you go, though," Alain said. "We do not want you returning to your people and letting them know that we are here."

"I understand," Malash replied. "I do not wish to return to my people or to the Empire. But I do not wish to fight against my people either. I cannot ask you to let me go and even if you did, I cannot simply wander the Federation. I do not imagine that I would be welcome. I do not know what is to become of me."

"Malash, we could put you to work with the army without asking you to fight your people," I said. "Have you any skills at healing or cooking?"

"You would not want to eat anything I cook," he replied. "I did get some basic training in healing when I was conscripted. I can render basic aid, and I would be very happy to learn more."

"There might be some difficulties if you work with our healers," Jaret noted. "Alain, would your Healers be willing to take him on?"

The king turned to Malash.

"You were raised on the stories of Mar. Could you work alongside my people?" he asked.

"If they will have me, I will work with them."

Alain gestured and an *Eldarin* soldier stepped out of an open doorway and joined us.

"Take this man to the Healers," the king commanded. "He is to work with them and learn from them. Have him watched until I say otherwise."

"Yes, Your Majesty," the soldier replied.

The king turned to Malash.

"You understand that I have to do that?"

"I do, Your Majesty. My thanks to you."

The next morning, I was just finishing my morning meal when Jaret arrived on horseback. He was accompanied by several Amersford soldiers, and a man dressed all in gray. That man seemed very familiar, but I struggled to put a name to his face until I noticed the white sash at his waist and the staff in his right hand. Then I recognized Olen, Master of the House of Wizards in Amersford.

To facilitate riding a horse, the wizard had traded his usual gray robe for a gray tunic and trousers. Olen was of average height and build, with jet black hair and wide set brown eyes. His staff was of rowan wood and was shod in copper. When I had met him nearly a round before, I'd found him pleasant and agreeable. I couldn't read his expression as his eyes found me in the small group of people outside the inn.

As Olen and Jaret approached, I sensed movement to my left and found Alain stepping up beside me. Together, we watched Jaret and the wizard dismount and hand their reins to one of the soldiers.

"Your Majesty," Jaret said. "I present Olen, Master of the House of Wizards in Amersford."

The chamberlain turned to the wizard.

"Master Olen, His Majesty Alain, son of Lorrestian and King of the *Eldar*."

Olen gave a slight bow, little more than a nod of his head.

"Your Majesty," the wizard said. "I confess that I find myself uncertain of how to proceed. I have spent my life certain in the knowledge that the Elves were oppressors of my people, but Jaret assures me that our histories are wrong and that you are here to help us."

"I understand your difficulties, Master Olen," the king replied. "Were I in your position, I would undoubtedly feel the same."

"It does a great deal to assuage my concerns that you handed the captive Kelmar over to Jaret and that I find only the south gate of this city fortified."

In response, Alain only nodded, but he had a slight smile on his face.

"I do hope that we can become friends," he said.

"Perhaps," Olen responded in a noncommittal tone.

The wizard turned to me.

"Lauren, son of Dalach and Minstrel of Alomar. You are why I am here," he said.

"Master Olen, my thanks to you for coming," I replied.

"I have been informed," he said, shooting a glance at Jaret, "that our transcriptions of *The Book of Kings* is inaccurate."

"The evidence that I have seen suggests that it is," I said.

"And that lawbreaker is only one translation of the original word."

"Yes. The original word was *endollin*, which can mean either lawbreaker or lawgiver."

"And which are you, minstrel?"

"I have only ever desired to make, Master Olen."

"Yet you bear a sword, contrary to the custom and traditions of our people."

"Master Olen, I did not choose the path that I am on. Some power to oppose Mar and the Keepers resides in me and whether I will it or not, I am fated to face them. This sword is part of that fate."

"You would turn away from that fate?" he asked.

"If I could, yes. But I do not believe that Mar and the Keepers would accept that. She has been searching for me. Her actions led to Ambrose's death. One of the Keepers led the attack on Songhaven. I lost friends there.

I lost the woman I loved there. Now they are attacking the Federation itself."

"You believe that the invasion of the Federation is about you?"

"Not entirely, no," I answered. "Mar has long wished to have the Alomar back under her dominion. But she also wishes to neutralize me. Alive, I am apparently a threat to her plans."

Olen brought his left hand up and scrubbed at the lower half of his face, gazing intently at me as he did so.

"The Kelmar have without cause invaded the Federation," he said. "They have murdered any leaders they could find and have made clear that they intend to do the same to our high king. I have heard rumors that wizards in the conquered cities have been imprisoned, perhaps worse. Ordinary people are living in fear. This is not the world I choose to live in. I have been told that only you can stand against the Keepers. Do you intend to do so?"

"If I can stop them, I will," I replied.

He stood considering my response for a moment and then said, "And what do you wish from me?"

"I seem to have power of some kind, but I do not know how to use it. And I need to know what this does," I said, gesturing toward *Endolsar.*

Olen glanced around the small group of people around us.

"Is there someplace private where we can work?" he asked.

"You can use the meeting room," Alain said.

In the time since our arrival, the *Eldar* had been repairing some of the places we were occupying. In the inn, scavenged materials had been used to construct a makeshift roof and a small backroom–possibly once a storeroom–had been cleaned out and furnished with a number of camp chairs. It was used to conduct meetings when there was a need for privacy. I led Olen there and we took up chairs facing one another.

"Lauren, you failed the *magenahr*. Why do you think you have powers?"

I frowned.

"How do you know that I failed the *magenahr*?"

He smiled.

"To give you one reason: you didn't train to be a wizard."

I nodded. I wasn't thinking. Had I passed, I would have become a wizard.

"To give you another reason: I was there when you were tested. I assisted in that test."

"I saw only Master Crom," I said.

"Nonetheless, I was there. So, I ask again: why do you think you have powers?"

I wanted to ask more about my test and Olen's role in it, but the needs of the moment demanded that I put my curiosity aside. I told the wizard about the falling tree when I was a boy and the deaths of the men who had tried to kill me. I told him as well about the sense of connection that I seemed to cause during celebrations of the change of seasons and the times that I had been guided by ethereal music. As I spoke, he leaned forward in his chair, an intent look on his face. When I finished, he sat up straight, his brows drawn together in thought.

"Lauren," he said finally, "are you familiar with the wizard's skill in Reading?"

"I've seen it done once," I said.

"With your permission, I would like to Read you," he said.

As I started to object, he raised a hand.

"I do not intend to rummage through your memories," he explained. "What I'm proposing is more of a sharing. I would like you to recall the events you described to me, and I will passively observe those memories.

I might learn something that would allow me to help you. I will not, however, insist. I will not do this without your consent."

"I understand," I said. "What do you need me to do?"

He nodded.

"We need to move our chairs closer together. I need to be able to touch you, preferably on the forehead."

We both stood and dragged our chairs closer together. I started to lean toward Olen, but he stopped me.

"I need you to relax. Lean back if you can do so comfortably."

I sat back and Olen leaned forward.

"I'm going to place my hand on your forehead," he said.

He brushed my hair from my forehead and laid his left hand just above my eyes.

"Close your eyes," he said quietly. When I complied, he said, "Now, remember the incident with the tree. Start with the events just before and leading up to it..."

We worked for nearly an hour. To my surprise, the last thing that Olen asked me to remember was my *magenahr*. When we were finished, I was unsettled from reliving the turmoil of the attack that led to Ambrose's death and the deaths of the eight men who attacked me. For his part, Olen was clearly exhausted from his exertions, his face strained and pale with dark smudges under his eyes. He looked as troubled as I felt.

"I could use some water," he said.

"I could, too," I answered. "You look exhausted. I'll go get some for both of us."

"Lauren," he said, stopping me. "I did see some things. I believe that the king and the chamberlain should hear them. How do you feel about that."

"I'll bring them when I return," I answered.

"May I examine the sword while you are gone?" he asked.

His eyes widened when I touched the hilt and the great pommel stone lit from within. I drew the sword and handed it to him hilt first. When I released it, the stone went dark again. He looked from it to me and then back again.

I returned a few moments later with a clay pitcher of water and two tin cups. Alain and Jaret were close behind me. Olen was slouching in his chair with *Endolsar* laying across his knees, his eyes closed. As we approached, he opened his eyes and sat up straighter. When he saw Alain, he started to rise, but the king gestured that he could remain seated.

As Alain and Jaret took seats, I poured out two cups of water and handed one to Olen. The wizard nodded his thanks and took a sip, paused, and then drank down half the cup.

"Lauren, would you mind taking back your sword?" he asked.

I retrieved *Endolsar* from his lap and slipped it into the sheath on my right hip. Then I sat and sipped my own water.

"That is a curious artifact," the wizard said. "I sense no magic in it, but I cannot understand how the stone does that.

"You on the other hand," he said, raising his cup in my direction, "I am certain that you do have some sort of power. Whatever it is, though, it is nothing like the powers that wizards possess. At your *magenahr*, Crom and I both thought we sensed something, but when we looked more closely, we saw nothing.

"Each time that your power has manifested," he continued, "it has done so on its own, somewhat like a reflex. There was no conscious intent on your part. What I could not determine from examining your memories is whether you could ever call it up intentionally."

He paused there to take several sips from his cup.

"I could try to teach you in the same way that we train wizards, but I do not know how effective that would be. A master and a novice wizard might differ in knowledge and practice, but they share a common perception, they can both sense the same sort of potential within themselves. You and I do not share that common perception."

"I see," I said, somewhat disappointed. Some part of me had been hoping that the wizards could be of assistance.

"There is one other thing," Olen said. "You know the standing stone in the center of the city?"

We all nodded.

"A round ago it woke..." his voice trailed off and he turned a wide-eyed gaze to me.

"You were involved in that. I remember now. You were there when it woke."

"I was," I agreed, puzzled.

Olen sat in silent contemplation for a moment.

"Lauren, through your memories, I got a sense of your power. It is similar to the power of that stone."

"But you said that stone was a thing of Dark Magic," I said. "Even the *Eldar* find it unchancy. I'm not like that." I looked around at my three companions. "Am I?"

"I did not say that it was the same," the wizard reminded me. "I said similar. It is like..." He paused for a moment, obviously hunting for words. "It is like the difference between red and white wine. They are similar because they are both wine, but they are clearly different. Whatever power you possess is of the same kind as that of the stone, but also clearly different."

"What does that mean?" I asked. "Was there once someone else like me? Is there someone else like me? Did that person raise the stone? Is that why Lorrestian's visions were so confused: are there two people with the power he saw?"

Alain leaned forward and rested his elbows on his knees.

"Nothing in his writings would suggest that," he said. "And when he spoke to me of the *Endollin*, he spoke only of a single individual."

"I feel that I know the three of you," Jaret said. "I need to stop you before you get lost in a deeply academic discussion. We need to focus on the main point. We were hoping that Lauren would be our defense against the Keepers. From what I've heard you say, it sounds as if our best bet is to stand him in front of the gates and when the Keepers try to annihilate him, hope that his own power annihilates them instead."

"The wording is a little more prosaic than I would have used, but yes," Olen said.

Jaret looked around our group, fear and resignation visible in his expression.

"Then I do not know how we win this war, my friends," he said.

A light rain fell overnight. I broke my fast and then spent the first few hours of the morning working with Olen, using every method known to the wizards to reach out to my power.

After a time, Olen suggested, "Gesture when you attempt to invoke your power."

"Gesture?"

"Yes. Observe."

He turned to the doorway to the room where a curtain had been hung to offer some semblance of privacy. He held his staff with his left hand and moved his right hand as if he was pushing aside the curtain. Across the room, the curtain moved to one side and then dropped back.

"What gesture should I make?" I asked.

"There is no prescribed set of gestures," the wizard answered. "It depends on what you wish to do. It really comes down to whatever helps you conceptualize the action you wish to take and focus your power on making that action happen."

I tried to copy his action of moving the curtain. I used several gestures and tried to focus on calling up whatever power resided in me, but I could not sense within myself the things that wizards could sense within themselves. An hour or so later and quite frustrated, we decided to suspend our efforts and take a walk. We hoped that taking a break would allow us to clear our minds and, perhaps, conceive of an approach that would work. Our wandering took us to the top of the south wall, where we stopped and leaned on the parapet. After a time, I brought up something that had been troubling me.

"Olen, you said that the standing stone is a thing of Dark Magic..." I began.

"I did," he said, cutting me off. "I said that because that is what my Masters taught me. They were taught the same thing by their Masters and so on as far back as we have records. In the past moon, however, everything that I know has been turned topside down. The Keepers, Mar's servants that we have always believed were there to protect and guide us, have attacked and killed defenseless minstrels at Songhaven and are aiding the Kelmar in destroying the Federated Kingdoms. The Elves have returned and instead of oppressing us, they are aiding us in resisting the Kelmar. You have what behaves somewhat like a magic sword, but I can sense no magic in it, and you have powers that I can barely sense and that we can't access. I would not trust my understanding if I were you. For all I know, that stone could be the source of all that's good in this world."

I knew the bitter tone in his voice. I had used that same tone myself. It signaled a sense of worthlessness.

"Olen, this is hard for everyone," I said. "We are all outside the bounds of our knowledge. I very much appreciate your help and knowledge."

He was about to reply, but a cry came from the top of one of the watch towers.

"Riders from the south!"

The cry was picked up by others and within moments the wall was swarming with *Eldarin* soldiers who were rapidly stringing bows and taking up positions near caches of arrows that had been placed at intervals along the parapet.

Olen and I strained to see. At first, all we could make out was motion on the horizon, but soon we could clearly see that a mounted force was approaching.

"Is it the Kelmar?" Olen asked me.

"I do not believe so," I replied. "The first scouts to spot them reported that only the Keepers were mounted. The Kelmar soldiers were on foot. These must be the *Cadwynir* who were left behind to ambush the Kelmar in the Echi Pass."

My guess was supported by the fact that, within a few moments, the *Eldarin* archers all along the parapet were relaxing and unstringing their bows. Soon, Olen and I could make out the individual riders. Suddenly, Olen gave a gasp of surprise and turned to me.

"They're riding unicorns," he exclaimed.

I smiled.

"I made the same mistake when I first saw them," I told him. "The *Eldar* call their mounts *aynekahrn*. The horns are strapped on. I've been told that they can use them in battle, but I have yet to see that."

Below us, I heard Alain order the gates opened and soon the square inside the gate was filling with mounted *Cadwynir*. I tried to count them as they entered, but lost track after about thirty. Instead, I turned to look down into the square, just in time to see Iseabail hand the reins of her mount to another *Cadwynir* and follow Alain, Jaret, Pyrett, and Konne into the inn. Just before they entered, Alain stopped and scanned the crowd in the square. Then his gaze climbed the wall and found me. He pointed at me and then at Olen and gestured for us to join them.

By the time we reached the inn, Rolugh had joined the others as had General Oscon, the leader of Amersford's armies. All the seats were taken, so Olen and I stood against one wall along with two other men, one in the livery of the high king and one in the livery of Amersford. I recognized them both as messengers who had been shuttling back and forth between Amersford and the Alomar army.

Alain glanced around the room, noting each of the people present and nodded. Then he turned to Iseabail.

"Second Captain, your report please," he said.

"Yes, your Majesty," she replied. "As ordered, one hundred and sixty of us remained at the Echi Pass. We spent over a quarter moon gathering wood to block the north end of the pass. Three days ago, our fellows who had been shadowing the Kelmar joined us and reported that the Kelmar army was a day from our position. Two days ago, we arrayed ourselves on the heights above the pass. The Kelmar entered. When those at the head of their army encountered the barrier, we lit it using fire arrows and began firing on the soldiers in the pass."

She paused for a moment, a stricken expression on her face.

"It was pandemonium down in the defile," she said. "The Kelmar could not mount an effective defense. I take no pride in what we did."

"I understand, Second Captain," the king said. "You did your duty. As the one who ordered it, any shame attaches to me."

The Alomar leaders appeared surprised by that exchange. Though many of them had been interacting with the *Eldar* for almost half a moon, they had been taught from birth that the Elves were evil.

"My thanks to you, Your Majesty," Iseabail said softly. She paused for a moment before continuing. "We continued firing until the Keepers rode up from the end of the Kelmar column. Without warning, they brought down part of the west side of the pass. I lost a dozen of my people in the collapse. As you ordered, I called for a retreat then. We pushed to get here as quickly as possible."

"You did well, Iseabail," the king said. "How soon will the Kelmar arrive?"

"I believe that it will take them another quarter moon," she replied.

The meeting broke up then. Jaret sent the messengers on their way to report to the high king and Marc of Amersford. Iseabail and Pyrett left to see the *Cadwynir* settled, and their mounts cared for.

Five days later, the Alomar army arrived at Amersford.

CHAPTER THREE

Alain, Ryan, and I had just finished our morning meal and were preparing to visit the Healers to check on Malash when a messenger arrived from Jaret.

"Your Majesty," the man said, "Duke Jaret wishes to inform you that the high king's army has arrived at Amersford. They plan to pause to take a meal and reorganize for the crossing. The high king would like to meet with you at midday."

"I would be glad to meet with him then," Alain replied. "Did he say where he would like to meet?"

"He suggested the park in the center of *Aennsrhyd*, Sire," the man replied.

"I and my people will be there," the king said. "Please convey my agreement to the high king."

"I will, Your Majesty. I was also tasked with asking whether there would be an objection if the Alomar army began crossing the bridge as soon as they are prepared."

"None at all," Alain replied.

"My thanks to you, Your Majesty."

The man bowed and then mounted his horse. As he turned to go, the king turned to Ryan and me and said, "I am afraid that we shall have to forego our visit to the Healers. I need to speak with Konne and Pyrett to prepare for this meeting. I would like you two to be there when I meet with the Alomar kings."

Several hours later, we set out for the center of the city. The king was in the lead, with Jorith to his left as the standard bearer. The *Cadwynir* proudly carried the *Eldarin* banner, *El an Arastalon*, a gold star on a field of deepest blue. To my surprise, the king insisted that I walk to his right. Behind us came Konne, Pyrett, Ryan, and several messengers. A short while later, we were standing in the park. During our time in *Aennsrhyd*, off-duty *Eldar* had cleared away the vines and underbrush that had grown unchecked since the Great War, revealing raised flowerbeds and paved paths that had long been hidden. In many places, trees had taken root in the flowerbeds and their roots had broken down the stone borders. Throughout the park, the rounds of neglect had toppled statues which had then been covered by the wild growth. It was easy to see, however, that it wouldn't take long to make the park a beautiful place of peace and reflection again.

The main path through the park ran north and south. In the very center of the park, the path widened into a circular plaza surrounding a standing stone. That was where our meeting with the high king would occur. We arrived first and the king and the others stepped into the open space but, leery of the stone, I held back. The last time that I had been in *Aennsrhyd*, the stone had awakened as I passed near it.

I stood just outside the circle, considering the menhir. It was twice the height of a man, its mottled gray surface rough and pitted. That's how it appeared to the eyes. The stone had a presence, though, that was sensed outside the normal senses, a presence that had led ancient authors to admonish their readers to avoid touching it. That presence was muted somehow. It put me in mind of a bright light seen through a heavy curtain.

"Lauren, are you well?" Ryan asked, his hand on my shoulder, breaking me out of my silent contemplation.

I shook my head to break my attention free of the stone's presence.

"I'm fine," I replied. "I was just remembering the last time we were here."

He nodded and glanced toward the stone.

"The high king's party is approaching. You'll need to join us, but I'd stay as far from the stone as you can."

"I agree with that," I replied.

Beyond the far end of the circle, I could make out the approaching party. Leading the group was High King Anders Sorren. On his right was a man I did not know carrying the high king's banner: the golden eagle of the Alomar high king, wings spread, outlined in deep green against a field of vertical stripes–indigo, pale blue, yellow, red, sky blue, and black–that each represented one of the Federated Kingdoms. On the king's left was my father, Dalach, son of Egan and War Duke of the Federated Kingdoms of Alomar. As they got closer, I could make out the people behind them. Marc, King of Amersford, was there with Jaret and Olen. I also recognized Roth, King of Canim and Moireach, the Queen of Marsden Forge. Roth's arm was in a sling. The other man with them had to be Marwynn, the king of Landfall. I had never seen the king of Landfall before. He was taller than anyone else in the high king's contingent with a lean, but not thin, build. He had a narrow, pointed face dominated by a long prominent nose. His salt-and-pepper hair was unbound and shoulder length and matched his beard. Even from a distance, I could make out the intense blue of his eyes, shaded under huge, bushy eyebrows. Behind the kings were several people that I recognized as messengers.

We walked forward to meet them halfway round the circle. The two groups stopped with Alain and Anders some five feet from each other. I saw the high king and his party take in the *Eldarin* banner. For a moment, no one spoke. The only sounds were the calls of birds in the trees, the buzzing of cicadas, and the gentle flapping of the banners in the breeze.

It was Alain who broke the silence. With his hands spread wide in welcome and well away from his sword hilt, he took a single step forward and said, "High King Anders Sorren, greetings. I am Alain, son of Lorrestian and King of the *Eldar*. *Selé il manana tul seli navoram.* We are honored by your presence."

"King Alain, son of Lorrestian, my thanks to you for your kind words," Anders replied. "I would like to reply in kind, but there is a great deal of history between your people and mine. We have much to discuss. The aid you have rendered so far says much in your favor. Set against that, however, is the fact that you come into my presence in the company of the man wanted for my father's murder."

Before Alain could reply, my father stepped forward.

"Your Majesty, may I speak to that charge?"

Anders turned to him.

"I believe that I know what you will say, War Duke. You do not believe that your son is guilty. That is what I would expect a father to say of his son."

"Sire, that is true, but I beg your indulgence for a moment."

Anders stood regarding him for a moment. The contrast between them was striking. They were of a height with one another, but the high king was slim, with long light brown hair and startlingly blue eyes. My father was broad-shouldered with arms that would not have been out of place on a blacksmith and with short black hair liberally salted with gray.

"Your service to me has earned that much," the high king replied. "Say what you have to say."

"Does it matter?" Marc said before my father could speak. "We know that the Lawbreaker killed your father, and the plan was to kill you as well so that snake Larsen could take the throne. Ambrose himself named Lauren the Lawbreaker. I was there. He said it to me. What more is there to say?"

My father's eyes narrowed, and he glared at Marc for a moment and then said, "Sire, you and I were both there. If Lauren had wanted you dead, all he would have had to do was stand still. Larsen would have killed you."

"True," Anders admitted. "But what about my father?"

"Sire, I have spoken with many people who were in the throne room that morning. They all agree in their reports. I do not seek to cause you pain, but if you would, recall the morning of your father's murder. Focus particularly on the figure in black and its actions."

A flicker of anguish flashed across the high king's face.

"Very well, War Duke, but I am unsure what this will accomplish. My indulgence will extend only so far."

"Bear with me, Sire," my father responded. Then he turned to me.

"Lauren, I see that you bear a sword," he said. He stepped between me and the high king and drew his own weapon. "Son, I want you to draw your sword but know that if you take even one step toward the king, I will strike you."

I nodded my understanding and carefully reached down and wrapped my left hand around the hilt of *Endolsar*. There were exclamations of surprise from the high king's party when the great pommel stone woke to my touch. I slowly drew the sword from its scabbard and held it with the point aimed at the ground. Then I froze and directed my gaze toward my father.

He nodded and turned to Anders.

"Do you see it, Sire?"

Anders looked from me to my father, a puzzled frown on his face.

"Compare what you see before you," my father said, pointing at me, "to the image in your mind."

Anders examined me, still frowning. Then comprehension lit his eyes, and he saw what my father was driving at.

"Lauren is left-handed," he said. "The figure in black was right-handed."

"Aye," was my father's only response.

The high king looked my way.

"Lauren, it was not you after all. I am glad to confirm that it was not you who murdered my father. It has been greatly troubling to me to believe that Ambrose could have so badly misjudged you all those years. Still, you do bear the tokens of the Lawbreaker."

That last came out as something between an observation and a question.

"Your Majesty," I replied. "I have learned a great deal since I last saw you. The original text of *The Book of Kings* used the word *endollin*. That word is a contranym that can mean either lawbreaker or lawgiver. Whatever scribe made the Alomar copies did not reflect that subtlety in the transcription."

"I will rescind the reward for your capture," Anders said after a moment's consideration. "Now, if you and your father will sheath your weapons, King Alain and I have much to discuss."

My father stepped across the distance between us as I returned *Endolsar* to its scabbard.

"You know how to use that?" he asked.

"I have worked out which end to point at the bad guys," I answered and smiled.

"He's much better than that," Pyrett said, joining us.

I hadn't heard her approach. My father looked at her, his expression guarded. They nodded to one another, their practiced eyes scanning the other and recognizing a kindred spirit.

"Father, this is Pyrett, Captain of the *Cadwynir*. You would call them the Elven Rangers. Pyrett, this is my father, Dalach, War Duke of the Federated Kingdoms."

"*Se en manana tul seli navoram*," she said. "I am honored by your presence. I have heard much about you, War Duke."

"So, you finally convinced my son to train," my father said, his tone neutral. He was clearly sizing her up, wondering what means of persuasion had been used. Like all the *Eldar*, Pyrett was beautiful.

"Nay," she responded. "There was no persuasion required on my part. Lauren requested training from the king when he felt that training was needed. I volunteered."

Just then, the kings called out to us, summoning us to their discussion. Anders began by introducing everyone in his party. Alain, in turn, introduced all the *Eldar*. Anders then turned to my father.

"Dalach, would you summarize the progress of the war thus far?" he asked.

My father stepped into the space between the groups and turned so that he could address both at once.

"As you all know, the Kelmar first attacked Han eight moons ago. We have no solid information concerning affairs in the Empire, so the attack was a surprise."

"If I may," Alain said. "Why is there no information from inside the Empire. Do you not have spies?"

Anders shook his head.

"Every spy that we've sent into Kelmar territory has vanished and we've never heard from them again," he answered.

"The Kelmar must be very good at identifying outsiders," Roth said.

"Or things are simply so much better there that our people choose to stay," Marwynn replied. "They do live with the goddess."

"That is not consistent with what we have learned," Jaret said then. Everyone turned to him. "The *Eldar* captured a Kelmar scout," he explained. "He has told us a great deal about affairs in the Empire. It is no paradise."

Alain nodded and Anders said, "Please continue, War Duke."

"As I said, the Kelmar attacked Han eight moons ago. Following a brief assault on the walls, they simply stopped. They would not accept a parley, but they also didn't leave. Instead, they steadily increased the size of the force camped in the pass. We know now that their purpose was to draw our forces north. In that, they succeeded. They gave us the time to move almost all our forces north and we obliged them. Then, a moon ago, they attacked Han in earnest. With the support of the Keepers, they breached the outer gates and, within less than an hour, the inner gates. We fled the city, hoping to stand at Badon, but..."

"My apologies, Father, Your Majesties," I said, with a slight bow to each. "What news of Houl of Han? I do not see him here."

A look of sadness flashed across Anders' face.

"Houl fell defending the inner gates of Han," he said. "Reports say that his son Mihangel took command of Han's army after that, but I've heard nothing more. None of Houl's family made it out of the city. I am sorry. I know that you were close to them."

"I didn't really know anyone but Pegara," I said, my voice strained. "I lost her in the attack on Songhaven. I once met Steafán in Badon when he was a member of your Guard."

Everyone was silent for a long moment.

"Many of us have cause to grieve," Anders said, looking around at everyone. "I wish we could do so properly, but we must focus on what is to come. Dalach, please continue."

My father resumed his summary of the war, recounting the fall of Badon and Canim. When he finished, Alain asked, "What of Meren and Marsden Forge?"

"We do not know the situation in Meren with any certainty," Anders answered. "Larsen is dead, and the bulk of his army is with us. Larsen was plotting with the Kelmar, though, so I think it prudent to assume that sympathizers are in control of the city."

Moireach stepped forward then. She was even thinner than I remembered. Her formerly close-cropped black hair was longer and shaggy, and the strain of the last few moons had etched lines into her young face.

"The Kelmar seem to have bypassed Marsden Forge," she said. "I suspect that they do not see it as an easy target. The city itself is not walled as are Han and Badon. Our defensive plan has always been to retreat into the mines. There are large caches of weapons and food hidden deep below ground and no one knows the mines as well as we do. It would be no simple matter to assault my people."

Alain nodded his understanding, and the conversation then turned to tactics and strategy. There was still a great deal of wariness on both sides and the conversation was careful, stilted, and—to my mind—overly polite. My attention soon began to wander. At first, I was wrapped up in memories of Peg, but then I drifted into wistful thoughts of Élan. After a time, something else began to intrude on my consciousness: the warped version of the *Arimë Daelyr* that I had been hearing in my sleep. I glanced around the group; no one else seemed to notice anything unusual. What I was hearing was not like the music I'd heard before, the ethereal inner music that had guided me to the dragon's cave, though I did seem to be the only one hearing it. Whatever it was, it was coming from outside me and the source was nearby. From deep within me came a flicker of emotion, mine and yet somehow alien. The music *offended* me. I slowly turned, seeking the source of that discordant tune.

I came to a stop facing the stone. It was the source of that ill-sounding song, but somehow so was whatever it was that muted it. I did not understand what I was sensing. Without realizing it, I began to drift slowly toward the stone, studying it intently, trying to understand. I came to a stop an arm's length from the stone, every nerve in my body jangling and irritated by its twisted music. Overhead, there was a long, growling roll of thunder, but I was only dimly aware of it.

I thought I could hear people calling my name, but they seemed to come from far away and that alien something inside me was driving my actions. I stretched out my left hand toward the stone, fingers spread and palm out. I encountered resistance a handspan from the stone, as if some invisible cushion lay between me and its surface. The thing inside me coiled and released, flowed up from my core and out my arm and pushed my hand forward into that invisible layer which suddenly shattered, falling away like shards of crystal. At the same instant, the thunder overhead reached a deafening climax that reverberated deep in my bones and echoed for long moments. I felt something like a silent explosion, and some force, some essence that had been bound suddenly ran free. My palm touched the pitted surface of the stone, and I sensed Mar's dark presence, her malevolence and something new: absolute panic. Then some force pushed me away from the stone, and I became aware of my surroundings again.

Behind me, I heard a confused babble of voices. I turned around and found my father, Pyrett, and Konne facing me, swords drawn. Behind them, Alain and Anders were staring at me, their mouths open in shock and surprise. Indeed, everyone in the plaza was staring at me, with one exception. Olen forced his way through the crowd and pushed past the warriors.

"What did you do?" he asked, his voice tinged with awe and wonder.

I shrugged, struggling to find words.

"I can..." Olen started and then stopped, at a loss for words himself.

"I have always been gifted at levitation," he said, "but even at my best, I could never lift more than a single iron coin, and that only with great effort and concentration. Now..."

He lifted his staff, and intense blue-white light flared along its length. I felt a lurch and found myself floating two feet above the ground. Olen lowered his staff, and the light died away. I dropped to the ground and stumbled forward.

"My apologies," Olen said. "I have never lifted anything so large as a person before. I could not. Lauren, what did you do?"

"I'm not sure," I replied. "There was some..." I shut my eyes in an effort to retain my perceptions while I searched for the words to describe them. "There was some binding on the stone. I pushed at it, and it broke."

Olen stood lost in thought. The warriors, convinced that there was no imminent threat to the kings, sheathed their swords. Alain and Anders stepped around them.

"What has happened?" the high king demanded.

"I am not sure," I answered.

"Nor am I," Olen said. "However, I now have access to a source of power that was not available to me before."

"Dark Magic?" Anders asked.

"I do not believe so, Sire," Olen replied. "What I feel is more an amplification of talents that I already possessed." He paused for a moment, his brows furrowed in concentration. "No. I believe Lauren's description was apt. My power was bound. It has now been freed. As I said a moment ago, I have always been gifted at levitation, but I can now lift much more than I ever could before. On the other hand, I have never been particularly skilled at casting glamours, and I do not feel that my ability to do so has increased."

"Rolf," Anders called over his shoulder.

One of the messengers stepped forward. "Yes, Your Majesty?"

"Go to the Wizard's House," the king said. "Find out if the others have experienced this increase in their powers."

"At once, Sire," the man replied and strode off.

Anders scanned the rest of the people crowding around us.

"We all heard the thunder and felt the... the... whatever that was. Did anyone else experience what Olen did?"

No one said anything for a moment. Then Alain spoke up.

"At the moment of the change, I felt a surge of energy," he said. "I feel invigorated, stronger and more alive than I have in many hundreds of rounds of the seasons."

"As do I," Pyrett added.

"I do as well," Ryan said. The other *Eldar* all nodded their agreement.

"I do not know what to make of this," Anders said. "Olen, this seems more a matter of magic than anything else. Do you have anything to say? Is there any guidance you can offer?"

"Your Majesty," the wizard replied, "I do not understand what has happened here. I might be able to say more after I've had an opportunity to confer with my colleagues. I do believe that if the other wizards have experienced the same thing that I have, we may be able to offer more in terms of opposing the Kelmar."

"Such aid would be welcome," Anders said. "Olen, please go meet with the other wizards. Let us know as soon as you can if your magic can aid us. For now, we need to plan as if such aid is not available."

"I will return as soon as I have an answer, Your Majesty."

Olen bowed and hurried off. Anders turned back to the rest of us.

"War Duke, what is the state of our plans?"

"Your Majesty," my father began, "even with the Elves..." He glanced at Alain and then started again. "Even with the *Eldar*, we are greatly outnumbered. In addition, the Keepers are with the Kelmar. In the assault on each city, the Kelmar troops have executed the first wave of the attack. If that does not prove to be successful–and it usually does not due to their inferior weapons and training–the Keepers step in and use their powers to blast down the gates. At that point, even with inferior weapons, the sheer numbers of the Kelmar overwhelm us.

"Because of that, we know that we cannot stand at Amersford. We have known that since Badon fell. We're already moving our army across the bridge and we're sending them west. The plan is to leave one hundred archers on the north wall of Amersford. We ask that the *Eldar* leave an equal number on the south wall of *Aennsrhyd*. The archers will hold off the initial assault for as long as they can, giving the main bulk of the army time to get further west. Our plan is to make our stand on the west end of the Dergun Causeway. They cannot come at us through the marsh and the causeway is only wide enough for five men side by side, so it will limit the impact of their greater numbers. Further, they will be strung out along the causeway which will leave them vulnerable to our archers."

"Speaking of archers, what of the ones we will be leaving in Amersford and *Aennsrhyd*?" Pyrett asked.

"We have ships enough to carry them all waiting at the wharf," my father answered. "The archers will hold off the Kelmar until it appears that the Keepers are going to engage. At that point, they will flee to the docks and take the ships downriver. They'll meet us west of the marsh."

"I cannot help believing that all of this is simply delaying the inevitable," Konne said.

"Konne?" Alain asked, turning to the leader of the *Eldarin* army.

"Your Majesty, by the time we stop to give battle, our forces will be beyond fatigued," Konne explained. "This plan might buy us some time but given their superior numbers and the power of the Keepers, we will eventually fall. I am not convinced that we could not last just as long–or longer–here where there are walls to protect us."

Alain looked at my father, but it was Anders who answered.

"Time may be all we need," he said. "Several moons ago, I sent a representative to Altiera asking for their aid. Their forces should be arriving in Landfall at about the time that we reach the western side of the marsh. We just need to hold out there until they join us."

"Reinforcements would change the calculations," Konne admitted.

"We also have the *aynekahrn*," Pyrett said. "They are quite hardy and exceedingly fast. We could use them to strike at the edges of the Kelmar army. If we were lucky, we might even take out some of their supply wagons. I doubt that we could do any significant damage, but we might slow them down." She paused, a thoughtful look on her face. "Are there any likely ambush spots ahead?"

"There is no likely place before the marsh," my father answered. "The Harbor Turnpike runs arrow straight from here to Landfall. The terrain is relatively flat and there are no significant forests or woods that straddle the roadway. Harrying the Kelmar with mounted troops is a good tactic, but I'm afraid we won't be ambushing them."

"I believe that we have covered the foreseeable eventualities," Anders said. "Would you agree Alain?"

At the use of his name, Alain looked up and smiled.

"I believe that we have, Anders," he replied.

"Then we should go," Anders said. "We need to be out of town as soon as possible. We believe that the Kelmar will reach here sometime tomorrow morning. The bigger a head start that we get, the better."

"As you say," Alain said and turned to go.

An hour later, I was in the stables checking on the well-being of my *aynekahrn, Yrtenstal.* I heard a boot scuff the ground behind me and turned to find my father standing there. His left hand was resting on the pommel of his sword in a relaxed pose, but he seemed anything but relaxed. The corners of his mouth were down, his eyebrows raised, and he was looking anywhere except directly at me. I had the decided impression that he was embarrassed. For a moment, neither of us spoke.

"You stood up for me with the high king," I said finally. "My thanks to you for that."

"You are my son," he replied.

I tried to smile, but I could feel the expression go awry. I remembered all too clearly the night that we had parted. I could still see his face, twisted in a drunken rage. He had struck his sister—my foster mother—and tried to kill me. He must have seen some of what I was thinking in my expression.

"It was the alcohol," he said haltingly, the first time I'd ever heard him speak that way. "But that's no excuse. What happened..." He faltered for a moment. "What happened that night should never have happened, even if I was drunk." He paused, his eyes on the ground. "I'm sorry. And I'm proud of you, Lauren. I kept track of you after you left. I figured that you would end up at Songhaven. I asked any minstrel that I encountered for word of you."

He raised his head, and his eyes finally met mine.

"You inspired me," he continued. "You left home with nothing and went to do what you really wanted to do. That gave me the courage to do the same myself. I haven't had a drink since you left. I dried myself out, went back to Badon and offered Aerman Sorren my sword. I would have been happy as a foot soldier, but he gave me back my position."

He was looking at me expectantly, but I didn't know how to respond to his version of my leaving. I hadn't really chosen to leave Cresswell; I was driven out. After a moment, his gaze flicked past me to my mount.

"Are those as fast as I've been told they are?" he asked, indicating *Yrtenstal* with his chin.

"I suppose," I answered. "Most of my riding experience has been on minstrels' horses. They're bred for endurance, not for speed. I did once ride the high king's post horses. The *aynekahrn* are much faster than that."

He nodded.

"I've been working with the Elves on a plan to hit the Kelmar. We'd like to take out some of their supply wagons. That would slow them down a bit."

"If it can be done, the *Eldar* will do it," I told him.

He gave me an odd look, as if I'd said something unintelligible.

"What?" I asked.

"I've heard them talking," he answered. "The Elves. I've heard them speaking the Alomar tongue with some of our people. They say that you're our only hope."

"I've heard the same thing from them," I replied. "They're here because they believe it."

"Is there anything you can do?"

I thought about everything I'd been told, everything I'd read. The dragon's words came back to me.

"I was told that the world is at stake," I said. "That terrible things could happen. I think they've already begun. I was told that I am the only one who can stop them."

"Can you?"

"I don't know," I answered. "I'll try. But I was also told that I will either save the world or destroy it."

That last statement hung in the air between us for several heartbeats.

"The last of the Alomar troops and the Elves are leaving now," he said. "I have to ride out with them to scout opportunities to delay the Kelmar. Stay safe, son." Then he turned and strode off.

That evening, I rode out of *Aennsrhyd* with Alain and Anders. We were headed to a small copse on the south bank of the Amer River that would offer concealment and provide a vantage point from which we could see both Amersford and *Aennsrhyd*. Each of the kings had brought ten of their personal guard with them. Ryan had joined us as well.

Scouts had come to Amersford bringing word that the Kelmar army would reach the city the next morning. Most of our forces had departed for the Dergun Marsh earlier in the day, but both kings wished to see what we were up against. And so, we were camped under a group of oaks on the riverbank. We were all clad in dull green to better conceal ourselves and we carried no banners. All of us were alert for any signs that Kelmar scouts were nearby.

The night passed quietly. We rose before the sun and broke our fast with cold biscuits and dried meat. The world was hushed; the nightbirds had gone to roost and the day birds were not yet about. Thin pockets of mist hung over the river. We sat silent and tense, some of us looking north to the far bank and the approach to Amersford, the rest south and the approach to *Aennsrhyd*.

The sun peeked above the eastern horizon in a blaze of red, foretelling a storm. By the time it was clear of the horizon, the mist over the river had dissipated. We strained our eyes peering into the growing light trying to catch sight of the approaching armies.

Ryan spotted them first. To my human eyes, the Kelmar army was nothing but a faint dark smudge on the northern horizon. Within an hour the leading edge of the horde was outside the gates of Amersford. I still could not see them as anything but a dark mass, but the keen-sighted *Eldar* could make out movement as the Kelmar soldiers took up their positions, though they could not make out the individuals. As we watched, the dark mass before the city gates grew.

"*Melse*," Alain said as the size of the Kelmar army became clear. I did not know that word, but from his intonation and the looks he got from the other *Eldar*, it was vulgar. I'd never heard him swear before that.

The approach of the southern force was spotted by Alain. Though we were closer to *Aennsrhyd*, I still could not make out individuals, but I could easily see the Kelmar army advance like a dark tide over the plain before the city gates. The flow stopped at a point that I surmised was just out of bowshot from the walls, but the crowd grew larger every moment as the Kelmar moved into position. The morning birds had gone silent and even the faint gurgling of the river seemed to fade away.

Then a flare went up from the northern Kelmar army. It streaked up into the sky trailing a plume of reddish smoke and exploded into dozens of brilliant crimson stars that drifted slowly down. Almost immediately, an answering flare rose over the southern force. Even from our distance, we could hear the battle cry that rose from the Kelmar forces as they surged forward. The assault had clearly begun.

"It is time we were away," Alain said quietly.

Anders nodded and we made our way to our mounts. Because the need for speed was so great, the *Eldar* had provided *aynekahrn* for everyone in our party. Within moments, we were galloping west as quickly as our mounts could run.

Once out of sight of the Twin Cities, we slowed the *aynekahrn* to a trot. Between the Corun Hills and the Amer River, the land was rolling and hilly and for the most part was covered in waist-high grass. There were few trees, but outcroppings of rock jutted out from the ground, islands of weathered gray afloat on a waving sea of green. At intervals, meandering streams flowed down from the hills to the river. The Harbor Turnpike, however, ran straight through the hilly terrain with minimal grades. The massive effort expended to construct the cuts and fills necessary to level the road was mute testimony to the builders' intent to make travel as easy as possible.

Somewhat over two hours later, we caught up with the combined army. After some searching, we found the leaders deep in conversation where the road crossed a shallow steam on a double arched stone culvert. Pyrett was scrambling up the slope from down below.

"Your Majesties," she said by way of acknowledgement, with a slight bow to each. Then she turned back to the rest of the group, which consisted of my father, several of the petty kings, and Konne. "We are fortunate that it has been a dry spring so far. The stream is only a few inches deep at most. Judging by the staining on the arches, if we'd had significant rain, it would be too deep for us to use."

"Use how?" Alain asked.

"The arches are high enough for mounted riders to shelter underneath them," the *Cadwynir* Captain explained. "I believe that four riders could conceal themselves under each arch. Three of each will be equipped with fire arrows. The fourth will hold a torch to light the arrows. They will wait for the Kelmar army to pass and then ride out, four on each side of the road, to try and set fire to as many supply wagons as possible. Because the Kelmar are not mounted, they should not be able to give chase."

"Do you expect to do much damage?" Anders asked.

"Perhaps not," my father replied. "It depends on how prepared they are to douse fires. They should not be expecting it, though. So far, we have not taken a single offensive action against them, and we have only tried to stand against them from behind city walls. If nothing else, it may force them to be more cautious and that will slow them down."

"It is the best we have so far," Konne added. "From here to the marsh there is little cover from which to stage a more effective ambush."

Anders nodded.

"Very well," he said. "Proceed. We'll be up ahead."

I spent the rest of the day riding at the head of the army with Anders and Alain. We halted for the day just as the sun dropped below the western horizon. After we ate the evening meal, I spent an hour or so working with Olen and several other wizards trying to unlock whatever power I possessed. I was anxious; the time was approaching when I would have to face Mar and the Keepers. For their part, the wizards were distracted; they had left behind colleagues who would try to reinforce the gates of the cities with their newly enhanced powers. The mind speech of those colleagues had fallen silent when the flares went up and they had not been heard from since. Not surprisingly, our efforts to access my power were unsuccessful.

It was fully dark when I finished with the wizards, so I laid down and tried to sleep. I couldn't get comfortable, though, and my mind wouldn't quiet. My father's questions echoed in my thoughts: was there anything I could do? Could I stop the terrible things that Lorrestian had seen? It occurred to me that Ambrose had also seen several possible dark futures after Aerman Sorren had been murdered. Haunted by his memory and afraid of what was to come, I finally rose and sat staring into the fire.

Something about my expression must have told people to leave me to myself; no one approached me though several people obviously noticed me sitting there.

The first quarter moon hung just above the horizon and the middle of the night was approaching when sentries heard riders approaching from the east. Anders and Alain were roused and went to meet the riders. I wasn't asked to accompany them, but I trailed along behind them. We had left eight *Cadwynir* to attack the Kelmar supply wagons, but I counted nine as the riders entered the circle of firelight. Iseabail had been in command of the party, and she was smiling widely as they dismounted.

"I take it that your mission was successful," Alain said.

"It was, Your Majesty," she answered. "At least a dozen Kelmar supply wagons were stuck by multiple fire arrows and were burning well when we had to break off our attack. Another three or four were hit by only one or two arrows and could possibly have been saved after we left."

"Excellent work, Second Captain" the king replied.

"Yes, well done," Anders agreed. Then he glanced toward the other riders. "Second Captain, I see that you have returned with more people than you started out with."

"We have, indeed, Your Majesty," she said. "We came across an Alomar scout who was returning and offered him our company. I believe that he has something interesting to report."

"I do, indeed, Your Majesty," the man said, stepping forward. He was dressed in a green and brown tunic with dark green trousers, sweat stained and covered in dust from the road. "My name is Trost, Your Majesty. I was assigned to observe the attack on *Aennsrhyd* and then to shadow the Kelmar after they left the city. I did so until early this afternoon."

Anders nodded his understanding.

"I was north of *Aennsrhyd* when the Kelmar crossed the bridge. Unlike our troops, the Kelmar marched through the city. I circled around outside the walls to observe them as they exited. That's when I noticed that the Keepers were no longer with them."

"The Keepers were no longer with them?" Anders asked in surprise.

"No, Majesty. I saw five of them cross the bridge into *Aennsrhyd*, but none of them left the city."

Anders and Alain traded glances.

"That is odd," the *Eldarin* king said.

"It is, indeed," Anders agreed. "You are sure of this, Trost?"

"I am, Sire. As I said, I shadowed them until this afternoon so that I could be certain. The Keepers were the only ones in the Kelmar army to ever be mounted. Unless they decided to walk, they were not there."

"Thank you, Trost," Anders said. "I am sure that you would welcome some food and rest. We will not keep you from them. You have our thanks."

"My thanks to you, Your Majesty."

Trost bowed and left. The kings began debriefing Iseabail, asking about all the details of her mission. I returned to my spot and wrapped myself in my blanket.

I was on the stage at Songhaven. Peg was there, lying on her back, her face streaked with soot and sweat. Flames were everywhere. Her eyes were closed, and she was trying not to cry out, but the flames tore a sound out of her, a deep, animal groan of pain and anguish. My heart shattered; I was there, I could see and hear her, but I was powerless to help her...

I woke with tears streaming down my face. The nearby fire had been banked, and the night was quiet. All around me I heard the quiet rustlings of sleeping soldiers. The man nearest me was breathing heavily, not quite a snore, but close. On the edge of the camp, a horse blew quietly and another nickered. Overhead, the stars were cold and remote. I found myself remembering my first trip away from Cresswell. I had seen eyes in the stars then, had heard them speak to me. I looked for them now, but there was no one there. I was still awake when dawn came.

It took us nearly three quarters of a moon to reach the Dergun Marsh. The Kelmar somehow managed to stay only a day behind us the entire way. The attack at the culvert had not slowed them down significantly; their scouts simply stayed farther out in front of the main body of their army. At random intervals, usually at night, *Eldarin* soldiers mounted on *aynekahrn* attacked the fringes of the Kelmar camps. We'd lost over a dozen people in those raids and a similar number were confined to the Healer's wagons with serious wounds. None of it slowed the Kelmar.

When we stopped and made camp in the evening, I spent time either sparring with Pyrett or working with the wizards. Then I'd roll myself up in my blanket and try to sleep. But I couldn't sleep. As soon as I laid down, I became acutely aware of every tiny pebble or root beneath me, every faint sound from the people near me. At the same time, my mind was racing, replaying every lesson from the wizards along with everything I had ever read about the *Endollin* and the coming confrontation with Mar. Lorrestian and Ambrose had both seen the world devasted, but neither had said whether that outcome arose from my failing to defeat Mar or from defeating her. She was a goddess. Was standing against her good or evil? I could find no answers.

After a time, I'd give up trying to sleep. I'd get up and sit staring at the fire, desiring sleep but unable to quiet my thoughts enough to rest. When I was finally exhausted enough to sleep, I'd drift off and I'd dream. At first, it was always the dream of Peg in the fire at Songhaven. Then, some nights, Élan would take Peg's place. Other times, I was alone in an endless dark, clutching the sword, knowing that somehow, I had ended the world and that all that remained was me and Lorrestian's ring and sword. I'd wake, sometimes crying, sometimes screaming. After the first few times, I began sleeping apart from everyone else to try and avoid disturbing them. Once I woke, I'd spend the rest of the night sitting up, staring up into the heavens, but even the North Star had no guidance for me.

Eventually, the lack of sleep took its toll. I became surly and irritable, and I began snapping at Pyrett and the wizards during our evening sessions. After a half moon, I was short with nearly everyone who interacted with me throughout the day and people began to avoid me. Several times I became aware of Ryan watching me, but I avoided him. I didn't want to hear what I knew he'd say.

The night before we were to reach the marsh, I was sitting by the fire, picking at my evening meal. My father approached from the other side of the fire and circled it to sit on my right side. He had what looked like a turkey leg in one hand. After a moment, he spoke.

"You're making my job harder."

I glanced at him but didn't answer.

"You're being an ass," he said, took a bite of his turkey leg, and continued with his mouth full. "You need to stop."

My exhaustion, my feelings of helplessness, my despair, and my anger toward him were dry tinder. His comment ignited them.

"And what do you know about it?" I demanded.

He finished chewing and swallowed before answering.

"I look at you and I see me from eight rounds ago. All you're missing is the bedamned ale pot."

He took another bite, watching me as he did. I started to respond, but memories of him from before I left Cresswell rose in my mind. He had a point.

"Lauren," he said. "You may not appreciate this, but you are the heart of this army. The Alomar were used to easily defeating Kelmar raiding parties, but then the Empire's whole army showed up with the Keepers–our supposed protectors–supporting them. No strategy that we have tried has worked. Even with the augmented power that you released, our wizards could not prevent the Keepers from blasting down the gates of Amersford. We just haven't been able to stand against them. Then the Elves showed up with you. They obviously believe in you; they've said that you're the only hope of standing against the Keepers. The Alomar are still wary of the Elves, but hope is a funny thing. It spread. When we set out from the Twin Cities, they all had faith in you. Now you're shaking that faith. In just a few days we have to stand against the Kelmar, and I need them to believe that we can win. An army convinced that it is going to lose will probably find a way to make that happen."

"But what if their hope is misplaced?" I asked. "We're going to stand against the Kelmar soon and I have no idea what to do."

"Neither do I," he said around another bite of turkey.

I glanced sharply at him, surprised, and he shrugged.

"I have a general idea of using the causeway to limit the effectiveness of the greater Kelmar numbers, but I haven't been to the site of the battle in over twenty rounds. And when I was there, I was simply riding through, not planning a battle. I won't be able to form a decent plan until I see what

I'm working with. All I can do is to prepare as best I can beforehand. That's what you've been doing. No one can do more."

"It's like preparing to perform," Ryan said quietly from behind us. I hadn't heard him approach. He sat down on my other side. "We can practice as much as we want beforehand, but I've never once played the exact set that I planned to play. I suspect that you haven't either."

"I haven't," I answered, just as quietly. I felt some of the fear and confusion dissipate. "My thanks to you both. A friend once told me that I was never alone. You've reminded me of that."

Ryan smiled. I turned to my father.

"Father, would you spar with me?"

He grinned and said, "On one condition."

"What?" I asked.

"When we're done, I'd like to hear you play."

Late in the afternoon of the next day, we reached the eastern edges of the Dergun Marsh. The marsh lay on either side of the Dergun River, which drained the basin that contained most of the northwestern section of the Elderwood. The exact course of the river and the depth of the water in the marsh changed depending on the season and the amount of rainfall and no reliable path across had ever been found. Even in the driest of conditions, mud was the most solid ground to be found, and the location of those mud islands shifted with the water levels and the strength of the flow. The marsh was populated by fish, birds, turtles, frogs, and several kinds of snakes, many of the later venomous. Larger animals could not find enough secure footing to survive, with one possible exception. Tales told of large reptiles that lived deep in the marsh; predators that could appear to be floating logs until prey came too close. Many people had drowned or been taken trying to find a way through.

As a result, the marsh was crossed in only one place: the Dergun Causeway. The causeway stretched a little over six miles across the width of the marsh and was in its own way as much a marvel as the Amersford Bridge. It was an ancient stone structure, a series of arched spans, some fifteen feet wide at the top, which was about seven feet above the surface of the water, depending on the season. There was a low stone wall on either side of the right of way, limiting the effective width to about eleven feet, just a little too narrow to allow two wagons heading in opposite directions to pass one another. Long ago, the Alomar had devised a system by which eastbound wagons crossed before midday and westbound after midday, but traders considered that restriction onerous and traffic eventually shifted to riverboats on the Amer. No one knew who built the Causeway. It was possible that the *Eldar* had constructed it when they first arrived at Landfall, but they had no record of doing so and it wasn't typical of their construction. It wasn't typical of Lost constructions either.

We set up camp about a mile from the east end of the causeway, hoping to avoid the attention of the mosquitoes and biting flies that lived in the marshlands. Ryan and I gave an impromptu concert and even though I still feared what was to come, I could sense a shift in the mood of the soldiers who heard us.

The next morning, as soon as it was light, we set out to cross the causeway. A mixed group of *Cadwynir* and Alomar scouts departed first, alert for possible ambush or trouble from the marsh. When they had covered about a mile, the kings–Alain, Anders, and the petty kings–set out, their banners flying side-by-side. Ryan and I rode with them, as did my father, Konne, and Pyrett.

The morning was cool, but not unpleasantly so, and the sky was clear. As the sun rose higher, I saw many different kinds of birds down amongst the cattails, sawgrass, and reeds. Within the first hour, I saw egrets, bitterns, cranes, several species of herons, redwing blackbirds, and an odd-looking bird with a red beak that Ryan said was called a swamphen. Riding close to the rail, I could see down into the water and the marsh was teeming with a multitude of fish. At one point, I saw the largest snapping turtle that I'd ever seen.

It took nearly an hour to cross the causeway, and we were halfway across when the mosquitoes and flies discovered us. The rest of the ride was spent swatting them, but despite our best efforts, we still ended up covered in red welts that itched almost as badly as the rash from poison ivy. I pitied those who followed us; they would be fighting the bugs the whole way across.

When we reached the western end of the causeway, the kings and the military leaders with them dismounted and began going over the lay of the land and making plans to engage the Kelmar. Ryan and I were somewhat at a loss for something to do until the first of the Healers' wagons reached us and the Healers began setting up their tents somewhat behind the proposed line of battle. Then he and I offered our help to care for those who had already been wounded.

In all of the combined army, the Healers were the first to let go of the ancient distrust between Alomar and *Eldar*. As a result, Ryan and I did not attract any particular attention when we walked into one of the Healers' tents together. An Alomar woman wearing a Healer's green sash approached us. The other Healer in the tent, a short, thin man, was working with an aide cleaning a wound.

"Is there something I can do for you?" the woman asked us.

"We have some knowledge of healing," Ryan answered. "We'd like to offer our assistance."

"Barth is cleaning an infected wound," she said, indicating the other Healer. "That's the only major issue just now. We could use help, though, changing bandages and checking on patients' progress."

"We would be pleased to help," Ryan said.

Ryan started in one corner of the tent, and I started in another. The first two people I saw had relatively minor injuries and were healing well. The third had been hit by a Kelmar arrow and I made sure to check the wound carefully for signs of infection. I had just finished placing a new bandage when someone behind me said, "Very nice work, Lauren."

I nodded to the person I'd been caring for and turned to find the young man who had been assisting Barth standing behind me.

"Do I know..." I started to say, and then my voice trailed off as I recognized him. "Malash?"

He smiled and nodded. He had filled out since his capture, and he no longer was the wary-eyed Kelmar scout he'd been when I first met him. His face was fuller, rounder; he was no longer gaunt and half-starved. He'd also shaved off his beard and adopted the Alomar style of dress.

"You've changed," I observed.

"I have left my people," he said. "I have given aid and comfort to Alomar and Elf, and I have questioned the teachings of the church and its leaders. They would say that I have turned my back on Mar and that I am no longer *kel Mar*. That would make me *alo Mar*."

"You don't seem particularly bothered by that."

For just an instant, the corners of his mouth tuned down and he blinked, as if fighting tears. Then he forced a neutral expression.

"I will miss my parents," he said. "Otherwise, I have nothing to return to. I have no wife, nor even the prospect of marriage and, as I've told you, nearly everything I had was taken for the church or the military. When I was conscripted, it saved me from starving."

I didn't know how to respond to that.

"Barth says that if we survive, he'll recommend me for training as a Healer. He says that I have the right instincts. That would be a good life, I think."

He looked around the tent, yearning clearly visible on his face.

"I hope that happens," I said.

He turned back to me.

"You can make it happen," he said quietly. "I have heard them talking. Save us, Lauren."

"Malash, I..." I started.

Just then Barth called from across the tent, "Malash, I can use your help here."

Malash shot me a pleading look and then hurried off, leaving me feeling flustered and speechless and unworthy of such confidence.

When I left the Healers' tent several hours later, the ground between it and the causeway had been transformed. We had been depleting our supplies and what was left had been consolidated, leaving many of our supply wagons empty. Those empty wagons had been turned on their sides in a wide arc around the foot of the causeway to provide cover for archers. Given how narrow the causeway was, a small number of soldiers–supported by archers–could hold out against the largest of armies.

I spent some time looking for Ryan but couldn't find him. No one I asked had seen him. The kings and the military leaders–including my father–were deep in planning; the Kelmar were expected to reach the east end of the causeway before nightfall. As a result, I ate the evening meal alone, though I was surrounded by Alomar and *Eldar* soldiers. Just as the sun set, one of the sentries who had remained at the east end of the causeway rode in to report that the Kelmar had arrived and were setting up camp.

I wandered around our camp, flitting from fire to fire like an earthbound moth. The tension was palpable; around each campfire the talk was a little too forced and the laughter a little too loud. Here and there I heard the quiet whisper of a whetstone on steel or a muttered prayer for protection. I found myself wondering which of those was going to be more effective.

I eventually found my way back to the tent I was sharing with Ryan. He wasn't there. I slipped my guitar out of its case and tried to play, but the music wouldn't come. I simply sat, fingering chords without strumming or wiping off specks of dust. I finally fingered an E chord and ran my thumb down the strings. The rich, full sound brought a sad smile to my lips, and I suddenly felt as if I was saying goodbye. The fear pent up in my heart ran free then and chilled my bones. We were going to face the Kelmar the next day and I still had no idea what to do.

About an hour later, Ryan came in. His eyes were downcast under drooping eyelids and the corners of his mouth were turned down. He saw me lying in my bedding staring at the canvas ceiling of the tent.

"You don't look happy," he said.

"Neither do you," I replied.

"I lost a friend today. I found him in one of the Healers' tents. He took an arrow in the shoulder during the raid several nights ago. It was early in the raid, so he just pulled it out and continued to fire at the Kelmar. By the time they got back, he'd lost a great deal of blood and literally fell out of his saddle. Then the wound festered."

He paused for a moment.

"I've known him since we were children."

I sat up.

"Ryan, I'm sorry."

He looked at me.

"How are you?" he asked.

For an instant, I considered telling him, but the grief evident on his face changed my mind.

"I'm fine," I said. "We should get some sleep."

Ryan undressed and snuffed out the candle. Soon, I heard him shift to the relaxed, deep breathing of a person asleep. I felt like I never got to sleep that night. I lay there in the darkness, unable to get comfortable, reviewing all the things that I had tried to unlock my power or to call power out of the ring or the sword, remembering that none of them had worked, and asking myself over and over if there was anything that I hadn't tried that might work. Then I'd tell myself that I needed to get some sleep, but the cycle would start again. Sometimes I'd become aware that I was dreaming and realize that I must have been asleep, but I still felt tense and unrested. When morning finally came, I was feeling groggy and exhausted. Before Ryan began to stir, I rose, dressed as quietly as I could, and then went looking for something to eat.

I had just finished a plateful of dried fruit and cheese when a ripple of excitement and concern washed through the camp. One of the sentries had just ridden in. A small group of mounted Kelmar were crossing the causeway under a parley banner.

CHAPTER FOUR

"H ow many?" Anders asked.

"Six, Your Majesty," the scout replied. "All of them mounted. The two in the lead are dressed as priests. Behind them is an older man carrying the parley banner. The other three appeared to be soldiers, but I saw no weapons."

The high king looked around our group: me, Alain, my father, Konne, and Pyrett.

"Thoughts," he asked?

"If they wish to talk, we should hear them," Alain said.

"In general, I agree," my father responded. "But I do not entirely trust this. They have not been willing to talk before now."

"I share your concern," Alain agreed. "We should be cautious."

"What do you suggest?" Anders asked.

"Let me get some of the archers in place," my father answered. "They can keep their bows down and out of sight but still be prepared to fire should it be necessary."

"That sounds reasonable," Anders said. "You'll need to be quick, though. They'll be in sight any moment now."

"Yes, Your Majesty," my father replied. He looked to Pyrett and nodded and together they strode off, shouting orders.

A short while later, the six of us were gathered at the foot of the causeway. We could make out riders in the distance. All eyes were on the Kelmar representatives as they approached. Within moments, we could discern the individual riders. Two of our sentries rode in the lead. Behind them came the two priests of Mar followed by an older man who was carrying the parley banner. He was followed by three men wearing Kelmar military uniforms. Several hundred feet from us, the Kelmar halted while the sentries continued forward until they reached us. They dismounted and one of them took the reins of both mounts and led them off to one side. The other came to us.

"Your Majesty," he said, bowing to Anders. "These Kelmar say that they wish to parley. We have searched them for weapons; they are not armed."

"My thanks to you," the high king replied. "We will hear them."

The sentry turned and motioned to the Kelmar. They dismounted and walked toward us. When they had covered half the distance between us and their mounts, they stopped and stood waiting. Anders looked at us, a questioning look on his face; he clearly had expected the Kelmar to come to us.

"Should we meet them halfway?" he asked.

"I mislike meeting them on the causeway," Alain responded. "Though there is some merit to the symbolism of meeting them halfway."

Anders nodded and started forward, the rest of us following. I took the opportunity to examine the Kelmar. I had never seen members of the Kelmar clergy before. Unlike the Alomar clergy, who were referred to collectively as the Repentant and who dressed exclusively in black, the Kelmar clergy were still in Mar's good graces and were considered the instruments of her will. Thus, they were referred to as the Hands of Mar or, simply, Hands. They were civil as well as religious leaders. The two leading the Kelmar delegation were so similar in appearance that they could almost have been twins, save that one had brown hair and the other black. They were of medium height and build. Their robes were the deep purple favored by Mar, edged at cuff and hem in black, and belted with a thin black cord with gold tassels. There were three black velvet stripes, edged in gold, on each sleeve. On their heads, the Hands wore purple mitres with black banding and, like all Kelmar men, the Hands wore neatly trimmed beards and mustaches. Each carried an ornate mace of carved wood, with a polished marble head.

Behind them came the banner carrier, a nondescript older man. Something about him seemed familiar, though as a Kelmar I would never have met him before. Almost as if he could sense my scrutiny, he turned his gaze to me but quickly looked away. As our eyes met, however, I got an impression of great age, a sense that he was far older than he appeared to be. My attention was diverted, however, when one of the Hands spoke.

"I am Bragin, Hand of Mar, and this is Valir, also Hand of Mar. We lead this host of the Kelmar, and we recognize that the situation here favors you. We do not wish to sacrifice lives needlessly. Will you treat with us?"

"I am Anders, son of Aerman, and high king of the Federated Kingdoms of the Alomar. We also do not wish to spend lives needlessly. We will hear what you propose."

I noticed that the banner carrier was now watching me. This time he did not look away when our eyes met. He was of average height and wore plain clothing, though the clothing did not fit him particularly well. The sense of familiarity grew, though I was sure that I had never seen his face before. I glanced at the high king and noticed that the Hands had slowly advanced as they spoke and the rest of my companions had retreated somewhat, so that I now stood behind the Kelmar leaders. Suddenly uneasy, I turned my attention back to the banner carrier and the parley banner he carried. The banner itself was a simple rectangle of plain yellow cloth. The pole it was mounted on, however, was quite ornate, made of some dark wood and shod with iron. In that instant, I knew him.

"Garth," I called out in warning, reaching for *Endolsar*, even as he jerked the parley banner from his staff and levelled it at me. I froze, suddenly unable to move.

The Keeper swung his staff to my left, toward the kings and I heard cries of alarm and confusion from that direction. He then turned to the three Kelmar soldiers.

"Seize him," he ordered, gesturing to me.

The three men swept me off my feet. As they lifted me, I got a quick glimpse of my companions on the other side of a wall of flame, then Garth touched his staff to my forehead, and everything went black.

Awareness returned slowly. At first, I was just a tiny point of awareness, floating in a vast void, lacking any bodily sensations. Slowly, light returned, and I became aware of my body, but I felt safe and warm. As I gradually eased back into myself, I became aware of an uncomfortable bump of some kind under the lower left part of my back and that my nose itched. I tried to scratch it, and my arm strained against some binding, and it all came flooding back...

I opened my eyes. In front of me was a stretch of canvas, clearly the wall of a tent, lit from behind by sunlight. I was lying on my back, and I couldn't move my arms or legs. By twisting my head around, I was able to see that I was tied down. Ropes across my chest, hips, knees, and ankles bound me to one wide, soot-stained plank and my wrists were bound to similar planks on either side, keeping my arms outstretched. The boards were angled so that my head was at about chest height and my feet nearly rested on the ground. I couldn't sense anyone nearby; I seemed to be alone in the tent.

I could hear the routine sounds of a camp outside, but no one entered. It grew warm in the tent and as it did, the smell of burning from the planks grew more pronounced, evoking memories of the attack on Songhaven. Sweat was running down my face into my eyes, but I couldn't wipe it away. Lying in one position was growing painful, especially with whatever was poking into my back, but I couldn't shift my position enough to relieve the pain.

I wasn't sure how long I had been unconscious, so I had no idea how long it had been since I had broken my fast. I was hurting enough, though, that I didn't feel hungry, but I grew thirsty, and I needed to urinate. I had no way to judge how much time was passing; all I could do was lie there with the smell of burning in my nose, trying not to think of Peg or the fullness of my bladder. Eventually, I had no choice, and I simply let go and the smell of urine mixed with the smell of burnt wood, and I fought down a gag.

I could hear sounds from outside the tent, distant conversations and the other daily sounds of a camp with an occasional shouted order. I had just noticed that the light shining through the canvas roof of the tent had dimmed somewhat and taken on a reddish hue–suggesting that evening was coming on–when I heard footsteps approaching from behind me. There was a rustling of canvas and Garth stepped into my view.

He was wearing a hooded robe of a blue very like the bright blue of a minstrel's sash, trimmed in black and belted with a black sash. Unlike the last time I had seen him–at the attack on the minstrels of Songhaven–his hood was down, and I got my first good look at him. His face was thin, with a sharply pointed chin and a large straight nose. His eyes were smokey green flecked with gold, like Ambrose's, and were full of power. His bushy eyebrows were grey, as were his beard and long hair, which was bound back with a leather tie. As he came to a stop in front of me, he sniffed conspicuously and then wrinkled his face at me in distaste.

"You are supposed to be civilized," he said, his tone soft, cultured, but subtly mocking. "I would have expected better.

"I hope that you do not find your accommodations too uncomfortable," he continued, tapping the bottom of one of the planks with the foot of his staff. "They were part of one of our wagons and I am afraid that they are a bit singed due to the hostile actions of your friends."

I noticed that he was not using the archaic speech forms he had used at Songhaven. He was speaking the Alomar tongue fluently, though his pronunciation and intonations were odd, ancient sounding. He waited expectantly for me to respond and, when I didn't, he frowned, stepped to my side, and reached behind me.

"Give that to me," he said to someone standing behind me.

When he stepped back into view, he was holding *Endolsar*. He slid the sword out of its sheath and examined it closely as he turned it back and forth.

"You attempted to attack me with this," he said. "Is this the fabled sword of the Lawbreaker?"

Again, I didn't respond, and I saw a quick flash of anger cross his face.

"Perhaps not," he said. "There is nothing special about this thing."

He sheathed the sword and tossed it to the floor in the corner.

"Perhaps the ring," he said. He looked behind me. "Remove it from his finger and give it to me."

A Kelmar soldier stepped into my view. The man attempted to remove the ring, but it did not come off.

"Relax your finger," the soldier ordered me.

"It is relaxed," I replied.

The soldier spent several minutes tugging at the ring and then turned to the Keeper.

"It will not come off, Your Holiness," he said.

Garth glared at me for a moment.

"Then remove his hand," he ordered the soldier.

Panic flared, clenching my gut, but then I remembered what had happened to Marc's soldiers.

"I wouldn't do that," I said to the man, my eyes locked on his.

He glanced at Garth, who simply nodded.

The soldier drew his sword. Even though I was sure that I knew what was going to happen, fear overwhelmed me, and I struggled against my bonds. He raised the sword and brought it down. I screamed, every muscle in my body tensed, and my eyes involuntarily closed. I felt some force explode out of me and for a brief instant it felt as if thousands of insects were crawling over my skin.

I heard a thud and then for a moment, there was no sound. I slowly opened my eyes. The soldier was lying on the ground, his eyes wide and unseeing and his limbs at odd angles. Garth was staring at the soldier, his eyes wide and his mouth open. He turned to me and took a nervous step back. He watched me for a moment and, when nothing happened, he frowned. Then he looked past me and called out, "Arkath, I need another soldier in here. Now."

A moment later, the tent flap rustled again and another Kelmar soldier stepped smartly into view. He hesitated when he saw his fallen comrade, but then he straightened and snapped out, "What is your will, Your Holiness?"

"This man is an enemy of Mar," Garth replied, pointing at me. "His very existence is an affront to the Goddess. He possesses a ring that he should not. Remove the hand with the ring."

The soldier turned to me, his face hard with anger. He drew his sword, never taking his eyes from my face. He raised his sword and shifted his gaze to my hand. He brought the sword down and the power erupted out of me again. The sword shattered. Gold fire engulfed the man, and he was flung back to land on his comrade. The hilt of his sword landed at Garth's feet.

"Interesting," Garth said. "You do have power, but you do not control it."

He turned and without even a glance at the fallen soldiers, he left me alone with the bodies. They had voided their bowels when they died, and the smell was overwhelming. Their eyes were wide open, and they seemed to be staring at something beyond my sight. At first, I thought that they looked surprised, but as the light failed, it seemed to me that they looked accusing. Guilt washed over me; I had now killed two more people.

Sometime after dark, I slipped into an uneasy sleep. I dreamed of searching for water. I could hear it running somewhere nearby but could never locate it. I'd wake to a raging thirst and lie listening to the quiet night sounds for a time and then slip back into sleep, only to dream again of unattainable water.

The sounds of someone entering woke me from my uneasy sleep. The dim gray morning light showed me that the tent was full of people. A pair of Kelmar soldiers picked up each of their fallen comrades and, with angry looks in my direction, carried them out. A fifth soldier held a tin cup of water up to my lips. I drained it quickly.

"My thanks to you," I said, my voice hoarse.

"Do not thank me, Lawbreaker," he replied, his voice hard. "Were it up to me, you could rot here. His Holiness ordered me to give you water. He will be in to see you soon and wishes that you be able to speak."

With that, he left.

Sometime later–I thought it was hours–Garth entered. Without speaking, he slowly walked a circle around me, examining me from every side. Then he stopped in front of me and simply stood there, his gaze locked on my face. Long minutes passed. Finally, I asked, "What do you want?"

"I do not *want* anything," he replied. Something in his tone chilled me to my core; I suddenly knew that his entire intent was to hurt me.

"Then let me go," I said. I tried to sound defiant, but my voice wavered. He smiled a thin, humorless smile.

"We both know that is not going to happen," he said, his voice quiet but adamant. "And you should not count on your friends to rescue you. I drove them back from the foot of the causeway and allowed my army across. Even now the Alomar and the Elves are fleeing toward Landfall where a very unpleasant surprise awaits them."

He stepped forward then and laid his hand on my forehead and I realized that he intended to Read me. I tried to dislodge his hand but could not move enough to do so. He closed his eyes and a faint light–a sickening parody of minstrel's blue–played along the length of his staff.

Olen had been gentle when he Read me; Garth was not. I felt a pressure in my head and memories rose, unbidden by me. At first, it was recent things: the snapping turtle I'd seen while crossing the causeway, Ryan telling me of the death of his childhood friend, and the moment that I'd first recognized Garth. I heard him chuckle.

The pressure increased, and I saw Élan's face, lit by starlight. She stepped into my arms, and we kissed. Suddenly, the pressure ceased.

Garth stepped back from me, his face twisted into an expression of disgust.

"You kissed an Elf," he said accusingly. "You are even more depraved than I realized."

He stepped forward and placed his hand on my forehead again. The pressure returned, but more intense and painful. I'm not sure how long Garth forced his way through my memories. He saw my father's attack on me and my lessons with Ambrose. He saw the first time I met Peg and the first time we made love. He saw the attack on Songhaven through my eyes and the grief-driven flight that ended in *Evendim*. He wandered back and forth through my life, taking what he wanted, but over and over again he returned to the times that my power had killed. Over and over, I relived the events that followed Ambrose's death and the death of the Kelmar soldiers the previous night. Then he returned to the attack on Songhaven, the figure in black, and the moment I fell unconscious. When he finally let go and stepped back, my head felt as if my skull was splitting in two and I could barely focus on him.

"Well," he said, his voice strained. "You have given me much to consider."

He started past me to exit the tent but then stopped and laid his hand on my shoulder.

"You seem quite taken with Pegara of Han," he said. "It is ironic that your own power prevented you from rescuing her."

I couldn't help but to turn my gaze toward him, shock robbing me of my breath.

"Perhaps it would interest you to know that she did not die there. One of my men recognized her at Songhaven. She has been my guest since then."

I looked up at him, hope and disbelief warring in my heart.

"I had thought her relatively plain," he continued. "You seem quite beguiled by her, though. Perhaps I will have her brought here and sample her charms myself. You seem eager to see her again; perhaps you could watch."

Before I could respond, he walked away.

For long moments, all I could think of was how much my head hurt. I tried resting it in different positions to try and ease the pain. That didn't really seem to help, but eventually the pain began to subside, and I could focus on other things. I was hungry and the single cup of water had not been enough to truly quench my thirst. There was nothing that I could do about either of those and thinking about them just seemed to make them worse.

Garth had said that Peg was alive and that the Kelmar had her. I wondered whether I could believe him. Part of me wanted to believe him, but I also knew that he wished to hurt me. Then my thoughts turned to Élan. If Peg was really still alive...

That line of thought faltered as another chilling realization hit me. Garth now not only knew of the existence of *Evendim*, he also knew where it was. I had put Élan in danger. Dismay flooded my veins like acid, followed by desperation. I had to get free; I had to find a way to stop him. I struggled against the ropes binding me, but they had clearly been tied by an expert; there was no give in them at all. It was dark when finally I gave up and fell into an exhausted sleep.

The surly guard was back the next morning to feed me a crusty heel of bread and pour a cup of water down my parched throat.

"My thanks to you," I said.

He glared at me, his face twisted in disgust.

"The princess will be here soon," he sneered. "His Holiness wishes you to keep your strength up."

He stalked off and I was left on my own for the rest of the day. Several times, though, people walked past the tent, speaking loud enough for me to hear. It seemed deliberate. They spoke with glee of Peg and what was going to happen to her when she arrived. They talked about the progress of the war; according to what I heard, the Alomar and *Eldarin* armies were in total rout before the Kelmar. The other Keepers had rejoined the Kelmar army, and no nonmagical tactic was successful against their power.

At one point, though, I heard two Kelmar talking outside the tent as they walked by. Unlike the others, these two did not seem to be aware that I could hear them, so I believed what I heard them say. They spoke of how their army was pursuing the Alomar through the Kalidin Sands. The Sands were a vast area of sand dunes to the southwest of Landfall. Inland, the dunes were dotted with patches of scrub; near the coast, the stunted trees gave way to beach grass. The northern end of the Kalidin Sands narrowed into a long peninsula–more an overgrown sandbar–that enclosed the huge deepwater harbor that served Landfall. That peninsula was known as Point Lookout. The Kelmar passed quickly, and I heard no more of their talk, but anxiety over the fate of my friends washed over me.

So passed the next several days. I'm not sure how many days it was; it was difficult to keep track. The Kelmar guard returned every morning with a tiny bit of stale bread and water and throughout the day I heard people outside talking about the depravities Peg would experience when she arrived and how poorly the war was going for the Alomar. I saw nothing of Garth. One night, in the middle of the night, I was awakened when Kelmar guards dumped several buckets of cold water over me.

"His Holiness wishes you to be clean when the princess arrives," they told me, laughing as they did so.

A gentle breeze whispered through the circle of pines standing all around me. Beyond the trees was nothing but black. Shallow streams flowed through the glade and wound their way around outcroppings of lichen covered rock. A woman clothed only in her long golden hair stood in front of me, a grave look on her face. To her right stood a woman in red and black and a man in white. To the woman's left were a man in gray and black and a woman in blue. I knew them: the greatest of the Old Ones: *Aenn, Saer, Ynes, Wyn,* and *Tael. Aenn* stepped toward me and smiled.

"*Ne astrynim, Endollin,*" she said.

I woke the next morning, the memory of my dream leaving me feeling oddly comforted, despite the fact that I did not understand what *Aenn* had said to me. Later that afternoon, Garth entered. He was accompanied by a soldier bearing a battered metal cup. The Keeper looked at me and smiled thinly.

"Well, Lawbreaker," he said, his words warm and welcoming, but his tone cold and smarmy. "I am afraid that I have been quite remiss as a host. You have been my guest for days, but I have yet to personally offer you my hospitality. I have come now to offer you some tea."

I was parched, but something in his tone told me that I did not want to drink whatever he'd brought. He gestured to the soldier, who held the cup up for me. It contained a brown-reddish liquid with an acrid odor. I gagged a little, but kept my mouth closed and turned my head away.

"Oh, come now, Lawbreaker," Garth said. "I really must insist that you try my tea."

He nodded and another soldier stepped into view. This one placed his hand on my forehead and kept me from turning away. With his other hand, he pinched my nose closed.

I tried to hold out, but I had to breathe. As soon as I opened my mouth, the first soldier stepped up and dumped the foul-smelling liquid into my mouth. He then forced my mouth shut and held it closed. I had no choice: I had to swallow.

There were small bits of stuff in the liquid, and I cannot begin to describe the taste. I can only say that it was vile and left an oily feel in my mouth after I swallowed. When they felt me swallow, the soldiers let me go. Garth smiled and nodded to them. In return, they bowed to him and left.

"Did you enjoy your drink, Lawbreaker?" Garth asked. I didn't respond. "Perhaps not," he continued. "In a few moments, though, you may alter your opinion."

Involuntarily, I frowned at him.

"The tea is my own concoction," he told me. "The primary ingredient comes from a plant the Altierans call the spirit vine. I boil it with the leaves of another Altieran plant, a bush if you're interested. It's not very tasty, I'm afraid, but the effects can be quite interesting."

I was beginning to feel vaguely nauseated.

"Those effects vary," he continued. "You may see or hear things that are not there. Your heart may race. And you may experience powerful emotions, either euphoria or anxiety and fear" He paused for a moment. "I am rather hoping for the latter and will try to steer you toward those."

He fell silent and stood watching me for a time. I still felt nauseated, but it didn't seem to be getting worse. I wondered whether I could will the nausea to increase and whether vomiting would protect me from the effects of the drink. Suddenly, I felt as if I was falling, and I tensed. Garth noticed and smiled.

"Feeling the effects, are you? Let me tell you a story."

The world seemed to be slowly spinning around me.

"The day after you became my guest, I sent my army across the causeway," Garth told me. "As they drew near the far end, archers began firing at them from behind wagons. The Kelmar are brave, however, and they pushed forward. At the foot of the causeway, they encountered a handful of Alomar and Elf soldiers. They engaged and their opponents fell back."

He frowned.

"It was a trap. As the Alomar fell back, my soldiers quite unwisely advanced off the causeway. But then additional Alomar soldiers moved in and cut my people off. The Alomar slaughtered them."

I had heard the plans and seen the preparations. I could see the battle in my mind.

"I took a hand, then," Garth told me. "I destroyed the wagons that were providing cover for the archers, and I drove back the archers and the people at the foot of the causeway. I held them off until hundreds of my soldiers were across. The Alomar lines broke and they fled. Many of them fell to my soldiers."

I could feel my heart racing and fear traced icy lines along my veins.

"The Alomar and their Elf allies have been driven to the very base of Point Lookout," he said. "We have them trapped there. My fellow Keepers are now with the Kelmar, and as soon as I join them, we will wipe the Alomar and Elf armies off the face of the world. With their leaders gone, the Alomar will have no choice but to turn back to Mar."

Panic bloomed in my chest, taking away my breath. I knew that it was fruitless, but I began struggling against my bonds. Some part of me knew that the panic I was feeling was the result of Garth's drug, but it didn't matter; that part of me was not in control. A wide smile split his face.

"When we have defeated your army, we will march on *Evendim* and destroy the remaining Elves. But before all of that, I intend to have some fun with your princess, and you will not be able to prevent it. I shall have her repeatedly and I will make you watch. And when I am done with her, I will offer her to my soldiers. How many do you think she can take? Will you still want her when we are done with her?"

With every word, my panic and my fear grew. The part of me that knew them as drug effects fled deeper inside of me, seeking refuge. Deep within, it found a place, a wall of glittering light, a shimmering veil, a door. I could sense safety on the other side, a power beyond belief. My power. I knew that it could save me, if I could just... Desperate, all doubt banished by need, I reached out...

And my power rushed through me, burning the drug from my veins, and leaving my mind clear. With a single flicker of thought, the ropes binding me flared into brilliance and turned to ash. I stood and Garth wrapped both his hands around his staff and raised it. Before he could act, I lunged forward and grabbed his wrists. With a thought, I blasted his staff to splinters. Then I surged across the contact between us and into his mind. I think I heard him scream.

What happened next took only a moment. I was acting entirely on instinct. Unsure of how I was doing what I was doing and not knowing how to select a specific one of his memories, I took them all.

He didn't have Peg. Until he Read me, he had never heard of her. His lies about having her and his threats to rape her were simply part of his efforts to break me. What he had told me about the army, however, was true. They were trapped at Point Lookout. I was going to have to do something about that. Garth must have picked up some of what I was thinking because the next thought was his own. It flickered through his consciousness in an instant, but I followed it and was led to other memories. The enormity of what I learned in that instant was staggering.

Well over a thousand rounds before, the Alomar had fled Mar's wrath through the Aeran Pass. They wandered into the lands to the west of the Breton Mountains and found a whole new world. They encountered the Elves–the *Eldar*–and learned of the Old Ones from them. Away from the control of Mar's Church, they also discovered that some gifted individuals were born with abilities that others did not possess. Some of them could move small objects with a thought or take on any appearance that they chose. Others could sense water or metal under the ground or see what was happening in distant locations. Almost all of them could speak to others like themselves across great distances. They were the first wizards, and their abilities were called magic. They established a school outside of the settlement of Amersford where the wizards could learn from one another and perfect their art.

For many rounds of the seasons, all was well with the Alomar. They established several kingdoms and traded with and learned from the Elves. Together with the Elves they built the Amersford Bridge and the Twin Cities to tend it. Both races sent their brightest children to *Calyth* to study and become minstrels.

The pride of the Alomar was the Wizard's College. The Elves surpassed the Alomar in nearly all crafts and arts, but only humans ever had the talents that made them wizards. And so, a thousand rounds before, the seven Masters of the college–the most skilled and powerful of the wizards–were extremely prideful people. As they became more skilled and knowledgeable, they discovered that the world itself was a source of magical energy, a power that enhanced and amplified their native abilities. Not understanding what they had found but realizing that it could be dangerous, they kept their new knowledge secret as they studied its use.

It was then that Mar had approached them. She told them that she had gifted them with their new abilities and that she had chosen them to usher in a new age of the world. If they helped her bring the Alomar back under her control, they could keep their new powers and would have prominent places in the reunited Kelmar Empire. They accepted her offer. It was the Masters of the Wizard's College who had sown the discord between the Alomar and the Elves, and it was the Masters themselves who destroyed the college and made it appear that the Elves were responsible.

I ripped my awareness out of Garth's mind, but I didn't release my hold on him. His eyes were wide, the corners of his mouth turned down, and he was whimpering. For power, he had deliberately driven a wedge between the Alomar and the *Eldar*. Thousands of the *Eldar* had died, and the rest had been robbed of their homes and driven into hiding so that he could maintain a grip on that power. He had murdered my friends at Songhaven and was preparing to help kill last of the *Eldar* and everyone in the Alomar army at Point Lookout.

Physically, I pushed him away from me, but I flung my power after him. He ignited with a white incandescence so bright that I had to narrow my eyes and then he was gone.

My power still filled me. I retrieved *Endolsar* from the ground where it had lain since Garth had tossed it aside. I belted it on, and flung my mind out, searching for the Alomar and *Eldarin* armies. I touched a familiar mind–Ryan–and stepped across the miles toward him.

When my foot came down, I was five feet over the ground at Point Lookout. I fell forward and sprawled face-first into the sand. For a moment, all I heard was an echo of something like thunder, but then all around me I heard exclamations of surprise. The sand scrunched beside me as someone stepped up to me, and a hand touched my shoulder.

"Lauren?" Ryan said hesitantly.

I rolled over. Ryan was crouched beside me, and I smiled up at him.

"It's me," I replied.

He stood and gave me a hand up.

"How?" he asked.

There was a thunder-like rumble from behind me, though there were no clouds in the sky. Ryan's head snapped up and his eyes moved from my face to some point behind me. Then I felt it: Mar's presence. She was there. I turned. I was far behind the Alomar front line. Beyond the ranks of soldiers ahead of me I could see *El an Arastalon*—the Star of *Arastalon*—and the high king's banner flying side by side.

"Ryan, she's here," I cried. "Mar is here. I have to get to the kings."

We began to push our way forward. Word that I was there spread quickly, and, after a few moments, the crowd began to part before us. Alain and Anders turned as I got closer. They smiled as they saw me, but then a cheer went up from the Kelmar lines, some two hundred feet away. We all turned and saw the Kelmar ranks part and a woman stepped into the open area between the armies.

The goddess Mar.

A hush fell over the field. Awe shone from the faces of the Kelmar; dismay etched the faces of the Alomar and the *Eldar*. The goddess was about my height or maybe an inch taller. Her waist length hair was jet black and framed a heart shaped face. Her lips were full and red, but it was her eyes that attracted attention. The irises of the goddess' almond-shaped eyes were a light bluish violet. She was thin, but curvaceous, and she wore a long, deep purple dress of silk that clung to and accented the curves of her body. The very low decolletage and slits up the sides supported Malash's claim that Mar wished to be the center of male attention. Mar was beautiful, but behind her beauty was something more: she radiated a barely contained sense of power and danger.

"She is a goddess," I whispered in awe.

When she had covered half the distance between the armies, she stopped and stood waiting expectantly.

Fear ran cold through my veins. My heart was pounding, and I suddenly could not conceive of standing against the power that I sensed in her. I glanced behind me at the kings. Anders looked dismayed. Alain looked resigned and sorrowful. The petty kings—arrayed on either side of them—looked afraid but determined. I turned back to Mar, and I quailed at the sight of her raw power. I closed my eyes, fighting to control my breathing. I heard the banners flapping in the breeze from off the ocean and I was suddenly standing in the torch-lit field outside *Evendim*, the *Eldarin* banner flapping above me, Élan in my arms. Then I was lying in the dark with Peg, speaking of marriage. I saw the lilacs in the Fountain Courtyard at Songhaven and mountain laurel blooming on the sides of Haven Mountain. More and more scenes of quiet beauty, all of them threatened by the being before me, flitted through my mind. I opened my eyes.

"I am afraid," I whispered to myself, but I wrapped the fingers of my right hand around the hilt of *Endolsar* and forced myself to step out to meet Mar. I slowly paced off the distance between us until I stood just a dozen feet from her. Then I stopped, my eyes on her face, fighting to quell the urge to turn and run.

"Lawbreaker," Mar said. Her voice was rich and melodious, but something in her tone reminded me of the song of the stone in *Aennsrhyd* and suddenly my fear died, replaced by a sense of irritation growing toward anger.

"You and I both know that the correct term is *Endollin*," I replied. She smiled; my words were defiant, but my voice wavered.

"And what do you know of what that word truly means?" she asked. "But come now, there is no need for us to be this way with one another. Despite what you may have heard, we do not have to be enemies."

I simply cocked my head and raised one eyebrow in response.

"You were meant to destroy the world," she said. "You know that. You do not want that, nor do I. Together, we can prevent it."

Suddenly, Mar's image shimmered, and Peg stood before me, but she had Mar's violet eyes.

"I can be anything you desire," she said. "And when you tire of one form..." She shimmered again and Élan took Peg's place. "...I can assume another."

She changed again to a woman I did not know, someone about my height who had shoulder length brown hair framing a long oval face. Something about that form felt true, but then she was back in her original form.

"We could rule this world together."

I heard her words, but in the back of my mind, I heard something else. I don't know whether she was using the wizard's Mind Speech or if some dream was echoing in my memory, but I heard her voice whispering, "Worship me."

I'm not sure whether I was responding to her spoken words or to the words in my mind, but I drew myself up and said, "No."

I was surprised; my tone was hard as steel. An expression of disbelief flickered across Mar's face and was instantly replaced with anger.

"You dare defy me?" she asked, her voice sounding like the hiss of a venomous snake.

"I do," I answered, my confidence growing.

Her eyes narrowed, and her lips twisted into a feral smile.

"Garth told me that you have no control over your powers," she said.

"And Garth is no longer with us," I answered.

Her eyes widened at that, and her face went a shade paler, but she reached up between us and took a two-handed grip on a massive black sword that materialized even as she reached for it.

Pyrett's training kicked in and I swept *Endolsar* from its sheath even as Mar began swinging the black sword at me. I called up my power and fed it into my sword. The blade went incandescent white, and the pommel stone flared red violet. I caught Mar's sword as she hacked down at me and the concussion from that clash seemed to rock the world. We spent several moments probing one another's defenses and then she cautiously stepped back.

"You are a better swordsman than I thought a minstrel would be," she admitted.

"I have had help from my friends," I told her.

She smiled that feral smile again.

"It will not matter."

Her dark sword vanished as she raised her arms high on either side of her head, palms toward me and fingers spread wide. Darkness flowed from her hands, spread above me, and crashed down on top of me with all the weight of the world.

"I'm sorry," I thought as I fell and then my consciousness went out.

I heard an unfamiliar sound. It pulsed and roared, sounding as if a giant wind gusted through a pine forest. I drifted in darkness and tried to understand what it was and could find nothing in my memory that matched what I was hearing. Then I realized that I was hearing, and I opened my eyes in surprise.

I was lying on my back, looking up at a canvas roof. For a moment, I feared that I was still Garth's captive, but I lifted my right arm and found that I was able to move.

"You're awake," said my father.

I sat up. I was lying near the rear wall of a large tent. My father sat on a camp stool to my right, between me and the entrance to the tent. Several other camp stools were unoccupied.

"Where am I?" I asked.

"The high king's tent," my father replied. "He had it set up for you."

"What is that sound?"

"The ocean," my father replied. "After you fell, Mar gave us twelve hours to surrender. Then she left and the Kelmar pushed us to the end of the peninsula. How are you feeling?"

For the first time since waking, I paid some attention to my body. I groaned.

"Parts of me hurt that I didn't even know that I had."

He gave a short laugh.

"I'm not surprised. When she struck you down, we thought you were dead."

I remembered the darkness crashing down.

"How long has it been?"

"About ten hours," he replied. "It's just past dawn."

My head spun and gray crowded the edges of my vision.

"I failed," I said quietly and hung my head.

My father stood and offered me a hand up.

"You didn't fail," he said as he pulled me to my feet. "You're still alive. We're still alive."

"But I put everything I had into my sword, and it wasn't enough."

My father stepped back from me and turned to where *Endolsar* lay on the floor, unsheathed. He picked it up and moved to the center of the tent. He sighted down the blade and then tried a few simple moves. Then he turned to me.

"Lauren, this may be the finest sword I have ever seen. The craftsmanship is excellent, and the balance is exquisite. But other than the fickle blinky on the pommel, I don't see anything special about it."

I frowned. Garth and the wizards had said much the same thing.

"Son, I don't know anything about magic or whatever power it is that you have, but I do know swords. It may be that 'putting everything you have into the sword' was the problem. Imagine me using a wooden training sword. If I use all my strength, I'm going to break the thing. So, I have to hold back. Could that be what happened with you?"

I thought back to my encounter with Mar. Was it possible that I had limited myself? As I considered that, Lorrestian's words came to mind: the ring and the sword were tokens of my power.

Just then there was a stirring outside the tent and Ryan entered, obviously excited. He saw that I was up and smiled widely.

"Lauren, I'm glad you're awake," he said. "I've been thinking about yesterday and there's one thing that I do not understand."

"What's that?" I asked.

"Why didn't Mar kill you?"

I wasn't expecting that, and I just stared at him, shaking my head slowly.

"She surely seemed to be trying," my father said.

"She did, indeed," Ryan replied. "But she didn't. I don't think that leaving Lauren alive was her choice, though. I don't think she can kill him. I think that if she could have, she would have."

"That makes sense," I said, thinking furiously. Mar couldn't kill me. The sword wasn't the answer. The lore said that I would face Mar and the

Keepers, and I hadn't done that yet. But I couldn't focus. One thought kept intruding.

"Is there anything to eat," I asked.

Ryan nodded and stepped to the entrance to the tent. He spoke quietly to someone outside and turned back to me and my father. I looked at them both.

"I know we don't have much time before the twelve hours are up," I said. "As soon as the food gets here, we need to go to the kings. There are things that you all need to know."

An *Eldarin* soldier stepped in carrying a cloth-wrapped packet and a wineskin.

"*Endollin*," he said, handing the items to me. "I am glad to see you well."

"My thanks to you," I replied.

He nodded and left the tent. I opened the packet to find a slice of stale bread along with a piece of fish that had obviously been cooked on a stick over an open fire. I wolfed them down quickly. The wineskin was only a third of the way full. I took several large sips, and offered it to Ryan and my father, both of whom declined. I dropped it to the floor alongside my sword.

"I need to go," I said.

"Aren't you taking that?" Ryan asked, pointing to *Endolsar*.

I glanced at my father, who just cocked his head.

"I don't think I'm going to need it," I responded.

I ducked out of the tent and froze. The ground below my feet was sand. The sky was full of gray clouds and the iron-gray sea crashed in on either hand. Ryan and my father stepped up on either side of me.

"Lauren, what is it?" Ryan asked.

"It's coming," I said. "The battle that Lorrestian foresaw." I gestured toward the sea. "I've dreamed of this place since I was a child."

"Tell me it wasn't a nightmare," my father muttered.

I shot a glance at him.

"I was afraid of that," he said.

"Where are the kings?" I asked.

"Follow me," my father said.

He started off across the sand, Ryan beside him. I had never walked on sand before. It shifted under my feet, twisting my ankles and knees, which were still aching from the beating I had taken from Mar and the days I spent immobilized by Garth. I stumbled after my father, grimacing with each step. I stopped when an Alomar soldier stepped up to me, leaning heavily on a long wooden staff.

"*Endollin*," he said hesitantly. "Did I say that right?"

"You did, friend," I replied. "What can I do for you?"

He was obviously exhausted, and his left leg was bandaged from thigh to ankle. He looked at me with an innocent expectancy.

"Do ye go to save us?" he asked. There was a faint note of pleading in his voice.

I looked around at the soldiers—Alomar and *Eldar*—camped on either side of us. They sat in small groups, their heads down, hardly speaking. Many bore bandages over minor wounds. Everyone I could see had dark circles around their eyes. I could feel hopelessness and exhaustion all around me. These people had faced defeat after defeat, and some had been retreating before the Kelmar since the fall of Han. I wasn't sure what else I could do, but I could at least try to kindle hope.

"I do," I said. I raised my right fist to the sky and touched the ring with my power, kindling a brilliant red-violet light that I flung at the clouds like a challenge. Thunder rolled. Heads turned toward us, and someone nearby called out, "*Endollin!*" I sent another blast of red-violet light toward the sky and people began to cheer. I turned back to the man before me. There was a light in his eyes that had not been there moments before.

"Take my staff, sir" he said. "The sand can be treacherous."

"I would be honored," I told him. "My thanks to you. I will see it returned to you."

"No worries, sir. It's just a stick. Save us and I'll find another."

The staff helped and a few moments later, we found Anders, Alain, the petty kings, Pyrett, and Konne near the front line. They looked as exhausted as the men I had seen near the high king's tent. They all looked at me intently as we approached.

"Was that you?" Anders asked, gesturing toward the sky.

I nodded.

"Anders, Alain," I said. "I know that time is short. Soon I must face Mar and the Keepers in the battle that Lorrestian foresaw."

Alain nodded, a guarded look on his face.

"You do not bear your sword," he observed.

"If you remember your father's words, the ring and the sword are simply tokens of my power. After yesterday, I no longer believe that the sword is required to defeat Mar."

The *Eldarin* king looked troubled at that, but I had no time.

"There are things that I've learned," I went on. "You need to know them. The Keepers are not supernatural beings. They are the last Masters of the College of Wizards. They found a way to augment their power; it has something to do with the stone in *Aennsrhyd*. They bound it–no Mar bound it for them–so that others couldn't do the same thing. I broke that binding when I touched the stone. Shortly after they discovered that power, Mar appeared to them and promised them eternal life and positions of power in the Empire if they helped her subdue the Alomar. They engineered the conflict between the Alomar and the *Eldar,* and they were the ones who destroyed the College. Mar has sustained them for the last thousand rounds, but they are nothing more than wizards with their power unbound."

When I finished speaking, Alain said, "That explains much that happened in the lead up to the war. My thanks to you for sharing it."

"And my thanks as well," Anders added. "However, we need to continue planning what we will do today. The time that Mar allotted us is nearly gone." He looked at me with hope in his eyes. "What will do you?"

"I am not sure," I replied.

"I have some thoughts," my father said.

As he began explaining, I turned to look across the open stretch of sand between us and the Kelmar. Mar and the remaining Keepers were over there somewhere; I could sense Mar's presence. Even if I was able to deal with Mar, we still faced the Keepers. They were missing one of their number, but any one of them was more powerful than all our wizards combined. And the Kelmar army still outnumbered us more than two to one.

One of Garth's memories came to mind then. He had planned to join the others at Point Lookout after he had finished tormenting me. He couldn't travel the way I had–he called it translocation–so he was going to Speak to one of the others and Mar was going to use her powers to bring him. If Mar could translocate others, could I? Could I possibly move the entire Kelmar army?

Even if I could, what could I do about Mar herself? If she couldn't kill me, I probably couldn't kill her, but as long as she was free...

Just then, a cheer went up from the Kelmar side. We turned and saw Mar and the remaining Keepers step out from the Kelmar line. They stopped just short of halfway between us with three of the Keepers lined up on either side of Mar. They wore hooded robes: black, gold, burnt orange, white, gray, and dull green. Their features were shadowed by their hoods. Each carried a tall, ornately carved wooden staff shod with iron.

"Your time is up," Mar said. She didn't shout, but her voice carried to the very end of the peninsula.

Every part of me ached and I still wasn't sure what I was going to do—what I could do—but I slowly walked forward, leaning heavily on my borrowed staff. Nonetheless, I felt nothing but calm and determination.

I stopped perhaps twenty feet from the goddess, who stepped forward a single step. She smiled, but the expression did not reach her eyes.

"Yesterday you faced me armed with a sword, and I swatted you down like a bug. Today you come against me armed only with a stick. Fool."

She spread her arms and black clouds appeared on the horizon all around and began to spread toward us, consuming the gray clouds as they came. Lightning flashed from cloud to cloud and a chaotic wind began to roil the sea. I could feel her power gathering but I ignored it. I slipped my mind past her to the men behind her. My consciousness spread, touching the mind of each man in the Kelmar army, finding his memory of home, and leaving a single thought: Leave the Alomar in peace. It took just moments—during which Mar continued to gather her power—and then with a thought, I sent the entire Kelmar army home.

Mar sensed it and stopped whatever it was that she had been doing. She lowered her arms and slowly turned to find that she and the Keepers were now facing me and the Alomar alone. She turned back to me, her face suddenly pale, but her expression was hard.

"Kill him," she shrieked at the Keepers. "Kill him."

I stood up straighter and tossed my staff aside. The Keepers raised their staves, which began to glow with eldritch light, the color matching their robes. I could feel a pulling sensation on my head and limbs; they were literally trying to pull me apart with magic. My power lashed out and they flared into blinding incandescence and were gone.

Mar screamed in rage and flung a bolt of pure, white-hot energy at me. I barely deflected it into the roiling clouds overhead. I couldn't kill her, but I couldn't leave her free. Acting purely on instinct, I began building a wall of power around her, locking her away from the world. When she sensed what I was doing, she tried to flee, but each time she tried, I pulled her back.

Far overhead, the sky shrieked as the world began to crack. Something was ripping at the very fabric of the world. Lorrestian had said that I might destroy the world, but whatever was happening up there did not feel like something that I was doing, though there was something familiar about it. I could perceive a will–one possessed of an obsessive anger and determination–behind it. I turned part of my power to forbidding whatever was out there from entering. A groan escaped me. I was stretched too far; there were too many things for me to attend to. I was going to lose both battles. Then I felt Mar become aware of the other power. She screamed, in fear this time, and ceased resisting me. I flung even more power at the crack in the sky and felt the being there withdraw. I was almost sure that I could feel it being pulled away rather than pushed away by me, but I couldn't think about that. I still had Mar to attend to.

She was nearly walled off completely, but I began to sense traces of her all around me and expanded my "wall" to include those, locking every shred of her and her power away from the world. When I could no longer sense Mar anywhere, I let my power drop, to find that I was standing with my arms raised.

The pulsing roar of the ocean seemed louder than it had been; the sea had been driven into a frenzy by Mar's storm and the attack from above. The wind hissed through the beach grass and snapped the banners of the kings. It was otherwise silent. I turned to find nearly everyone staring at me. Ryan was on his knees, his head down and his face covered by his long hair. As I ran my eyes over the army, it was clear that there were far fewer people than there had been moments before. *El an Arastalon* was lying on the ground. Then I noticed that I could see none of the *Eldar*, except Ryan. My father crossed the distance between us, shock and awe mixed on his face.

"They're gone," he said in response to my unasked question. "You saved us, but the Elves are gone. The *aynekahrn*, too. They vanished when you did..." He looked around frantically, as if searching for the words. "When you did whatever it was that you did."

I couldn't speak. My mind was reeling, my breath was coming in quick gasps, and the edges of my vision went gray. My father placed a hand on my shoulder for a moment, then turned and walked slowly back to our front line. Ryan looked up as he approached, and my father gave him a hand up. I watched as Ryan awkwardly hobbled toward me. The waves crashed in on either hand and overhead the black clouds churned. Thunder rumbled. Ryan stumbled to a halt in front of me. His face was pale and drawn with pain.

"They're gone," I said, my voice choked with horror. "They're all gone. Élan..." For a moment, I couldn't speak; I was struggling to breathe. "I lost her, Ryan. I tried, but I lost her."

"They're not dead," he said, so quietly that I could hardly hear him over the pounding of the surf. "I am half *Eldarin* and that part of me is wherever they are, wherever you sent Mar."

"I don't understand," I said.

Before Ryan could answer, I felt a stirring behind me, something that felt like an echo of power. I turned to find a woman standing there. Her long black hair was unbound, and she was clad in a long red robe, with the hem and the cuffs edged in black. With a start, I realized that she wasn't really there, that I could see through her to the sand and beach grass behind her. Then I recognized her: *Saer*, the embodiment of Fire. One of the Old Ones.

"Is this the ending you wished, *Endollin*?" she asked, her voice quiet and dispassionate.

"No," I answered, my voice broken by grief. "No, but I don't know what to do."

"It is not my place to tell you what to do," she replied. "But to make that choice, you need to know. Hear me, *Endollin*. I do not have much time. Like the others, I am going quiescent."

She reached out toward me, but her hand was fading even as she did.

"Seek the dragons," she whispered. "Wake the Old Ones."

Part Five

A Song of Creation

What do you tell forever's children
When it's their turn to hurt and heal
Whatever spins a grim tornado
Can also turn the potter's wheel

- from Potter's Wheel
- Bill Danoff

CHAPTER FIVE

Hours later, I was sitting at the very end of Point Lookout, star-ing into the foam-clad gray waves crashing in from seemingly all around me. Though the black clouds had dissipated, the sea was still in turmoil. So was I.

I had faced Mar and–in a sense–defeated her. I hadn't destroyed the world, but it was changed. Broken. I could sense that much, though I couldn't identify all the changes. Everything seemed somehow flat, empty. Something essential, something that had always been there, unnoticed, was now gone. One thing, though, I knew with certainty. The *Eldar* were gone, banished somehow when I banished Mar. I had banished Élan. I loved her, I wanted to protect her, and I had sent her into some other place with Mar. The crashing waves almost seemed to roar the word "gone" at me.

I felt a hand on my left shoulder and looked up to find that my father had come up from behind me.

"The high king requests that you join us for the midday meal," he said. "There is much that we need to discuss."

I nodded and he offered me a hand up. As we walked through the camp, I noticed that there were even fewer people than there had been before.

"Where is everyone?" I asked.

"When you…" He paused and glanced sidelong at me. "When you sent the Kelmar away, their wagons and supplies remained here. We've got people going through them to see if there's anything there we can use and to tend to the animals."

We walked in silence for a moment.

"Are the Kelmar…" he started.

"They're alive," I said, cutting him off. "I sent them all back to their homes."

Just ahead of us, Olen and Ryan emerged from a tent. Ryan was wrapped in a blanket and was leaning heavily on the wizard. They joined us and we walked without speaking, though I took up a place on Ryan's left to add my assistance to Olen's.

A circle of camp chairs had been set up near the former front line. Anders and the petty kings were seated there, obviously waiting for us. Anders had a bloody bandage on his left hand, but he was still waving it around to emphasize some point he was making. Roth's eye patch was missing, and he and Moireach were both spattered with blood, apparently not their own. Roth's arm was no longer in a sling, but he had a bandage wrapped around his head. Marwynn was without a shirt, and he had a bandage wrapped around his chest and a blanket draped over his shoulders. Like the soldiers that I had seen earlier, their faces were haggard, and they all had dark circles under their eyes.

They saw us approaching and fell silent. Anders glanced around the circle, and they all rose and faced us.

"*Endollin*," the high king said, and they all bowed. "We owe you our lives."

I glanced at Olen to ensure that he had a firm hold on Ryan and then stepped forward. I returned their bows.

"High King Anders Sorren," I said. "Your Highnesses. You do me far more honor than I deserve."

"Perhaps," Anders said. "But I am reasonably certain that had you not done what you did, we would not be here to have this conversation."

He gestured to the chairs.

"But come. Join us. Food will be coming shortly. We have much to discuss."

We all took seats. I was sitting directly across the circle from Anders with Ryan to my left and Olen beyond him. My father sat to my right. At that moment, several people arrived with food, a hastily prepared fish stew.

"*Endollin...*" Anders started, but I cut him off.

"My apologies, Your Majesty, but I would very much prefer to be called Lauren."

"Then I am Anders," he responded. "Please, we would all like to hear what it is that you did this morning."

I looked around the circle. Some of the others were watching me, the rest were slurping the stew from wooden bowls.

"I would be happy to tell you what I can," I said. "But before I do that, I would like to hear how you all ended up here. What happened at the causeway? Why did you not stand in Landfall? And where are the Altierans?"

While I was speaking, Anders had taken a bite of his stew and was occupied chewing a particularly tough piece of something, so my father answered.

"Losing you demoralized everyone," he said. "Especially the Elves. The only one of them who continued to express optimism was Alain, but his optimism was desperate in tone. Despite that, our plan at the causeway went well at first. The Kelmar came across the causeway in force, but because it was so narrow, only five or so of them could engage us at once. Our archers were firing almost continuously and were taking a tremendous toll. As planned, our front line engaged and allowed the Kelmar to push them back. When nearly two dozen of them were off the causeway, riders pushed in from each side to cut them off and additional swordsmen blocked the foot of the causeway. We quickly dealt with the trapped Kelmar, but then Garth overwhelmed us. He set fire to the wagons protecting the archers and pushed us back with the same kind of barrier he used when they took you. He kept us apart until a huge number of the Kelmar were off the causeway, then he dropped the barrier. Our line crumbled, and we couldn't stand against them. We broke and ran for Landfall. We lost a large number of people and most of our supplies were left behind."

Marwynn took over the story then.

"He won't say it, but Dalach rallied us," he said. His voice was deep, and his intonation brought to mind the rolling cadence of the sea chanties I had learned. "He pulled us all back into some kind of order so that it wasn't a complete rout. When night came, the Kelmar let up, so we were able to get some rest. Shortly after we stopped, a couple of our advance riders returned from the west. They had gone ahead to apprise my Steward of our approach."

He paused and took a sip from a battered tin cup. When he spoke again, his voice was strained.

"My queen died in childbirth a round ago and my boy is still a child. So, when I departed Landfall, I left Torlen, my Steward, in command of the city. Torlen has been with me many tens of rounds; he was my first mate aboard the *Stormwind* when I was but a captain. When the Kelmar drove us south of Badon, I sent a messenger to Torlen to ready the city should we be driven so far. I never heard back. In the chaos of the retreat from Badon, the messenger slipped my mind.

"When our advance riders came to Landfall, they found the gates closed. Torlen was hanging from the wall above the gates. Our riders could not understand what had happened and they called out for entry. The men on the walls told them that Bredwyr–that's Torlen's son and a devout follower of Mar–had declared his father apostate. Together with the Repentant in the city, he roused the devout against his own father for his support of us. Bredwyr said that we were defying Mar's will and so true followers could not in good conscience aid us. They hung Torlen and Bredwyr named himself Steward of the city. I can only assume that they killed or imprisoned my messenger."

No one spoke for several moments, but then Anders–who had finally spit out whatever he'd been chewing on–finished the story.

"We did not have enough soldiers nor enough time or supplies to lay siege to the city," he explained. "So, the Kelmar drove us past the city into the Kalidin Sands. That's where you found us."

At a nod from Anders, Olen spoke next.

"I do not have much to add to the tale," he said. "We in Amersford heard nothing of the insurrection from the wizards in Landfall. I would like to believe that had they been able, they would have warned us. Looking back, it is odd that we did not hear from them after the incident with the standing stone. I fear that they may be dead."

He bowed his head for a moment.

"Now, I have no way of knowing. Our powers are gone. They faded as you did whatever it was that you did to Mar."

He hung his head. No one else spoke. My stomach rumbled and I looked at my bowl of stew but couldn't summon the will to raise it to my lips. A gull landed in the center of the circle and turned a greedy yellow eye on our bowls.

"You all saw Garth take me," I said. I felt as if I was forcing the words to come. "I woke in a tent, bound to timbers from one of the wagons we burned. Garth had taken *Endolsar* from me. He tried to take the ring, and two soldiers died in the trying. Then Garth Read me." I glanced quickly at Olen, but his head was still down. "He found out about Peg and…"

"Peg?" Marwynn asked, looking around the circle.

"Pegara of Han," I answered. "We were promised to one another."

Marwynn nodded his understanding.

"Garth found out about Peg and Élan, Alain's daughter. He began trying to break me then. He withheld all but the barest minimum of food and drink. He claimed to have captured Peg at Songhaven, and he threatened to rape her and to have his soldiers rape her. He threatened to destroy *Evendim* and to kill Élan. He told me what was happening to all of you.

"After days of that didn't wear me down, he drugged me. The drug was meant to induce fear and panic, and it did. It was also supposed to cause hallucinations, but as I started to experience those, I reached for the one thing that my heart knew could save me: my powers as the *Endollin*."

Ryan turned to me at that. His face was very pale and dark circles ringed his eyes. Nonetheless, he smiled faintly.

"What is it, Ryan?" I asked.

"Your wording," he replied, his voice weak and wavering. "That's the first time that I have heard you firmly and definitively accept who you are and what you can do."

He paused for a moment, breathing heavily.

"Lauren, is it possible that the reason you could not consciously access your powers was that in your deepest core you did not believe that you had them?"

He stopped and looked at me expectantly.

"You may be right," I replied after a moment's consideration. "In that moment I knew beyond all doubt that I had power and that it could save me. The rational part of my mind, the part that said that I did not, was silenced by the drug. And my power did save me. It burned away the drug. I was acting purely on instinct at that point. I freed myself from my bonds and I took Garth's memories. All of them. The ones that I've actually brought to mind are still with me, but I feel as if the rest are fading quickly. I'm not sure that I'll be able to access them much longer."

"That is typical for a Reading," Olen said. "Any memories that are not actively consolidated into the Reader's memory fade quickly."

I nodded my acknowledgement.

"Garth was one of the seven Masters of the College of Wizards," I told them. "They were prideful and vain. They were the most gifted and powerful of the wizards, but they were frustrated by the effort it took to do even the slightest of magic. After years of study, they discovered that the world itself was a source of power that augmented their own abilities and allowed them to do far more than they had ever dreamed they could do.

"They kept their knowledge secret. Partly that was because they realized that unlimited power could be dangerous, and they felt that no one but they could safely navigate those dangers. Mostly it was because they delighted in being more powerful than their colleagues and they relished the respect and adulation that their power brought them. That was when Mar came to them."

I paused then. What I had just said brought one of Garth's memories to mind.

"When she first came to them, it was pronounced M'ar," I said. "Over hundreds of rounds she had it changed. I'm not sure why." I felt myself frowning. "Garth was always careful to avoid the old pronunciation."

I took a moment and sipped a bit of the broth from my bowl of stew.

"Mar claimed that she had gifted the Masters with their newfound powers and made them an offer: if they would assist her in subjugating the Alomar, they would keep their powers and be granted positions just below hers in the new order.

"The goddess had an irrational hatred of the *Eldar*," I continued. "The Masters, envious of the skills of the *Eldar*, shared that sentiment. Most of the Alomar, however, valued their *Eldarin* friends and neighbors, and would not willingly turn against them. Mar and the wizards realized that to take control of the Alomar would require separating them from the *Eldar*. They started by creating a new religious order, the Repentant, and gave them a new holy book: the *Torun Mar*. The Repentant were charged with preaching Mar's word to the people and—as you know—the *Torun Mar* casts the *Eldar* as ignorant, evil sprites whose only purpose is to lead people away from Mar's worship. At the same time, the wizards began a campaign to drive a wedge between the Alomar and the *Eldar*."

I looked around the circle.

"We all learned about Denbyr," I said quietly. They all nodded. "We learned that a band of *Eldar* pillaged the village and slaughtered every man, woman, and child. Everyone knows that the *Eldar* were responsible because the body of one of the *Eldarin* soldiers was found there. But it was the wizards. They ambushed an *Eldarin* soldier and killed him. Then they hired mercenaries to kill the villagers, and they left the body of the soldier there. That was the beginning of the strife between the Alomar and the *Eldar*.

"The end of it was when they burned the College of Wizards and made it appear that they and all the other wizards had been murdered by the *Eldar*. When they reappeared, it was in the guise of the Keepers at the fall of *Elsgard*. They spent the next thousand rounds of the seasons vilifying the *Eldar* and sowing strife and discord amongst the Alomar."

I stopped and took several more bites of my stew. The others exchanged glances and then turned back to me.

"The history lesson is nice," my father said. "But, son, what did you do to Mar? Why did the Elves disappear?"

I had gotten a particularly tough piece of some kind of vegetable, so I waved at him to wait. After I forced down whatever it was, I answered.

"Before I faced her again," I said, "I thought about what Ryan said. If Mar couldn't kill me, I figured that I probably couldn't kill her either. But as long as she was in the world, she was not going to allow the Alomar to live in peace. She was not going to allow me to live in peace. So, I walled her off from the world. I don't know why the *Eldar* are gone or why the wizards lost their powers."

"Lauren," Ryan said, exhaustion making his voice raspy. "Do you remember that I once told you that the *Eldar* do not do magic, that they are magic?"

"I do," I answered. "That seems like a long time ago."

"It does. Consider this. The *Eldar* are magic. The wizards had magic. The *Eldar* and the wizards' power both disappeared when Mar did. Could Mar somehow be the source of magic?"

Olen's head snapped up at that. I nodded.

"That makes sense," I agreed. Then the implication hit me. "So, to get the *Eldar* back, I have to bring Mar back?"

No one responded. I hung my head and spent a moment digging into the sand with the toe of my boot. Then I looked up to Anders.

"There's one last thing that I got from Garth. The Kelmar campaign was designed to accomplish one major thing before you all were killed: it was meant to humiliate you and undermine the confidence of the Alomar in their hereditary leaders. That part of the campaign started many rounds ago when Mar began blighting crops and warping animals."

I paused there for a moment and looked around the circle. Garth's memory told me that my birth had sent a shockwave of power across the world and Mar had done what she did in reaction to that. I wondered if I should share that. I chose not to. I cleared my throat and continued.

"The Repentant began subtly suggesting that failures of the kings of the Alomar were responsible for the blighting of the land. Those attacks continued for many rounds of the seasons and that brings us to the present. Mar and the Keepers planned to eliminate the high king's line. Then the entirety of the Kelmar army–with the aid of the Keepers–would drive the petty kings before them, defeating them at every turn and forcing them to run time and time again. They wanted to show the people that the kings were ineffective, that they could offer no safety or protection. They believed that the Alomar would willingly submit to her rule after that."

"Humiliate us and then kill us," Roth said, his voice raw and ragged. "Were the Keepers not supposed to keep us safe, protect us, and lead us back to Mar?"

"Aye, they were," Moireach agreed.

"I'm not feeling all that safe," Marc said. "They tried to kill me by treachery in my own home." He looked at me. "And all of this was done with Mar's blessing?"

"It was," I confirmed. "You saw. She stood with them at the end."

No one responded to that, and I wasn't sure what else to say, so I focused on eating my stew. The others chose to eat then as well. As we were all finishing up, Roth wiped his mouth with the back of his hand and said, "We've been lied to all our lives. Our people have been lied to for over a thousand rounds. We cannot allow that to continue. We need to purge the Federation of the church and the Repentant."

"I wouldn't do that," I replied. "I don't think it would be wise to turn on our own people. The Repentant were lied to just as the rest of us were. They've spent their lives following what they believed was a true calling and studying the *Torun Mar*. And just like us, when they found inconsistencies and raised questions, they were told to have faith in Mar's love or that the frequent atrocities described in the stories were the fault of the Alomar, that it was the Alomar people who drove Mar to those lengths. They couldn't know—any more than we did—that their entire calling was based on a lie."

"Are you saying that Mar is not truly a goddess?" Marwynn asked.

We all turned to him. In my mind, I could hear myself, face to face with her power, whispering to myself, "She is a goddess."

"I..." I started but couldn't find words to continue. "That's not..."

I stopped then to try and gather my thoughts. At Ryan's insistence, I had studied the *Torun Mar*. I had seen firsthand how Mar had treated the *Eldar* and the Alomar.

"I don't know," I said finally. "I guess it depends on what you mean by 'goddess.'"

Marwynn barked out a short, sharp laugh.

"Spoken like a true minstrel," he said.

I just shook my head at that.

"She is a very powerful being," I explained. "But think about what we've seen of her and what is written in the *Torun Mar*. We've seen her destroy the land and everything that grows on it. In the stories, she—or one of her surrogates—is always killing someone, destroying something, or taking things away from people. She claims that she made the world and everything in it, but all we have ever seen her do is wreak destruction on it. Consider Jorlith, your forefather. Even the most devoted of the faithful suffer. Does that make her a goddess?"

Marwynn looked thoughtful and several of the others were nodding. I felt as if articulating that thought had solidified a belief that I hadn't known that I had.

"Lauren, if I may?" Olen asked.

"Certainly, my friend."

"During your battle with Mar, something happened in the sky. What was that?"

"I don't know," I replied. "It felt as if something was trying to break through from somewhere else. I don't know what it was or where it would have been coming from, but something about it felt very familiar. Whatever it was, it was powerful."

"How were you able to prevent it from coming through?"

"I'm not sure that I did, Olen. I was trying to wall off Mar and hold out against that thing and I could feel myself beginning to fail at both. But then Mar became aware of whatever it was. It scared her, enough that she stopped resisting me and I was able to shift my focus to that thing. But even then, I might have failed, but it felt as if something else pulled it away."

"And the woman in red," Anders said. "Who was that?"

"That was not just a woman," I answered. "That was *Saer*. She is one of the greatest of the Old Ones, the embodiment of Fire."

"She told you to seek the dragons and wake the Old Ones," Marc said. "What did she mean by that? If she's an Old One, why would she tell you to wake them? She didn't look like she needed waking."

"I don't know," I said. "I've met a dragon in the southern Bretons, and it vanished. I don't know where it went. Now I've met one of the Old Ones..."

"That was a sending," Ryan cut in. "She wasn't truly here."

I simply nodded to acknowledge Ryan's statement and continued.

"Still, I don't have any idea where to even begin searching for either the dragons or the Old Ones. I know that there are five major Old Ones, and I know of several minor ones. How many are there? And how many dragons are there?"

Just then a soldier in the black and gold of the high king's Guard stepped into our circle. He bowed to Anders.

"Your Majesty," he said. "My apologies for interrupting. Sails have been sighted to the east. We believe they are coming from Landfall."

"Ships?" Anders asked. "How many?"

"It is difficult to say, Your Majesty. They are still quite far out. It does appear to be a great many, though."

Marwynn stood, his expression grim.

"That can only be my fleet," he said. "No one else has more than one or two ships in Orismay Bay. The question is whether the captains of those ships are loyal to me or to Bredwyr."

He turned to the guardsman.

"Take me to where we can see the ships," he ordered.

The guardsman, surprised, looked to Anders, who gave a quick, sharp nod.

"If you'll follow me, Your Highness," the man said.

The guardsman led Marwynn through the camp to the eastern beach with the rest of us trailing along behind. When we reached the water's edge, a small crowd of people already stood there. One of them–clearly one of Marwynn's soldiers–approached.

"Your Highness," he said. "Those must be our ships. The wind is against them, but they should still reach here within the hour."

"Aye, they will," Marwynn agreed.

"I can't be sure at this distance, but I think there are more ships out there than we had in the harbor, though."

Marwynn spent a few moments peering intently into the distance, his eyes scrunched up, leaning forward as if those few extra inches would help him see more clearly. Then he turned back to his man.

"I believe you're right," he said. "They must have commandeered everything in the harbor that could float."

"But who are they?" Anders asked.

Marwynn simply shrugged and shook his head.

Anders turned to his guardsman and said, "Bring the rest of the Guard here. Make sure that they're armed. I want a couple of companies of archers, too. And have my banner brought here as well."

The man nodded and left to carry out the high king's orders. The rest of us stayed there on the beach, watching as the ships drew ever closer. I had wanted to speak with Ryan about how he was doing but he was so exhausted and weak that he spread the blanket that he'd been wrapped in on the sand and went to sleep. I was just thinking about going to find something to eat that wasn't fish stew when Marwynn gave an exclamation of surprise and turned to his soldier.

"Are those orange sails that I see out in front of the fleet?" he asked.

The man squinted his eyes and peered into the distance.

"I believe so, Your Highness."

The king of Landfall turned to us.

"That's the *Black Marlin*," he told us, smiling broadly. "My personal racing schooner. I had her built to compete for the Merchant's Cup. She's the only one on the water with orange sails. She's faster than anything else in the fleet, so she'll be here first. If that bastard Bredwyr has taken her, I'll have his mangy head off his shoulders."

We all watched anxiously as the fleet slowly drew nearer. Far out in front of the other ships, the *Black Marlin* tacked back and forth against the west wind, gaining ground with every passing moment. Eventually, she was close enough for us to begin making out details.

"She's flying Landfall's banner," Roth observed.

"That's not definitive," Marwynn replied. "Bredwyr considered himself the ruler of Landfall. He'd fly our banner."

"True," Roth countered. "But would he come to us without surrounding himself with several ships full of soldiers?"

The *Black Marlin* turned directly into the wind and the schooner coasted to a stop some six hundred feet from shore. The anchor was dropped, and the crew set about furling the sails and lowering a small dinghy into the water. Seven people climbed into the small craft. Six of them took up oars and began rowing toward shore.

"That looks like Trefor, my Fleet Captain, there in the back of the dinghy," Marwynn said. "I do not believe that he would serve Bredwyr..."

His voice trailed off, but he moved his hand to rest on his sword hilt.

As the dinghy neared shore, several Landfall soldiers warily waded in to help beach the boat. The archers had their bows strung and were ready to draw and fire at the first sign of trouble. In a moment, the prow of the boat touched the sand and–obviously impatient–Trefor slipped over the stern into waist deep water and waded ashore. He scanned the people on the beach, spotted the high king's banner, and trotted across the sand toward us.

The fleet captain was of average height and build. His long blond hair was tied back and fell nearly to his waist. His eyes were a deep sea blue under prominent blonde eyebrows and the lower half of his face was covered in pale stubble. He wore a navy-blue uniform coat marked with a good deal of gold braid over what appeared to be soiled civilian clothing. His face lit in a smile when he saw Marwynn.

"Your Highness," he said and bowed. "We saw your signals. We came as soon as we could."

Marwynn looked confused.

"My signals?"

The fleet captain raised an eyebrow.

"This morning. Lookouts reported two flares, one after the other."

Marwynn looked at me and raised his eyebrows.

"That was me," I said sheepishly.

Trefor's look hardened.

"And who is it that I scrambled the fleet for?"

Marwynn made a "keep quiet" gesture at me and answered Trefor himself.

"Trefor, this is Lauren of the Minstrels, son of War Duke Dalach Egan-son. He is known to the Elves as the *Endollin* and this morning he saved us all from the Kelmar army."

Trefor's expression softened as Marwynn spoke and he began looking toward the base of the peninsula.

"And where is the Kelmar army?" he asked.

"Back in the Empire," Marwynn answered. "All of them."

Trefor's eyes grew wide at that.

"How?"

"I'm not sure that I understand it myself," Marwynn replied. "Let's save that for another time."

He turned to Anders.

"Your Majesty, I present Fleet Captain Trefor Mabin-son. Fleet Captain, this is Anders Sorren, High King of the Alomar."

Trefor bowed to Anders.

"Your Majesty," he said. "I offer my apologies. I should have realized who you were when I saw your banner. I intended no disrespect."

Anders smiled.

"No disrespect was perceived, Fleet Captain," he said. "Your timely arrival is most appreciated. Had things gone differently this morning your quick response may have saved us all."

"Trefor," Marwynn said. "Given what I've heard, I cannot believe that Bredwyr would have let you come, signal or no. What has been happening in the city? How did Bredwyr manage to take over?"

"You knew the self-righteous little twit was a devout follower of Mar? He probably spent more time at the temple with the Repentant than he did in his own home."

"Aye."

"Well, after you left to join the high king, Torlen began preparing to support the army should it be necessary. He was laying in extra stores of food and medicine. He had the smiths forging swords and arrow heads. None of us expected you to be pushed back so far, but he wished to be prepared.

"That's when the Repentant began speaking out. They said that anyone who supported the high king and the Lawbreaker would be damned to the outer darkness, apart from Mar forever. Bredwyr himself began speaking out against his father, saying that Torlen was leading the faithful astray. Some people paid them heed, but most just went about their business.

"Your Highness, you left Torlen five companies of soldiers to keep order in the city. At first, things seemed normal; watch was kept from the walls, and the hourly patrols through the city proceeded as usual. But as time went on, it seemed as if there were more and more soldiers in the city. They appeared to be everywhere. Eventually, I realized that I didn't recognize most of them and I went to the palace to investigate. That was the day that the high king's messenger arrived. Torlen received him and offered him passage on one of our ships that was leaving for Altiera the next day. The messenger left the throne room with two soldiers that I knew, but I never saw any of them again. When the ship left the next morning, the messenger was not aboard."

Anders spoke up.

"Trefor, I very much want to hear the rest of this. Please give me a moment to arrange some refreshment for you and your crew."

The high king gestured to one of his guardsmen.

"Your Majesty?" the man asked.

"Jelor, have the archers and the Guard stand down. We are not being attacked. Ask the crew of that boat if they need anything and, if they do, see if we can provide it. Then see if you can find some wine and some cups and bring them here to us."

"At once, Your Majesty."

He bowed and strode off toward the archers. Anders turned back to Trefor and nodded.

"After the messenger left, things seemed to settle down," the Fleet Captain continued. "There were still more soldiers around than I thought there should be, and I tried to share that with Torlen, but he was so tied up organizing things that he rarely if ever left the palace. All the men serving there were old familiar faces, and I think it was easy for him to believe that I didn't recognize the soldiers because I serve in the fleet rather than the army.

"Then the wizards brought word that Badon had fallen and that you all were fleeing toward Amersford with a plan to make a stand near Landfall. Torlen stepped up his preparations. In response, the Repentant joined Bredwyr in his attacks on his father. Their preaching to the crowds started to hint at violence against unbelievers and Torlen was called an unbeliever."

A soldier in the blue and white of Amersford approached, carrying an assortment of cups and a wine of unknown vintage. Trefor paused as the cups were distributed and the man explained that the bottle had come from one of the Kelmar supply wagons. After taking a sip and frowning at the taste–it was an abysmal wine–Trefor continued.

"I remember the day that a rider came from Amersford with word that you were on your way and that there were Elves fighting alongside you. That very night, I was just sitting down to my evening meal when soldiers came pounding on my door. My wife answered. The men outside were wearing our uniforms. Without a word, they shoved her aside and dragged me out of the house. They took me down to that abandoned livestock barn on the north wharf. Many of the fleet sailors were already being held there. As the soldiers brought more sailors in, the new arrivals told us what was going on in the city. Under the command of Bredwyr and the Repentant, soldiers in our uniforms had marched into the palace and slaughtered the soldiers who remained there. They took Torlen to the wall above the main gates and hung him as a traitor and an apostate.

"It was while I was being held that I finally figured out who the soldiers were. They didn't speak much around us, but from the few times that they did, I recognized the accent. They weren't our people. They were from Meren. As near as I can figure from bits and pieces I got from the others while we were being held, fighters from Meren have been drifting into the city for over a round. The Repentant found them housing and Bredwyr supplied them with uniforms and weapons. They've been planning this for a long time."

Anders' face could have been carved from stone. His eyes were narrowed, and his mouth set in a straight line.

"So, Meren's complicity with Mar's plot was deeper than we knew," the high king said. The tone of his voice carried the ring of steel. "Not only did Larsen send someone to poison Marc, not only did he position himself to kill me and take my throne after Mar murdered my father, he sent people to take Landfall and hold it against us. Larsen may be dead, but others in Meren must have aided him and willingly followed his orders. I think it is past time to deal definitively with the problem of Meren."

The other ships were now drawing close. One by one, they turned into the wind and dropped their anchors.

"Your Majesty, Your Highness," Trefor said, looking at Anders and Marwynn in turn. "The fleet is ready to either send men ashore to fight or to send boats to bring you all aboard. I must signal them some command. Which is it to be?"

Anders and Marwynn exchanged glances, and Anders cocked his head in an unspoken question.

"I would suggest that we take ship back to Landfall," Marwynn suggested. "I offer the hospitality of my city to the combined army of the Alomar. You're welcome to rest and recover until you're ready to return to your homes."

"My thanks to you," the high king responded. "I, however, wish to take a boat upriver to Amersford. I should return to Badon as soon as possible. Dalach and my Guard will travel with me; I'll leave Trahern in command of Badon's troops."

"If it is not too much trouble, I would like to travel to Amersford with the high king," I said. "I need to begin my search for the Old Ones and the dragons. The wizard's library in Amersford is second to none. I might learn something of use there."

Anders started to reply, but my father cut him off.

"Your Majesty," he said. "It has been an honor to serve you and to fight at your side. I hope that I may do so again in the future, but I cannot go to Badon now."

Anders turned to him with a quizzical look but didn't say anything.

"I cannot say why, exactly," my father explained, his face twisted into a puzzled frown, "but I must accompany Lauren. For the duration of his quest, where he goes, I go."

"And me as well," Ryan added.

Anders gave me an odd, vaguely disapproving look and then turned to Trefor. Before he could speak, though, Marwynn spoke up.

"Your Majesty, I understand your desire for speed and taking a boat upriver is not going to meet your need."

"Why not?"

"Remember, you'll be going against the current. If you were lucky enough to have a following wind the entire time, you could reach Amersford in about eight days. It would take you just as long on horseback. You are not, however, likely to be lucky with the winds and chances are that you would take longer to reach Amersford by boat. If I'm right, we have ships out there that could carry your horses. We can get you across the bay and you can ride from there."

"Very well. Have them send boats to bring us and our mounts aboard," the high king said.

"That will take some time," Marwynn noted. "Trefor, after you send the command, I would like to hear how it is that you are here and not locked in a livestock barn."

Trefor went back down the beach to his boat and spoke to the crew. One of them retrieved a set of flags from inside the dinghy and began waving them in a complex pattern at the ships offshore. Sailors on the nearest ships responded with flags of their own and I could see the message being passed from the nearest ships to those further out. In a flurry of activity, each ship began lowering additional dinghies into the water. Satisfied with what he was seeing, Trefor returned to our group. He picked up his cup, took another sip, and scowled again.

"That is nasty," he said.

"Aye, but it's wet and it's alcoholic," Marc responded.

Anders smiled.

"You were locked in a warehouse..." Marwynn prompted.

"I was," Trefor said. "I was in there for over half a moon. They fed us, not as much as we would have liked and not particularly good stuff, but they fed us. Occasionally, they'd round up another sailor–most of the ones who hadn't been taken yet were in hiding–and we'd get news from outside. Our people do not lightly accept the strictures of the church, never have. Many were troubled when Bredwyr hung Torlen. They grew even more so when he began treating the pronouncements of the Repentant as law. Individual Penitents, backed by soldiers, began entering people's homes and taking whatever they wished 'for the church.' Then your messengers arrived, Your Highness, requesting aid at the Dergun Causeway. Bredwyr conspicuously refused to send anyone. When people saw the combined army march past, with your banner among those at its head, their anger finally boiled over. The idea that their king could be beggared in his own home was too much.

"The next morning, the people armed themselves. Right at dawn they swarmed out of their homes and cut down anyone in a soldier's uniform or a Penitent's robes. By midday, they reached the palace. They found Bredwyr hiding under your bed, Your Highness. They dragged him outside the gates and hung him. Toward the end of the fighting, a group found us and turned us loose. I was the highest-ranking person left in the city, so I took command with the fleet sailors to back up my orders. It didn't take long to restore order. I've been acting as steward until you could return. Then, this morning, we saw those signals. I commandeered every ship in the harbor to augment the Fleet ships that were in port and ordered them to get underway at once."

An hour later, Ryan, my father, and I followed the high king and Marwynn down to the water where the *Black Marlin's* dinghy had been beached. Ryan had ensured that my guitar and other belongings had not gone astray after my capture, so I had my instrument strapped on my back and my pack over one shoulder. *Endolsar* hung in its scabbard on my right hip. I waded the slight distance out to the boat and handed my guitar over to one of the sailors.

"Have a care with that," I said. "It's fragile."

"Aye, master minstrel," he answered. "I've shipped with minstrels before."

I waded back to shore and took Ryan's guitar from him.

"I'll carry that, Master," I said.

"My thanks to you, Lauren," he answered. Then, with my father's assistance, he waded into the water. I watched them as they made their way to the dinghy; I had never seen my father behaving so solicitously toward anyone before. When they were aboard the dinghy, I waded out and handed Ryan's guitar up to him and climbed aboard myself. I settled in on a seat in the stern next to Ryan and my father. The sailor who had taken my guitar from me returned it and took his place at the oars.

"Oars!" he called.

The sailors all placed their oars at the ready.

"Back astern starboard!"

The rowers on the right side of the boat began rowing backwards, which had the effect of turning us toward the open sea. The lead sailor kept watch over his shoulder and when the bow was pointed toward the *Black Marlin* he called out, "Right lads, give way together."

He then fell into a rhythmic, sing-song chant that helped them keep time. I listened carefully, but there seemed to be no real words to the chant, just nonsense syllables that followed no pattern that I could discern. After a few moments, I gave that up in favor of looking around me. I had never been on a boat before.

The sea had calmed considerably since the morning turmoil. Sunlight glinted from the wavetops all around, tiny diamond pinpoints that winked into existence and then were gone. The west wind carried the scent of brine and whipped my hair across my face. The slop of the waves against the hull provided an erratic counterpoint to the sailors' chant and I felt that for the first time I understood the sea songs that I had learned at Songhaven.

Soon, we were drawing alongside the *Black Marlin*. She was a gaff-rigged schooner, built for speed to compete in the annual Merchant's Cup race carrying oranges, bananas, and other fruit from *Cha Peraluda* to Meren. Consistent with her name, the hull was black, with a green antifouling coating below the waterline. She looked fast, even at rest, and I wondered that she had yet to win the Cup.

Ryan and I handed up our instruments and then were helped aboard. My father followed with his own belongings and Ryan's pack. The sailors began preparations to lift the dinghy out of the water. As we stood looking around the deck, a woman approached.

"*Endollin*, War Duke, Minstrel of Alomar, welcome aboard," she said. "I am Adaryn. His Highness has asked that I show you where you can stow your belongings. It will take us less than two hours to reach Landfall, but we can't have loose gear rolling across the deck should things get rough."

We followed her below to a small cabin with two cramped bunks and several storage lockers. We stowed our packs in one of the lockers and Ryan and I laid our guitars on one of the bunks. Then we followed Adaryn back to the deck where she left us together at the starboard side rail.

The dinghy had been brought aboard and lashed upside down on top of the cabin that was located amidships. The anchor had been raised, and sailors were working in groups to raise the sails. At a shouted command from Marwynn, Adaryn joined one of those. As they rose, the sails caught the wind, and we began to move. It took what seemed to be to be an inordinate amount of work to get the ship turned toward the east, but when the turn was completed, the wind filled the sails, and the *Black Marlin* began to race across the water. Behind me at the helm, Marwynn gave an inarticulate cry of joy and excitement.

"This is exhilarating," Ryan said weakly, "But I think I'd like to go below and lie down."

I shot a quick glance at my father–who nodded to me in response–and said, "I'll go with you, Master."

I took Ryan's arm and together we worked our way back to the small cabin below decks. Ryan lay down on the empty bunk, his face pale and pinched, eyes sunken into his skull and shadowed with dark circles.

"What have I done to you, Master," I asked softly, mostly to myself, but Ryan heard me.

"I feel as if I have been torn in two," he answered. "The *Eldarin* half of me is somehow in that other place at the same time my human half is here. It saps me of my vitality and even the simplest of actions exhaust me. And it hurts, Lauren, though the pain seems to be decreasing."

"Then should you really make this journey with me? I do not know where it will lead, but I suspect that I have far to go. It will not be easy for you. You could remain in Amersford under the care of Healers. Or, I know a Healer in Cammford. I would trust her with my life. She would provide excellent care for you."

He smiled wanly.

"I will admit that I am tempted, but like your father, my heart is telling me that I must accompany you."

Feelings that I had been holding at bay surfaced.

"Why?" I demanded. "What's the point? The trial came and I failed. I chose the wrong note in the Song, and I broke the world."

"Lauren," he said weakly and laid his hand on my arm. Even that effort was too much, and he paused for a moment to rest. "I believe that the battle that Lorrestian saw is the one we just went through, and scholars have often called it the Final Battle. But Lorrestian also saw other events, some that frightened him and some that gave him hope. I believe that those events have yet to happen. You are not finished, my friend. You have not yet chosen your note in the Song, and I feel that you will need to hear from both me and your father before you do."

I started to reply, but his gaze went soft, the lids of his eyes drifted down, and his breathing became deep and regular. I took the blanket from the other bunk and covered him. Then I went back up to the deck.

The *Black Marlin* was running before the wind, her orange sails straining against the spars and lines. Marwynn was shouting orders to adjust the trim, the joy in his voice clear evidence of a man in his element. Anders and my father were standing on either side of Landfall's king at the helm and one of Anders' guardsmen was standing at the rail behind them. The bulk of the high king's Guard and our horses were on board a pair of ships that were following us, but they were falling farther and farther behind. I saw Marwynn glance their way and laugh.

I went to stand at the rail near the port side of the bow. Several gulls were keeping pace with us, screaming disappointment that we were dropping no food for them to scavenge. A faint mist of saltwater kissed my cheeks and was quickly dried by the sun. I stood there savoring the sensations and doing my best to keep my thoughts and emotions at bay. It took effort to avoid noticing how flat the world felt and when I failed, thoughts of the *Eldar*–of Élan–tore through my mind and larger drops of saltwater rolled through the thin crust of salt on my cheeks. Within an hour we were coasting up to the wharf in Landfall.

We spent the night in the palace in Landfall. I don't really remember leaving the *Black Marlin* or the walk through the city. I clearly remember, though, the effort it took for Ryan to rouse himself and stagger up to the deck of the ship. Watching him broke loose a despair that slowly extended its black, sticky tendrils throughout my mind as we walked, robbing me of my awareness of my surroundings. When we reached the palace, Marwynn ordered that a feast be prepared for us, but I begged his forbearance and went to my room instead. The weight of my failures, the weight of what I had done, tore at my spirit until I felt as if I was being ripped to shreds. I had torn Ryan apart. I had forced the *Eldar* from the world. I had lost Peg by not knowing who and what I was and, when I finally knew, I banished Élan. I had killed ten men. I had erased seven ancient wizards from existence with no more than a thought. I looked at my hands, half expecting them to be red with blood. I wasn't fit to be around people, couldn't bear to be with people who were grateful for the terrible things I had done.

I managed enough politeness to thank the page who guided me to my room, a young girl still obviously in awe of the responsibilities she had been given. I didn't choose to light a candle; I sat in darkness near the west-facing window watching a storm roll in over Orismay Bay. The roiling black clouds were shot through with lightning and the long growling peals of thunder seemed to echo throughout the city.

I'm not sure how long I sat there, watching the turmoil in the sky that seemed so perfectly matched to the turmoil inside me. I watched and the storm never seemed to break, never found release in a driving rain. Eventually, I gave it up and flung myself down on the bed still fully dressed. Failure stung my eyes, but no tears came to wash away the hurt.

I was standing alone on Point Lookout. Overhead, lightning lit night black clouds from within. Massive waves roared in, pounding the beach so hard that the earth shook. I turned toward the east and found myself rising into the air. Faster than the wind, faster than any bird, I began flying east. In moments, I was climbing higher to soar over the Breton Mountains and then swooped down to alight on unfamiliar ground.

The Kelmar Empire.

All around me was horror. Men were half embedded in the ground or in trees or in cattle or in the walls of buildings or cities. Women in sackcloth dresses and hoods and groups of half-starved children surrounded each man, wailing their grief. I had caused it. I had grabbed the men on Point Lookout and sent them here, but I hadn't known what I was doing. Now thousands of them were gone. And thousands of women were widowed, and many thousands of children deprived of their fathers and all of them witness to the gruesome way that the men had died. I raised my face to the cloud-filled sky and cried out in horror at what I had done...

I woke face down on the bed, clenching the blanket with both hands. The muscles in my neck and shoulders were strained and sore and their stiffness merged into a headache that made me vaguely nauseated. Despite that, I was ravenously hungry; I hadn't had anything to eat since the meeting on Point Lookout the day before.

I rose and stretched, which seemed to help my headache a little. The images from my nightmare rose in my mind and my stomach lurched. I dug into my pack to find my medications and pulled out a couple of pieces of willow bark and began chewing them. The taste was bitter, but the soreness in my shoulders and neck began to ease and my headache faded. My nausea faded along with it. When I felt that I had extracted all the good that I could get from the bark, I spit the chewed pieces into the chamber pot.

When I opened the door, I found the page who had guided me to my room curled up on the floor outside my door, her head cradled on her arms. She woke almost at once and scrambled to her feet.

"Good morning to you, sir," she said, trying to tug her clothing into better order. "How many I assist you?"

I ignored her question and asked, "What's your name?"

"Goriwyn, sir," she answered, "but everyone calls me Gori."

"Gori, have you been out here all night?"

"Yes, sir. I was told to make sure that you had anything you wanted."

"Well, Gori, I want you to take me to someplace where I can get a bath, then someplace I can get something to eat, and then I want you to go to your bed and get some sleep."

"But, sir..."

"Anything I want, right?" I countered.

"Yes..."

I think she was going to add a "sir" to that, but a huge yawn broke through her control.

"Well, it troubles me that you spent the night on a cold floor outside my room and I want you to get some rest. I will make sure that your king knows that you discharged your duties well."

"My thanks to you, sir. If you'll follow me, I'll take you to the bathing room."

It wasn't far from my room to a room with a bathing pool and less than that to the kitchen. There I was handed a plate full of eggs, sausage, fried potato slices, and a large hunk of bread. Gori then led me out the far door of the kitchen into the dining hall.

When we entered, the hall was empty except for two small groups of people sitting at opposite ends of the room. At a table on the far end of the room, four sailors in the uniform of Landfall's merchant fleet were quietly eating. Nearby, my father, Moireach, and Ryan were sitting at a table near a large window. They were deep in discussion and didn't seem to see me when I entered.

"Gori, my thanks to you," I said. "Now please, go get some rest. I know the people at that table. I'll be able to manage on my own now."

She nodded and went back through the kitchen. As I drew near to their table, I heard Ryan say, "My favorite of those is *Ironton*."

I stopped and stood quietly. I didn't want to interrupt their conversation. I was also wondering what they were talking about. *Ironton* was a long historical story song that told of a battle outside Marsden Forge. In the 879th round of the seasons after the founding of the Federation, the high king, a man named Roth, had levied a tax on the Alomar kingdoms to raise funds to repair the Great South Road between Badon and Amersford. Almost two rounds of the seasons later, the people of Marsden Forge, unhappy at having to pay for a road they felt they got no use from, revolted. Roth, at the cost of his life, put down the rebellion. The final engagement was fought at a tiny village called Ironton. Alternate verses of the song expressed one of two points of view: the narrator and a common soldier who fought in the battle. I was surprised by Ryan's comment; I had never heard him mention the song before.

"That is a favorite of mine, as well," my father said. "I've always liked how everything changes between the alternate verses: the key, the chord patterns, the timing, everything. It's quite an impressive piece when it's performed well."

I was surprised again. I'd never heard my father express appreciation for any piece of music, and he had never shown me that he had any knowledge of the intricacies of music. I must have made some sound because Ryan looked up and saw me.

"Lauren, come, join us," he said, smiling.

I took the seat next to my father.

"Don't let me interrupt your conversation," I said. "You were speaking of *Ironton*."

"Well, we were speaking more generally of the historical story songs," Ryan said. "Many of them are about battles. I was just saying that of those, *Ironton* is my favorite."

I nodded, but then noted, "You seem to be feeling better, Master."

He nodded.

"I do still feel weak," he explained. "But after a great deal of sleep, I seem to be adjusting. I cannot say for sure, but I think what I am experiencing may be similar to the adjustment that people go through when they lose a limb."

We were all silent for a moment; everyone chose that instant to take a bite of their food or a sip of their drink.

"So, the imagery in *Ironton* is very compelling," my father said. "The soldier's part is a fairly accurate description of the sights and sounds and emotions of a battle."

"It is said that the historical details in the narrator's part are quite accurate as well," Ryan added.

My father and Moireach both snorted derisively.

"What?" Ryan asked, looking puzzled.

"The topography described in the song doesn't match the most likely site of the battle," Moireach said. "We can't be entirely sure, though. My ancestor, Reigin, became king when his father fell in the battle. Reigin was appalled that his father and the high king had fallen in a fight over money, and he believed that the Alomar were stronger standing as one people. He made peace with Roth's son Artos. The two of them did not want Ironton to become a reminder of division or a rallying point for one faction or another, so they ordered it utterly destroyed. They left no two stones of the town standing on one another and all records of the village were destroyed. All that's left is the song."

"The author of the song was also pretty clearly attempting to aggrandize High King Roth and his troops," my father said. "He claims that the high king was outnumbered more than five to one, but Marsden Forge could never have fielded a force that large."

Moireach nodded her agreement and was about to say something more, but at that moment, a woman in the sable and gold uniform of the High King's Guard entered the room. She spotted us and headed in our direction at a brisk pace. When she reached our table, she hesitated, glancing back and forth between Moireach and me, clearly trying to decide which of us had the higher rank. A quick frown passed over her face and then she decided.

"*Endollin*. Your Highness," she said, sketching a quick bow to each of us. "War Duke. Minstrel of Alomar. The high king has sent for you. The horses are being readied, and it is nearly time for us to depart."

The four of us stood, Moireach somewhat stiffly. She had taken a wound during a skirmish on the Kaladin Sands, a long, shallow cut on the back of her left thigh, and it had begun to fester. She had come with us to Landfall to receive better treatment than could be provided in the field and would be staying in the city until her troops arrived.

"Your Highness, it was a delightful conversation," Ryan said to her. "My thanks to you."

"And to you as well, Ryan of the Minstrels. Travel safely and may Garth..."

She broke off and flicked a glance in my direction.

"I suppose that Garth isn't watching over anyone anymore," she said.

"Fat lot of good it did us when he was," the King's Guard muttered.

We stood, uncertain what to say in response to that.

"I must go fetch my things," I said finally, breaking the silence. "I hope I can find my way back to my room."

"Our rooms are near yours," my father said, gesturing toward Ryan. "We'll guide you back."

A short time later, we entered the square inside the landward gates of the city. The members of the High King's Guard were all mounted, but Anders was still on foot, talking with Marwynn. Three stableboys stood nearby holding the reins of horses for me, Ryan, and my father.

"Lauren," Marwynn called as we approached. Then a slight frown wrinkled his face.

"I see that my page has abandoned her duties."

"She has not, Your Highness," I said. "Goriwyn acquitted herself quite well."

The king of Landfall shook his head.

"I ordered her to stay with you..."

"You ordered her to see that I had anything I wanted," I cut in. "To fulfill your orders, Gori spent the night on the floor outside my room, a fact that I did not discover until this morning. The poor child was dead on her feet, so I ordered her to her bed. She refused at first, but I claimed that I'd be displeased if she didn't get any rest. Only then did she leave me. You are fortunate to have her in your service."

"I will tell her that you spoke highly of her," Marwynn said.

The high king stepped closer.

"The day is passing rapidly," he said. "We should go. It would be best if we were well past the causeway before we break for the midday meal."

I wondered briefly at that, but Marwynn bowed to me, distracting me from the king's comment.

"I am in your debt, Lauren *Endollin,*" he said formally. "Should you ever require anything of me, you have only to ask."

"My thanks to you, Marwynn, King of Landfall," I replied.

Marwynn then turned to Anders and bowed deeply.

"Safe travels, Your Majesty," he said. "I will see to it that your people are well cared for when they arrive here. And I will root out any remaining traces of Meren's treachery."

Anders simply nodded and turned to mount his horse. My father and Ryan each spoke a brief word of farewell to Marwynn. Then we mounted up and, following the high king, we rode out of Landfall.

CHAPTER SIX

I t had rained during the night and wide shallow puddles dotted the road. Tattered scraps of mist still hung in the dips and hollows and clung to the low-hanging branches in stands of trees. The sun was a faint white disc behind the silver-gray clouds in the east. As soon as we cleared the city, the Guard arranged itself to protect the high king. Three of them rode out ahead and three more dropped behind. The rest arrayed themselves in a broad circle around us. Hagan, their captain, rode just behind the king, who was speaking with Ryan and my father. I dropped back to ride by myself and for the next couple of hours I rode alone, lost in my thoughts.

Though I was surrounded by people, I felt alone. No one seemed to recognize it, but I had failed. I was supposed to be some powerful being who could save the world, but I had failed. True, I had stood up to Mar, but the cost of that defiance was too high. The *Eldar* were gone. Élan was gone. Magic was gone. And I had caused all that. I'd hurt Ryan beyond my ability to understand. Before that, my ignorance had permitted Peg to die. I closed my eyes and fought back tears. People I loved had died because of me. And I had killed. I was the only minstrel in recorded history to have killed another person. I had possibly killed thousands. My minstrel's sash was still tied around my waist, but I no longer deserved to wear it. I opened my eyes and spent a moment focused on the bright blue cloth. I had worked so hard to earn it, but the right to wear it was no longer mine.

I was just reaching to untie my sash when a quick, sharp pain shot through my mind. It left behind a dull sense of pressure, an ache behind my eyes. I swayed in my saddle as I tried to make sense of what I was feeling. It took a moment to clear my head, but then I recognized Mar's touch. She was struggling against the barrier I had built around her. But there was something else as well. With a shock, I realized that the thing that had been trying to break through from beyond the world was also probing the patch that I had put on that rent. My task wasn't done. In time, they would break through, and the world would be destroyed. I had to find another answer.

"Lauren, are you well?"

At the sound of my father's voice, I turned my attention outward. He rode to my left, Ryan on my right.

"Son, what is it? You look like you're about to fall out of your saddle."

"I..." I started but faltered. I was holding the reins with my left hand. The fingertips of my right hand brushed my sash. "I'm fine. It's Mar. She's trying to break through. So is whatever that other thing was. I'm holding them off for now, but I won't be able to do that forever. I've got to find another solution."

"*Saer* said that you should wake the Old Ones," Ryan said. I nodded my agreement, and he continued. "I was born long after contact between the *Eldar* and the Old Ones stopped. Until yesterday, I had never seen one of them before. I do know that the *Eldar* had more dealings with *Aenn* than any of the others. I don't believe that I've ever seen anything that even hinted at where she might live, but it seems reasonable to assume that she is somehow connected with the river."

"Which river," my father asked.

"The Amer," I answered. "The *Eldar* call it the *Aenn.*"

"I see," my father responded. He glanced toward the north; the river was a day's ride in that direction. "I don't think it makes sense to search between Amersford and the delta. There is too much traffic on the river for any being to stay hidden there for long. We should search east of Amersford up into the mountains."

"I agree," Ryan said. "That's still a great deal of river to search, though."

My father snorted. "Aye, it is." He looked back at me. "What about the dragons?" he asked. "Didn't the Old One say something about dragons?"

"She told me to seek the dragons," I answered. "I don't know why or even where to begin."

I paused. Once again, I was faced with the fact that although I knew a great deal, I didn't know enough.

"Lorrestian saw me end the world. Maybe I have no choice."

"Lorrestian also saw you save the world," Ryan reminded me. "You can choose the note you sing."

I didn't answer. In the silence that followed, I became aware that the people around us were slowly falling silent. The jovial conversations and good-natured japing of the morning were replaced with a sober silence. I looked around but noticed nothing unusual about our surroundings except that a large number of birds—most likely vultures—were circling in the sky ahead of us. Then I understood: we were approaching the Dergun Fens and the site of the battle at the causeway.

Within a quarter of an hour, we came upon the first bodies. The passing of our advance riders had scattered the scavengers, but it was clear that animals had been at the bodies. As we drew nearer to the causeway, the number of bodies increased until it seemed that whole companies of men—Alomar and Kelmar—lay there. Emboldened by their numbers, the scavengers did not flee at our approach. Vultures and ravens, foxes and rats were all feeding upon the dead. Clouds of flies hung in air thick with the sickly-sweet smell of rotting meat. The hissing of the vultures, the yips of the foxes, and the buzzing of the flies did little to cover the horrid ripping and sucking sounds of the animals feeding. I gagged, fighting to keep my morning meal down. Several of the Guard failed and the sound of their retching almost cost me my control.

"Halt," the high king ordered, his quiet command a virtual shout in our near silence. He turned his mount to face us and gestured for our escorts to draw nearer.

"I wish that we could take the time to honor the fallen with a proper burial," Anders said. "But I must get to Badon. The Federation needs its leader. I did make arrangements with Marwynn, and he will be sending teams to bury the people lost here. I do not wish to pass without acknowledging the fallen, though, so let us take a moment for silent reflection."

We sat silent, our heads bowed. Even our mounts were quiet, as if they had picked up the somber mood of their riders. After several moments, I glanced at Ryan. He nodded his understanding of my intent and together we sang *The Parting Song*. One by one, the others joined in. Moved by an impulse I didn't understand, I reached into the pocket on the side of my guitar's leather case and pulled out my wooden flute. As the last notes of *The Parting Song* faded, I put the flute to my lips and played the *Arimë Daelyr*.

I felt my power stir deep inside and Ryan gave a quick, sharp exclamation of surprise and seemed to sit straighter in his saddle. The pressure in my mind seemed to fade a little. All around me, my companions turned toward me, their eyes wet with tears. When I finished, the field was completely silent; even the animals stood with their eyes on me, their gruesome meals temporarily forgotten.

The high king nodded at me, his face grave, and then turned his horse toward the causeway. As the rest of us urged our mounts into motion to follow him, Ryan glanced my way. His expression told me that he wanted to talk. We were halfway across the causeway when he finally spoke.

"Lauren, what was that?"

"I told you about it back in *Evendim*," I reminded him. "I never got the chance to play it for you, though. It's called the *Arimë Daelyr*."

"I've never heard anything else like it. Where did you learn it?"

"A villager in Noweth taught it to me. He's the one who gave me this flute."

Ryan was frowning as he considered my answer.

"The name of the song sounds like the True Speech, but I do not know those words. Where would a backcountry villager learn such a thing?"

"He said that it has passed from parent to child in his family for as long as anyone could remember."

Ryan looked thoughtful.

"Minstrels have never given much attention to simple instruments like your flute," he said. "It may be time to reconsider that."

Later that night, I was sitting around a fire with Ryan and my father, finishing our evening meal. Conversations in the camp were subdued. What we'd seen earlier in the day was still with us.

"Dalach," Ryan said quietly. "What we saw today. *Ironton* doesn't do that justice. My thanks to you for being a shield for the rest of us against that."

My father only nodded. Ryan turned to me.

"Lauren, will you come with me? Bring your guitar."

I retrieved my instrument from the place where I'd laid out my bedding; the night was warm, and we weren't using tents. I followed Ryan away from camp. When the campfires were barely visible, we stopped.

"Lauren, you've never asked, but did you wonder why I never introduced you to my father while we were in *Evendim*."

"I did," I answered. "I believed that you had a reason."

"You know that my mother was gravely ill?"

"Yes." I could hear a piercing pain in his voice.

"My father was caring for her. He was doing everything he could to keep her alive, even though she no longer recognized him or me. He couldn't bear to let her go, but he knew that he was going to lose her. I didn't want to intrude on that grief."

"I understand," I said softly.

"Then take out your guitar and sing *The Parting Song* with me, my friend," he asked.

"Ryan, your father isn't dead, he's with the rest of the *Eldar* in that other place."

"Not for my father, Lauren," he answered me so quietly I could barely hear him. "He was caring for my human mother. When the *Eldar* went to that other place, she would have been left alone in *Evendim* with no one to care for her. She..." His voice faltered. "She wouldn't survive there alone."

Waves of dismay and grief flowed out of my heart and ran down my arms and my vision went gray at the edges.

"Ryan..." I started, but he cut me off.

"Sing for her, Lauren. Sing for her with me."

I settled my guitar into playing position and together we sang. And while we sang, the weight of one more lost soul settled on my heart.

Late in the afternoon, two days later, we reached a place where the road crossed a small river on a stone arch bridge. We could have pushed on, but the horses were still recovering from the long retreat and Anders, Hagen, and my father thought it best to rest them. We set up camp on the crest of a low, broad-topped hill on the south side of the road.

Though I'd bathed in Landfall, some part of me still felt soiled from my time as Garth's captive. I decided to take the opportunity to bathe in the river. I pulled a set of clean clothes out of my pack and then rooted around for the cake of soap that I knew was in there. I couldn't locate it, so I upended the pack and dumped the contents onto my blanket. One of the items there caught my eye.

The Lost artifact that I had found in *Elsgard*.

It was a decahedron carved of wood. Five of the faces had beautifully rendered images of dragons, their colors as bright and vibrant as if the paint had just been applied. The other five faces bore abstract symbols, a dot surrounded by a partial circle over what must have been some kind of letters or numbers.

I turned the object one way and another, wondering again what its purpose was. Each dragon face was on the opposite side of the object from a symbol face. One of the dragons was green and gold, another blue and green. A third...

I froze, my breath catching in my throat. The third was red with a line of upright black scales down its back. It was the dragon that had warded *Endolsar* at Lorrestian's bidding. And if that dragon was real...

I turned my attention to the symbol faces. Each had a dot in the center of a partial circle. As I examined each of the faces, I realized that the center dots were not truly dots. Each was roughly oval in shape, with angled upper edges and a flattened bottom. I froze again as the realization hit me.

They were all identical. They were all a silhouette of the standing stone in *Aennsrhyd*.

I quickly examined each of the five symbol faces. On each, the arc defining the partial circle began directly above the stone. To the north, I thought. The arcs then extended different distances around the stone. On a hunch, I turned to the face opposite the red dragon. The arc ended to the southeast. I called to mind a map of the Federation that included the *Eldarin* lands. As near as I could tell, a line drawn toward the southeast from the stone pointed approximately toward the cave where I'd met the dragon. I stood and looked around for my father and Ryan.

"Father! Ryan!" I called, my bath forgotten.

They looked up from where they sat talking with Hagen and a couple of the other members of the High King's Guard. I began walking quickly in their direction. They both stood, a look of alarm on their faces. The Guards watched us with concern.

"Do either of you have a map," I asked as I got closer.

Ryan shook his head, but my father nodded, a look of curiosity on his face.

"I do," he said. "Why?"

"I think I've figured out what this is," I answered, holding up the decahedron.

"What is that?" my father asked.

"It's a child's toy," Ryan answered. Then his tone became carefully neutral. "I did not know that you had that."

My father had taken a few steps to his bedding and was digging around in his belongings. I turned to Ryan to find his face set in a guarded expression.

"Is it a problem that I have it?" I asked.

"I am unsure," he answered. "Had you asked, I have no doubt that Alain would have given it to you. You are the *Endollin*. I do believe, though, that people should have known that you had it."

"Ryan, I'm sorry. If I can bring the *Eldar* back, I'll return it."

Ryan nodded.

"What do you think that it is?" he asked as my father returned.

"A map," I answered.

"A map?" Ryan echoed, his eyebrows raised in surprise.

"Yes. Father, let's have a look at your map."

He unrolled it and used small stones at the corners to hold it flat.

"Look," I said, showing them the red dragon. "This is the dragon that was guarding *Endolsar*. On the opposite face, there are these symbols. If you look carefully, this thing in the center is the standing stone in *Aennsrhyd*. If I'm correct, the arc should point to the cave where I found the sword."

I held the object over the map and the three of us compared the two. My excitement died; compared to the approximate location of the cave, the angle indicated by the decahedron pointed in a more southerly direction.

"I guess I was wrong," I said.

"No, Lauren, you're not," Ryan responded. "It's not pointing to where you found the sword. Look where it is pointing, though."

I looked at the map, but all I saw was open space until the line intersected the Gray Mountains.

"You think there's a cave in the Gray Mountains?" I asked.

"No. Look beyond the Federation and the *Eldarin* lands," Ryan told me. It's in Altiera. Lauren, it's pointing to Fire Vale."

Suddenly, the pieces fell together in my mind. The dragon was red and black, and *Saer* wore red and black. Their voices rose together in my memory; they were the same. From farther back in my mind came a memory of the Lost settlement near Cresswell and the painting of dragons and human-like figures standing side by side. *Endolsar* had been guarded by fire, not by the fire of a dragon, but by the very embodiment of Fire. I looked up at Ryan and my father.

"They're the same," I said, my voice trembling with excitement. "The Old Ones and the dragons. They're the same beings. And this is a map to find them."

Ryan had been crouching over the map; he dropped to the ground with a thud, his eyes wide with surprise. My father looked puzzled.

"So, we know where to go now?" he asked.

"Almost," I answered. "We know what direction to go in, but not how far to go. I have an idea about that: the other markings must be the distance."

"That seems a reasonable assumption," Ryan said. "Will we be able to decode them, though? Would the Lost have measured distance the same way we do?"

I smiled.

"All we can do is try."

We spent several minutes in silence, Ryan and I studying the map and my father peering intently at the decahedron.

"How far is it from..." he started. "*Aennsrhyd*," he said slowly and carefully, "to Fire Vale?"

"About 900 miles," Ryan answered. "It depends on where in the Vale you mean."

My father nodded as if Ryan's answer confirmed something he'd been thinking.

"And is there any place due west of *Aennsrhyd* where a dragon might live that is a multiple of one hundred miles from the city?"

"Due west of *Aennsrhyd* would take us straight down the Harbor Turnpike," Ryan responded. "It's about 600 miles to Landfall and I don't recall…" His voice trailed off. He was looking intently at the map.

"*Ech Numen*," he said quietly.

"*Ech Numen*?" my father asked.

"Shade's Isle," I told him. "What are you thinking?"

He held the decahedron so that we could see the face he'd been studying.

"This vertical line here–I think it represents zero and the two dots to its right mean two zeros. Note that it's one of two symbols on this face. The same is true for the face pointing due west. Now this one…"

He rotated the decahedron to show us another face.

"This one has three symbols, but there's only one dot next to the vertical line. I think that's a single zero."

Ryan and I both nodded in agreement.

"That would make this symbol a seven and this one a nine," Ryan said. "That would locate *Saer* in Fire Vale and *Ynes* on Shade's Isle."

I held out my hand to Ryan and he handed me the decahedron. I studied the other three symbol faces. Of those, one only had two symbols, one of them a double zero. I compared it to the map and identified the dragon associated with it. The blue one.

"Would it make sense that *Tael* would be here?" I said, pointing to the map. "Here where the mountains border Gorthin Mear?"

"There could be a cave in the cliffs above the lake," Ryan answered. "What made you think of that?"

"It's in the right direction and there are only two symbols on that face, one of them the double zero. It looks to me like Gorthin Mear is about 800 miles from *Aennsrhyd*."

"If that's correct," my father said, "the symbol for nine looks like a combination of the symbols for seven and eight."

Ryan and I nodded our agreement and then we all fell silent, contemplating the map and the Lost artifact. I got up to find some water. When I returned, Ryan was staring intently at the map.

"Why is it that we don't know exactly where the headwaters of the *Aenn* are?" he asked.

"Master?"

"The line representing the river ends where the mountains begin. This map should show the headwaters, but it doesn't. I don't believe that I've ever seen a map that does."

"I don't believe that I ever have either," my father said, a puzzled expression bringing his eyebrows together.

I glanced at the decahedron and suddenly Ryan's point got through.

"*Aenn*," I said. "She's there."

Ryan nodded.

"I think so. There are three digits on the distance to *Aenn* and the last one is a zero. Just guessing at the approximate location of the headwaters, it looks like they'd be about three hundred and fifty miles from *Aennsrhyd*."

"That gives us two more symbols, then," my father noted. "Three and five. If we assume that–similarly to nine–six is a combination of four and five, this symbol would be a six."

"That's all of them, then," Ryan said.

"Aye, it is," my father responded.

"So, we have the distance to all of the major Old Ones," Ryan said. "It's nine hundred miles to Fire Vale, and that's as the eagle flies. We would have to go through *Seldenawé*. It would take us most of a moon to ride there and most of a moon to get back. Could you..." He turned to me. "What did you call it? Could you translocate us there?"

"I... I don't know," I told him.

I closed my eyes. I had translocated to Point Lookout by sensing Ryan's mind. I tried then to locate another mind—even Ryan's—but could find nothing. I could sense my power deep inside me, but it was dormant, unresponsive. I probed deeper and felt a faint brush of fear that grew stronger the harder I pushed. I stopped and opened my eyes.

"I don't think I can," I answered. "When I did it before, I was desperate and acting on instinct. I sensed your mind, Ryan, and simply stepped toward you. Right now, I sense nothing." I didn't mention my fear, despite the fact that it was clenching a cold iron fist around my heart. "I didn't know what I was doing. Even though I made it to Point Lookout in one piece, I arrived five feet over the ground. Suppose that I materialized us in the heart of a mountain?"

My voice broke on that thought.

Both Ryan and my father caught that, and concern wrinkled their brows.

"Lauren, are you well?" Ryan asked.

I tried to stay silent, but my feelings poured out in a flood that I couldn't stop.

"Ryan, what if I killed them all? What if I..."

He cut me off.

"Lauren, I've told you. The *Eldar* are not dead. I can still sense them. You can bring them back."

"I don't know how," I cried. "And even if I do, they're going to hate me. Élan will hate me. I banished them. But I'm not talking about the *Eldar*. I'm talking about the Kelmar. I translocated them all. What if I sent them into rocks or mountains or the middle of a river? Ryan, I might have killed thousands of people."

For a moment, neither of them spoke. I felt tears welling in my eyes.

"Lauren," Ryan started, but my father raised a hand to stop him. He stood and offered me a hand up.

"Come with me, son," he said.

I took the help up and followed him away from the camp. We walked down the hill toward the river and stopped on a stone shelf that gave a good view of the water. Away from the noise of camp, it was quiet, with just a hint of a breeze whispering ever so softly through the grass.

"Son, I've seen you notice the help that I've given Ryan. You seem puzzled by it. Are you wondering why I've helped him?"

I was surprised by the question; I'd been expecting some sort of lecture. I had been wondering, though.

"I have been," I admitted.

"I owe him a great debt," my father said by way of explanation.

I turned toward him, my brows crunched with puzzlement.

"I don't understand. Did he somehow save you in battle or heal some wound I haven't heard about?"

"Neither of those. He was your Master. He taught you. He did more to make you who and what you are than I ever did. You are such a man that any father would be proud to call his son, a man that I am proud to call my son, and I owe that to Ryan.

"Lauren, maybe you did kill every soldier in the Kelmar army. I doubt that you did, but even if you did, they were soldiers. Every one of them knew that death was a possibility when they marched out on campaign. And it's actually a good thing that you feel guilt over the killing. It's when a soldier stops feeling bad about killing that he ought to hang up his sword and go home."

He pointed back toward the camp.

"Every one of those people–including the high king–is alive because of you. All of the people we left at Point Lookout are alive because of you.

Had you not done what you did, they'd all be dead and the Kelmar would be hunting down any leaders they had missed. Those people are now safe. You single-handedly saved countless Alomar lives. You saved the Federated Kingdoms."

What he'd said made sense and I understood it with my mind, but it did nothing to dispel the horror clenched around my heart. He saw that.

"Why is it that you think you killed all the Kelmar? That's not what you told me right after you sent them back."

I hesitated to explain, but I couldn't avoid answering.

"I saw it in a dream," I admitted.

Annoyance flashed across his face and for just an instant I caught a glimpse of the man I had fled from all those rounds before. His next words, therefore, surprised me.

"Lauren, what's bothering you clearly goes deeper than a nightmare. It's been obvious since you banished Mar. Whatever it is has undermined your confidence in yourself. It's eating away at you. What is it?"

I struggled to find the words.

"It's a memory that Garth pulled up. At Songhaven, during the attack, I saw a figure in black. I knew that it was the power behind what was happening. I intended to smash my guitar over its head to try and stop the attack, but I passed out."

He nodded but didn't otherwise respond.

"I know now that the figure was Mar. Garth explained what happened. To prevent a confrontation with Mar, to protect me, my power rendered me unconscious. My own power prevented me from saving Peg."

"I see," he said. "And why do you think you can trust anything Garth told you?"

"Not everything he told me was a lie," I replied.

"But everything he told you was intended to hurt you, to break you."

"I can sense the truth of this, though."

"Son, you didn't attack Songhaven. Garth and Mar did that. They are responsible for Peg's death. Have you considered what would have happened had you faced Mar prematurely? That might have been how you destroyed the world."

I shook my head, but the iron fist around my heart eased its grip somewhat.

"You've suffered losses, son. There's no denying that. You lost Peg and you will never get her back. But you could bring back the Elves. You could get Élan back. That won't happen, though, if you let yourself be paralyzed by guilt and fear."

My father stood watching me, his head cocked slightly to one side. He was apparently happy with whatever he saw in my face. He nodded and said, "Come back when you're ready."

He turned and headed back to camp. I turned and looked down the hillside at the river. The sun was low in the sky behind me and warmed my back, but a whisper-soft breeze cooled my face. Below me, a great blue heron glided in and landed on the near bank of the river. I wasn't sure, but it seemed to be looking at me. We stood motionless for long moments, then it spread its wings and took to the air. I turned and went back to camp.

Six days later, we rode into Amersford. Anders sent a couple of his Guard ahead to alert whoever was in charge at Marc's mansion of the high king's coming. As we entered the Southgate, the men were waiting for us.

"Your Majesty," one of them said as we reined in. "Chamberlain Jaret bids you welcome and is making ready for your arrival."

Anders looked as surprised as I felt.

"And how is it that Duke Jaret survived the Kelmar?" he asked.

"We do not have the particulars, Your Majesty," the Guardsman answered, "but rumor has it that the chamberlain grew out his beard and posed as the proprietor of an inn whose owner had fled the city."

The high king simply shook his head, a bemused smile on his face.

"The chamberlain says that he has sufficient space in the manor house to accommodate our entire party," the Guardsman informed us.

I urged my mount closer to the high king.

"Your Majesty," I said. "With your permission, my father, Ryan, and I will take our leave of you here. I am feeling a need for haste. Mar is testing the boundary I imposed, and I do not know how much longer I can hold out against her. I must find the Old Ones and learn why they wish me to seek them out before she breaks through."

"I understand," Anders said. "Will you not stay at the king's manor?"

"I think not," I replied. "I'd like to be on our way early tomorrow, the earlier the better, so we need to spend the rest of the day gathering supplies and making ready for the journey. That might be difficult surrounded by Marc's courtiers."

The high king smiled.

"You are probably right about that," he said. "Where will you be staying?"

"The Minstrel's Haven. They are used to accommodating the odd hours kept by minstrels."

"Very well. Safe travels, Lauren *Endollin*. Know that you will always be welcome in Badon."

"My thanks to you, Your Majesty. It has been an honor."

The horses that Ryan and I had been riding belonged to the Alomar army, so we removed our belongings and slung the saddlebags over our own shoulders. My father's horse—he called him Steadfast—belonged to my father. Ryan and I were going to have to find mounts of our own. We stood watching as the high king and his party rode north toward Marc's manor house, then we set out for the Minstrel's Haven.

When we reached it, the inn was nearly empty. The innkeeper was a former member of the High King's Guard named Kaitrin. She was one of the largest people I had ever met, taller even than Ryan, and well-muscled. She had a rather plain face with brown eyes and a crooked nose. She perpetually looked as if she was ready to shout orders at someone, but a smile lit her face when she saw us enter; she was obviously glad to see us. When we asked for lodging, she told us that we were the only ones staying the night and she gave us our pick of the rooms. Because no one else was staying, we didn't have to double up and each of us got our own room. Until that moment, I hadn't realized that I hadn't been alone in a very long time. I was looking forward to some time to myself that evening.

We spent the afternoon searching the markets for food, horses, and other supplies. The Alomar troops had taken a great deal of Amersford's food reserves with them when they pulled out and the Kelmar took much of what the army had left. As a result, food was scarce. Horses were even scarcer. The few we found were in miserable shape and terribly overpriced. By the time we returned to the Minstrel's Haven, we had managed to locate and purchase only a couple of small wheels of cheese, several loaves of travel bread, and some dried fruit. We had found reasonable deals on a small tent for each of us and my father had found a serviceable longbow with a quiver of arrows.

"If we can't find food to take with us," he said, "I'll just have to hunt. It may slow us down some, but there's no help for it. We need to eat."

We returned to the inn just as Kaitrin was lighting torches beside the door to welcome in travelers, though she muttered under her breath as we passed that she wasn't expecting anyone besides us. The minstrels had all been recalled to Songhaven after the attack on the college and had not yet come out again. The Kelmar invasion had put an end to other travel and even though the occupiers were gone, it had been too soon, and people were not venturing far from home. Only one table in the main room was occupied. Still, the smell of fresh-baked bread and roasting meat wafted out of the kitchen and my stomach rumbled.

"Those two are waiting for you," Kaitrin rumbled, pointing to the men at the table.

"We'll go find out what they want," Ryan said. "Would you bring us meals and some ale."

"Aye," Kaitrin responded and headed for the kitchen.

The men looked up as we approached. They looked similar enough to be brothers, with shaggy brown hair framing round faces brown from the sun. Their eyes were dark brown and set wide on either side of large lumpy noses. Neither had shaved in several days and when they reached for their mugs, it was clear that they hadn't washed their hands recently either. When they recognized us, they scrambled to their feet.

"War Duke Dalach," the one on the left said. He looked completely flustered and was wringing his hands as if he expected to be reprimanded for speaking.

"Don't I know you two?" my father asked.

"Aye, sir," the man answered. "We're stable hands for King Marc. I'm Alyn and this is my brother Joff."

"You were looking for us?"

"Aye, sir." Alyn peered past my father at me and Ryan. His gaze settled on me. "You are Lauren of the Minstrels?"

"I am," I answered, puzzled. I had no idea why one of Marc's stable hands would be looking for me. "Is there something I can do for you?"

"Oh, no sir. You and Ambrose left your horses with us last round. We've been caring for them ever since. Duke Jaret sent us to return them to you."

Relief flooded through me, and I felt a grin spread across my face.

"You've got Windsfoal and Realmstrider?" I asked.

"Aye, sir. All settled in the stables here at the inn," Alyn answered.

"The high king also had us bring you a pack horse," Joff added quietly. "He thought that you might have need of one."

At that moment, Kaitrin returned with our food, thick slices of roasted beef with carrots and potatoes, all of them covered in a thick brown gravy. There was also an entire loaf of some dark bread and a large crock of butter. I suddenly became aware of how hungry I was. I turned to Alyn and Joff, who were eying the food with interest.

"Have you two eaten?" I asked. "Would you care to join us?"

"No, sir," Alyn replied reluctantly. "We haven't eaten. But now that we've given you the horses, we must get back to the king's stables. We've been waiting here quite a while, and we have duties to attend to before we can take the evening meal."

"I'm sorry that we've kept you from your duties," I said. "My thanks to you for your patience."

They both simply nodded in response and then departed, leaving the three of us as the only patrons in the room. Ordinarily, the common room of the Minstrel's Haven was crowded with travelers and locals enjoying the excellent food and listening to whatever minstrel happened to be performing.

"It feels strange to see this place so empty," Ryan said as we sat down.

The meal—as could be expected from Kaitrin's inn—was excellent. Freed from the prospect of having to undertake the journey to find the Old Ones on foot, we were able to relax and enjoy our meal. Our conversation was light and easy and focused entirely on the routine events of the day, especially the bowyer who somehow overlooked the Warrior's sash around my father's waist and who had endeavored to instruct him on the proper use of a bow.

After the meal, we visited the inn's bathing pool and then retired to our rooms. Alone and not facing imminent danger, I simply sat and let my thoughts wander. Memory after memory skittered through my mind: Élan smiling up at me with stars shining in her eyes, the brief trip on the *Black Marlin*, the visions I'd had of *Aenn*, the smile Peg gave me the first time she and I had sung together, weather lore I'd learned from sea chanties. I felt as if there was a song hidden in my thoughts and so I pulled my guitar from its case and played some soft meditative chords, but the constant nagging pressure from Mar and that other being distracted me and I couldn't pull my thoughts together into coherent lyrics. After a time, I gave up and packed away my guitar, extinguished the oil lamp beside my bed, and went to sleep.

Well before dawn the next morning, I was awakened by a persistent knocking on the door to my room. I hastily pulled on my tunic and opened the door to find my father standing there, fully dressed and with his fully laden pack slung over one shoulder.

"You said that you wanted to get an early start," he said, his tone somewhere between puzzled and apologetic.

"I did," I answered. "Give me a few moments and I'll meet you in the common room."

I hadn't unpacked the night before, so it didn't take me long to get dressed and carry my pack and guitar down to the common room. My father and Ryan were already there, and Kaitrin arrived a few moments later with three plates filled with eggs, thick slices of ham, and finely chopped potatoes, all of it fried. The potatoes appeared to have onions and red peppers mixed in with cheese melted over the top. A young man I hadn't seen before accompanied Kaitrin; he was carrying three mugs and a pot of a strong black Altieran tea.

"You're all up early," the innkeeper noted.

"We have a long way to go," Ryan answered.

"When do you not, Ryan?" Kaitrin replied. "Listen, I have a great deal of bread from two days ago. I have to bake fresh each day in case travelers arrive, but if they don't, I'm stuck with it. Would you all like some of it to take with you?"

"That would be helpful," Ryan said. "Our thanks to you, Kaitrin."

"I usually give it to the Repentant to share with the poor, but they've shut themselves up in the temple and will see no one."

The young man set down the tea pot and looked directly at me then with an odd expression on his face.

"That's because of what you did," he said. "I heard from some people last night that you fought the goddess, that you killed her."

I looked to my father and Ryan, but their faces were frozen in carefully neutral expressions, and they did not speak. I glanced at Kaitrin, but she just said, "This is my nephew Kivyn."

"Mar's not dead, Kivyn," I told him. "She's locked away."

"Locked away? Where? How?"

"That's hard to explain."

"Why? Why would you do such a thing? Mar is the source of all that's good. Why would you fight her? I cannot believe that someone who would fight against the source of good is here in Amersford..."

"Was Mar truly good?" I countered. "Perhaps you haven't heard, but Mar killed High King Aerman Sorren. Her actions led to Ambrose's death.

She ordered and participated in the attack on Songhaven and innocent people–including someone I loved–died there. She was trying to murder all the Alomar leadership and everyone in the Alomar army. She had been looking for me since I was a child so that she could kill me. Do I need to go on? Does that sound like the source of all that's good to you?"

Kivyn's eyes were wide, and his mouth was open in a silent "O" of surprise. Without a word, he turned and fled toward the kitchen. To his credit, he didn't run, but it was close.

"A bit defensive, aren't you?" Kaitrin asked.

"Perhaps a little," I replied, feeling a little embarrassed. "Please give him my apologies."

"He's not alone in how he feels," she told me. "People are torn. They're glad that the Kelmar are gone, but they're not sure how they feel about a sword-wielding minstrel who killed the goddess."

"She's not dead," I repeated. "And if I can't figure out another answer, she'll be back. I cannot believe that her return will be pleasant for the Alomar."

For a moment, Kaitrin didn't answer. Then she said, "You'd best eat before it gets cold. I'll be back in a little with the bread."

We ate quickly and in silence. In less than half an hour we were hauling our belongings to the inn's stable. In the pale early morning light, I made out Kivyn sitting on a bale of hay near our horses' stalls. He stood as we drew near, his gaze fixed on me.

"You said that Mar intended to kill everyone in the Alomar army," he said.

"She did," I answered.

Kivyn turned to Ryan.

"Ryan, Minstrel of Alomar, does he speak truly?"

"He does," Ryan confirmed.

"Then I owe you an apology," Kivyn said, turning back to me.

"There's no need for that, but my thanks to you."

"No, Lauren. My thanks to you. I am working with Aunt Kaitrin because my father marched out with the army. I know that he may have died before you fought Mar, but if he didn't, you saved his life."

He walked past us on his way out of the stables.

"I wish I could tell him that his father was coming home," I said as I watched him go. "Do either of you know the man?"

They shook their heads.

"I guess we'd better go then," I said, but I looked in the direction Kivyn had gone and sent a silent wish for his father's return after him.

We rode out of the South Gate just as dawn began to brighten the eastern sky. We stayed close to the river, each of us lost in our own thoughts. Just after midday, the sound of our horses' hooves changed and when we dismounted soon after so that my father could relieve himself, I discovered traces of an old road beneath the grass.

"There was a road here," I said in surprise.

"There was," Ryan confirmed. "Do you not know the story?"

"No, I don't."

"After High King Roth died putting down the revolt in Marsden Forge, the throne went to his son, Artos. Artos V was a reasonably good ruler for the first five rounds or so of his reign, but then his wife and infant son died of a fever. Artos was never the same after that. He began spending more and more time in his chambers creating paintings that he destroyed as soon as he finished them. He spent less and less time governing, but he refused to allow anyone else to make decisions.

"The petty kings began to quarrel amongst themselves and there was no strong central leader to keep them in line. The chaos disrupted trade between the kingdoms, so food and other goods began to grow scarce. As tensions mounted, the petty kings began conscripting men into their armies. In the midst of that tension, a group of people, primarily from Amersford, Cammford, and the villages in between, decided to remove themselves from the rule of the petty kings. They formed an independent village similar to Durning, on the river east of Amersford. They settled at the point where the Amer turns to the north. They called the village Great Bend."

My father finished and we mounted up and nudged our horses into motion. After a few moments, Ryan continued the story.

"The village did well for six or seven rounds of the seasons. They built homes and planted fields. Enough people came to visit that they even built an inn. Then suddenly, all communication stopped. The king of Amersford eventually sent people to Great Bend to find out why. When they arrived, they found everyone dead. No one knows for sure, but all the evidence pointed to a particularly virulent illness."

"Everyone died?" my father asked.

"That's what they assumed. The soldiers from Amersford found no one alive."

"And no one lives there now?" I asked.

"No. The soldiers rounded up the livestock that was still living and took it back to Amersford. Before long, stories started spreading that Great Bend was haunted by the spirits of the people who had died there. It didn't help that most of the animals brought back died soon after reaching Amersford. It was most likely the effects of starvation and neglect, but many believed that the spirits of Great Bend came to reclaim their animals.

After that, no one was willing to go live in a haunted place, so the village was abandoned."

We reached the site of the abandoned village late in the afternoon. Great Bend had been built on a low bluff that looked over the bend in the Amer. Like my home village of Cresswell, a low dirt wall had been built around the village, but nearly one hundred and thirty rounds of neglect had allowed it to erode and much of the wall had settled back into the earth. Beyond what was left of the wall, we could see stone foundations topped by the skeletal remains of the homes, the weathered gray wood splintered and broken by time. I felt like I was looking at the ghost of Cresswell and I shivered a bit at the thought. I glanced past Ryan to my father and found him looking at me. It was clear that we were thinking the same thing.

"I think that I'd like to go further before we stop for the night," I said.

"I agree," my father responded.

As one, we turned our horses away from the ruins of Great Bend. We didn't stop until the abandoned village had dropped below the horizon and the light began to fail.

Three days later in the afternoon, we crossed Tolan Creek and began to climb into the mountains. I had come to think of the Bretons as home and I couldn't help but to think of Songhaven and *Evendim*. I did not sleep well that night. My sleep was troubled by dreams in which either Élan or Peg was burning at Songhaven or in which I was sitting alone knowing that they were gone. Every hour or so, I woke, my heart aching with loss and tears running down my face. For a time, I'd lie looking at the stars overhead, seeking solace and guidance, but the North Star was hidden behind tall trees, leaving me lost in the darkness. Lying awake and staring up at the slow nightly dance of the stars, I was very aware of the pressure on the boundaries I had set. Eventually, though, I'd drift off to sleep, only to wake again a short time later.

We spent the next day working our way upward around moss-covered boulders and fallen trees. Several times we had to wade across tributary streams. The air was thick with the clean metallic smell of damp rock. As the way grew steeper, the river narrowed and became wilder, and the susurrating sound of the water rushing through its rock-lined channel grew ever louder. As we climbed, I slowly became aware of a new sensation, a faint echo of power. It felt a little like Mar, but there was a difference I could not identify. If I opened myself enough, it made me want to turn around and go back the way we had come, so I held it at a distance and tried to understand its source.

We had to leave the river that evening to find a place dry enough and flat enough to make camp. As Ryan and I gathered wood for a fire, my father took his bow and left us. He returned a short time later with a pair of squirrels, so we had fresh meat for our evening meal. After we ate, I took my guitar out of its case and walked away from camp. When I felt as if I was far enough away that I wouldn't be heard if I played quietly, I found a fallen log and sat down. The light had gone gray, and the diurnal animals and birds were falling silent. My dreams of the night before had stayed with me all day and the feelings they aroused were aching to be put into words.

I tried a few chords and a simple finger-picking pattern. A G chord at first, then I moved two fingers to form a modified C chord. My brief time aboard Marwynn's ship came to mind. I repeated the chord pattern, and a few words flowed:

A red sky at morning is a lovely sight to see

> But to sailors it's a warning of a storm
> that's soon to be.□
> Now with all the things I know, don't
> it seem a little strange
> That though a storm was coming, I
> never sensed the change.
> Now the absence of her smile and this
> emptiness inside
> Have left me here to founder, adrift
> upon the tide...

I stopped. A ship that had foundered had sunk and wouldn't be drifting. I continued to finger the chord pattern, and another line of lyrics came:

> It would be no use to shoot the stars,
> to see where I may be
> 'Cause I know they'd only tell me that
> I was lost at sea

The chord pattern changed slightly.

> My surest guide is the starlight in her
> eyes.

I wasn't sure what to do with what I had, but I thought that I could make a song of it. I repeated the first six lines again, to make sure that I remembered them. As I finished, Ryan asked quietly, "Élan?"

I jumped slightly and stopped playing. I hadn't heard him approach.

"Yes," I answered just as quietly. "And Peg. Being back in the mountains brought them to mind. I dreamed of losing them last night."

"Lauren, I'm sorry," he said. He was silent for a moment. "I've been told that grief gets easier to bear with time."

I peered at him through the growing darkness. He hadn't mentioned his mother since we sang *The Parting Song* for her.

"Perhaps we can learn to bear it together," I said softly.

Neither of us spoke for a time, but then Ryan said, "Several times today your father and I felt a strong urge to turn back. Did you feel that?"

"Not so strongly that I would have called it an urge," I answered. "I did feel a power. It feels similar to Mar's, but very weak."

"Could it be *Aenn*?"

"Possibly. If she had set a compulsion to make people turn back, that would explain why no one has ever been to the headwaters of the river. Why would it be fading now, though?"

"Didn't *Saer* say that the Old Ones were going quiescent?" he asked.

"She did. Perhaps they must be active for their power to be effective."

I think he nodded slightly, but it was getting hard to see.

"We should get back before it gets too dark," he said.

I stood and followed him back to our camp.

Late the next morning, the river split, one branch coming from almost exactly due south and the other from the northwest.

"Which way?" my father asked.

He and Ryan both looked at me. I looked up each branch. There was no visible sign either way. Then I closed my eyes and tried to extend my awareness up the south branch. I felt nothing. I turned my attention to the north branch and there I felt it: the barest hint of a compulsion to turn away. I opened my eyes.

"North," I said, pointing.

Several more times that morning I had to decide which way to go as tributaries flowed out of hollows and the stream we were following divided again and yet again. The air was thick with the clean scent of pine and the forest floor was thick with a carpet of fallen needles, muffling the sound of the horses' hooves. I heard no birds, but only the rippling, ever-changing murmur of the stream. Lichen-covered rocks jutted up from the forest floor. I had never been here before, but I felt a growing sense of familiarity. Then the stream we were following split into three smaller streams that ran roughly parallel to one another ahead of us.

"Lauren," Ryan said softly. "The compulsion to stop is too strong. I can't go on from here."

"Nor can I," my father said.

I dismounted and handed Windsfoal's reins to Ryan.

"Wait here. I feel as if I know this place."

I walked slowly forward following the center stream, glancing over my shoulder at my father and Ryan every few paces. Just as I lost sight of them, I entered a circular clearing. The three streams all flowed through the clearing, two to the left and one to right, filling it with the soft gurgling sound of water flowing over stone. Across the clearing, a nude woman lay curled up in a moss-lined depression at the foot of a large stone.

Aenn.

CHAPTER SEVEN

I walked slowly across the clearing. *Aenn* did not stir as I approached. At first glance, she appeared to be an ordinary woman. I guessed that standing she would be an inch or two shorter than me. She had a diamond-shaped face, with high rounded cheekbones and a long straight nose. Her eyes were wide and set close to her nose. Her lips were full and turned down as if she were unhappy. Her long golden hair was wavy and disheveled. She wasn't thin, but she carried no extra weight either. Her breasts were full, and her hips were...

With a start, I realized that I was losing focus. *Aenn* was the essence of the earth, of life, of growth, and fertility. Even quiescent, her presence had an effect on me. I clamped down on my feelings and stepped a little closer.

She seemed completely inert; I couldn't see any sign that that she was even breathing. I was supposed to wake her.

"*Aenn*," I called softly.

She didn't respond.

"*Aenn*," I called more loudly. I knelt down beside her. I could still see no sign that she was breathing. I reached out and set my hand on her shoulder. She was warm, but my touch didn't rouse her. I tried to rock her, but she was as rigid and unmoving as the rock she slept under.

Stymied, I took back my hand. She looked somehow fragile, vulnerable, and I found myself feeling protective of her. Her legs were long and shapely, and I wanted to run my hand down the length of one. I placed my hand on her hip...

"No," I whispered to myself fiercely and drew back my hand. "No. I must wake her."

Not sure why, I slipped my guitar off my back and pulled my flute out of its pouch. I laid my guitar aside, raised the flute to my lips, and the haunting melody of the *Arimë Daelyr* filled the clearing. Deep within, I felt my power stir, and a wisp of it slipped away toward *Aenn* and formed a bond between us. A moment later, her eyes opened. The irises were the rich dark brown of fertile soil, flecked with traces of brilliant green. She sat up and fixed her gaze on me. Asleep, *Aenn's* beauty had been captivating. Awake and animated, she was eliciting feelings I could barely control. She raised both hands to push back her hair, emphasizing her breasts. I forced my gaze away from her. She noticed and an indulgent smile raised the corners of her lips. She did nothing that I could see, but I was suddenly a bit less aware of her as a woman.

"It has been many eons since I have heard that song played the way it was meant to be played," she said. "*Vorath, Endollin.*"

"*Vorath, Aenn,*" I replied.

She smiled again.

"*Aenn* is the name the *Enwilion Arastalon* gave me. My true name is *Ëyn.*"

I nodded.

"I am honored to meet you, *Ëyn.*"

She paused for a moment and her gaze grew distant and unfocused. Then she was back with me.

"I am the first you have visited. That was well done. I am the eldest."

"I was told to wake the Old Ones," I said. "Why?"

"*Endollin*, there is much that you need to know. I will answer your questions, but first I must tell you a story. Will you hear me?"

"I will," I answered, nodding.

"In the Void between the worlds dwell the *Arimë*. No one knows how many there are. The *Arimë* are known on many worlds as the Makers and with their thoughts and dreams they spin worlds out of the Void. Among the *Arimë* there is only one Law: once Made no world may be broken. Perfection is their goal, yet across the eons, no one of the *Arimë* ever Made a world that did not ultimately fail. Every Making seemed to have some unforeseen flaw that finally led to its self-destruction. Great was their puzzlement and greater still their efforts to achieve perfection, but still every world Made was in time Unmade from within.

"The greatest of the *Arimë* were two siblings, twins. One, known to us only as the Creator, was a loner, who labored unceasingly to Make the perfect world. His worlds, among them all, came the closest to perfection and all acknowledged that his worlds were the most exquisitely beautiful of all the creations of the *Arimë*. The twin, a sister, never seemed to Make worlds of her own, but was open and friendly and assisted all the others in their Makings.

"Then came the time when the Creator set himself to the greatest Making he had ever attempted. All his skills and passion were poured into crafting a world that was so achingly beautiful that the others all ceased their own Makings to watch. His sister offered her aid, which the Creator gratefully accepted. It was then, in that most observed Making of all, that the awful truth became known: the sister was found planting the seeds of entropy in her brother's world. While the Creator struggled to right the wrong, the other *Arimë* rose up against his sister, calling her *Melcurie-ar*, the Unmaker. In a last effort to save herself, she insinuated herself into her brother's world just as the final phrases of the Making were being sung. The world was coming to life, and the Creator could not stop the process. The *Arimë* could not reach the Unmaker, for to do so would break the new world and their only Law. At the same time, the Unmaker was bound within the world, unable to free herself from its confines. Enraged that his sister had put herself beyond the justice of the *Arimë*, the Creator altered the final lyrics of the Making. With an extra final phrase, he created a jewel and poured a measure of his own Power into it. It was a thing of rare beauty, that jewel, and it glittered violet, blue, and red in response to the Power contained within it."

I glanced at the ring glittering on my right hand.

"The Creator flung the jewel into the world, the last thing to be added. It blazed across the sky like a sun falling from the heavens. It shattered and spilled the Creator's own Power into the world. That Power dissipated and hid itself. In time, though, it would reside in a single individual, a frail, flawed being who, in attempting to use it, would destroy the world and release his sister to the justice of the *Arimë*. Thus, he ensured the destruction of his own world."

Ëyn paused, and then added, "And thus was he corrupted..."

My heart sank. My feelings must have been mirrored on my face. *Ëyn* frowned.

"The tale disturbs you, *Endollin?*"

"My name is Lauren," I answered. "And, yes, it disturbs me. Mar was not lying, then, when she said that I was meant to destroy the world."

"It is not so simple," *Ëyn* said. "*Melcurie-ar's* presence changed the world, made it different from what the Creator intended. She entered the world in the midst of the Making and the forces of creation shredded her. The *Arimë* are immortal. They cannot be killed, but the fabric of her being was torn asunder and integrated into the world. Her power became part of the structure of the world, and it changed things."

"Such as?"

"The *Enwilion Arastalon* became tied to that power. It gave them some of the creative power of *Arimë*."

"You've mentioned them before. Who are the *Enwilion Arastalon*?"

"The Children of the Stars. You know them as the Elves."

"So, when I banished Mar and all traces of her power, the *Eldar* were banished as well because they are tied to that power."

"Yes."

"You said *things* were changed. What else is different?"

"Another of those differences is my existence, the existence of those you call the Old Ones. We are the thoughts of the Creator, somehow given physical form by the presence of *Melcurie-ar's* power. We call ourselves the *Cogen*.

"We do not understand how we came to be, but we were not intended to be part of this world. Like the *Enwilion Arastalon*, we are bound to *Melcurie-ar's* power. But we are also tied to the world for we are the thoughts that shaped it. When you locked away the Unmaker, we were deprived of that which animates us, and we went quiescent."

"How are you awake now, then?"

"You have the power of the *Arimë*. Your will woke me, and I am now bound to you."

She smiled and her eyes locked onto mine. My heart melted. In that moment, thoughts of making love to her nearly overwhelmed me.

"Would you stop that?"

The words were meant to be a demand but came out more like a plea.

"Perhaps this form would be easier for you."

I took several steps back as she moved to stand. As she did, her form shimmered, and a green and gold dragon stood where the woman had been.

"You prefer this form?" she asked.

"No," I admitted. "But desiring you makes it hard to talk with you."

Her form shimmered again, and the woman was back. Her long golden hair now spilled down the front of her, covering her breasts, but that somehow made me even more aware of them. Her hair also reached far enough down to act as a frame for the golden triangle between her legs. I pulled my gaze upward to stare over her left shoulder. She noticed.

"My apologies to you, *Endollin*. Life and lust and fertility are part of what I am. I shall do what I can to suppress that part of my nature."

"My thanks to you, *Ëyn*," I said. Then my curiosity got the best of me. "How is it that the *Cogen* have two forms? Or can you take any form you choose?"

"We each have only two. All of us have a human form. For most of us, our second form is that of a dragon. We have long pondered why we have the forms we do, but we have no answer."

We stood silent a moment as I considered what to ask next. There was so much that I wanted to know, but much of it was just to satisfy my own curiosity. I set those questions aside and returned to an earlier point.

"So, I truly was meant to destroy the world?"

"Yes. But as I said, the world is not what it was meant to be. *Melcurie-ar* is here. *You* are here. You have all the power of the *Arimë*. You can choose to make the world what it was meant to be. You have power but lack the knowledge to use it. By some strange quirk of fate, the *Cogen* are here as well. We can give you what you lack. We can show you how the world was meant to be. Will you let me show you?"

She stretched out her hand. I took it.

Deep within me, some small speck of my power was bonded to *Ëyn*. That speck blossomed out until she filled me, a joyful union shot through with barely sensed music. Then I perceived the world as she did. I was the unbending granite bones of the Bretons, fleshed out with the rich loam of ancient forests. I was the loam and the worm pushing its way through me. I was a fawn, just rising to take my first faltering steps. My awareness spread and I could sense the near consciousness of the Elderwood, the scraping of miners digging for metals in the guts of the Iron Hills. I felt the wind whistle between the towering, snow-covered peaks of the Gray Mountains. Still further, I sensed the dense life in the jungles of southern Altiera and–beyond the Bretons–I could feel the agony of the overworked fields in the Kelmar Empire. More–I could sense the Kelmar soldiers. All of them. I hadn't killed thousands. Beyond the Empire, another mountain range, and beyond that, vast grasslands that trembled to the thunder of thousands of huge, shaggy beasts that *Ëyn* called bison. The world–*Ëyn* called it –was far larger than I had ever even imagined. Beyond the plains, there were more mountains and beyond those, a land filled with people living in cities that were ancient when the *Eldar* first landed. Some of those cities were built on the shores of another ocean. Or maybe the other side of the ocean I knew...

I think maybe I cried out, whether in joy or agony I am not sure. I was the entire world, and I was creatures so small that they could not even be seen. And, in the middle of it, piercing me to my heart, was the splinter of a massive bone, the last physical remnant of *Melcurie-ar's* physical form. Only the tip remained visible above my crust.

The stone in the center of *Aennsrhyd*.

The effects of *Melcurie-ar's* presence were everywhere, subtle warps at the core of everything...

When I came back to myself, I was lying on the ground, my head cradled on *Ëyn's* breast, her arms wrapped around me. I sat up, feeling dizzy and disoriented, but the feeling faded quickly.

"You now know all in my domain," *Ëyn* said softly. "I can rouse the others under my sway. You will need to visit the other four. I suggest that my opposite be your final visit."

"*Wyn*, Air?"

She smiled.

"*Ùyne*. You would know him as *Ynes*, Time. He is one of us, but his thoughts are strange and unsettling. You would do well to go before him knowing all that the rest of us know."

"My thanks to you, *Ëyn*," I replied. I stood and retrieved my guitar and slipped the strap of the case over my shoulder. *Ëyn* stood and came to me. Before I could react, she wrapped her arms around me and kissed me. My body reacted on its own. I wrapped my arms around her and kissed her back.

"*Ne astrynim, Endollin*," she said as she stepped back.

I now knew more of the True Speech. It meant "be strong."

"I will try," I said as I turned and walked away. I didn't look back.

It had been late morning when I left Ryan and my father. The sun was now halfway to the horizon. I had been with *Ëyn* for hours. I found Ryan and my father waiting where I had left them. They seemed upset.

"Lauren, are you well?" my father asked when I reached them. He and Ryan both looked haggard and worn.

I nodded.

"Shortly after you left," Ryan said. "The compulsion to leave became almost overwhelming. It has been difficult to even remain here."

"That must be when I roused *Ëyn*," I said.

"*Ëyn*?" Ryan asked.

"*Aenn's* true name," I explained.

"You found her, then?" my father asked. I nodded in response.

"We heard you scream," Ryan said. "We tried to follow you then, but we couldn't overcome the forbidding. What happened?"

"I'll tell you what I learned," I said, "But I would like to put some distance between us and here before we settle in for the night."

We mounted up and retraced our path for an hour before stopping. While Ryan and I tended to the horses, my father started a fire and prepared a meal. The sun dropped below the tree line as we sat down to eat, and it rapidly grew dark. I told them much of what I had learned from *Ëyn*.

"She thinks that I can make the world what the Creator intended it to be," I finished.

"Can you?" my father asked?

"Maybe after I learn from the others," I answered. "But I don't see how. Anything I can do, *Melcurie-ar* can counter. I'll never be able to make things right as long as she is in the world."

"Can you force her out?" my father asked. "Can you kill her?"

"I can't kill her. According to *Ëyn*, the *Arimë* cannot be killed. I don't know if I can force her out. Even if I could do either of those, I would lose magic and the *Eldar*. If I bring her back, she'll continue to attack the Alomar and everyone else. I have no doubt that eventually she'd rule the world."

I felt despair sliding through my gut like an ice-cold snake. For a while, no one spoke. I listened to the cracking of the fire and tried to find a solution.

"I don't know what to do," I told them. "Even if I find a way to defeat her, I lose precious parts of the world. I lose Élan." I looked at Ryan. "Is this what Lorrestian saw? Did he see me give up and destroy the world because there simply was no good answer?"

"I don't believe that," he answered me. His voice was quiet, but there was steel in it. "Lauren, remember who you are. Remember what you are."

Despair turned to frustration and anger in an instant.

"I'm a minstrel," I nearly shouted. "I should be playing my guitar in an inn somewhere, not battling a being capable of creating entire worlds out of nothing." I paused as the frustration dissipated and despair returned. "Ryan, I can't win!"

"Then the best that you can hope for," my father said quietly, "is not to lose."

He must have seen my confusion mirrored on my face.

"Have you read the works of Sloanne?" he asked me.

"No."

"She's required reading for anyone wanting to take the Red," he explained. "She wrote that there are times when you know that you cannot win but the cost of losing is too high. In those situations, the best that you hope for is to fight your opponent to a standstill. Are you familiar with the battles of the Fifth Meren Treachery?"

"Somewhat," I answered. "High King Aran Sorren was murdered by a spy from Meren. His son Alwyn assumed the throne and led Federation troops in the battles that came after. The ruling family in Meren was deposed and Meren became a principality."

My father nodded.

"That's accurate as far as it goes, but it lacks detail. Alwyn led Federation forces into Meren's territory to put down the rebellion. Despite an overwhelming numerical superiority, he lost the first two battles and retreated back into Federation territory. Had King Farnir of Meren left it at that, he would have ruled over an independent Meren. Instead, he decided that he had to win, that he had to not only defeat the Federation forces, but he had to seize Federation land as well. He pursued the high king, who managed to rally his troops. In his home territory, Alwyn used his familiarity with the terrain to set an ambush and was able to lure Farnir into it. That battle broke Meren's strength. What was left of Farnir's troops fled back toward home. They tried to avoid engaging, but Alwyn caught them up before they could reach the Sorden where they could have just disappeared into the forest. Farnir's men were dispirited and disorganized and he couldn't pull them together. The last two battles were total routs. Farnir himself died in the last one. Lauren, he didn't have to win in the sense of defeating Alwyn. He could have won by simply fighting Alwyn to a standstill."

"This Sloanne sounds like she is worth reading," Ryan said.

My father nodded in Ryan's direction and then looked to me, a questioning look on his face.

"My thanks to you for sharing that," I said. "It gives me something more to consider. One thought does occur to me now, though. *Melcurie-ar* is immortal. I am not. Even if I could fight her to a stalemate now, what happens when I am gone?"

Neither of them had an answer to that and I chose to change the subject.

"I did learn to translocate," I told them. I sounded weary, even to myself. "I need to be familiar with my destination, though."

"Where are we going?" Ryan asked.

"Han," I answered. "*Wyn* is the closest and according to the Lost artifact, he should be close to Han. I've never been there, though. I could probably find what I need in what I absorbed from *Ëyn*, but I can't be sure that I could find it quickly."

"So, we need to ride," Ryan responded.

"Not necessarily," I said, not looking at either of them. "I could Read one of you."

When I finally looked up, Ryan was watching my father, who was staring into the fire, a troubled frown on his face and tension in every line of his body. Ryan shifted his gaze to me.

"You can Read me," he said. My father visibly relaxed.

"My thanks to you, Master," I replied. "I won't be rummaging through your memories. I'll just need you to think of a place in Han or–better–just outside the city. I'll Read only that."

"When would you like to start?"

"I don't want to arrive in Han in the dark. Let's go first thing in the morning."

We were up before sunrise the next morning. We ate a cold breakfast of dried fruit and salted meat and then packed the few things that we had used overnight away. Then Ryan and I sat on the ground facing one another.

"I need to lay a hand on your forehead," I said quietly.

He nodded. I placed my hand on his forehead and said, "Just think of a place in Han, open enough that we can appear there without risk of landing in a building or down a well."

"There's a broad field outside the western gate between the road and the river. Will that do?"

"Yes," I replied. "Close your eyes and concentrate on an image of that field."

I closed my eyes and slipped into Ryan's mind. His was a disciplined mind and the image I saw was clear and vivid. Just before I let slip the bond between us, though, I sensed something else. He was in pain. Though he had learned to function in spite of the pain caused when I separated the world, the loss of the *Eldar* half of his being still hurt him. Guilt colored my cheeks and leaked across the bond between us before I could let go and sit back.

We opened our eyes at the same time.

"I felt that," he said. "Lauren, you didn't mean for it to happen and you're doing your best to heal it."

"I will heal it," I insisted. "Whatever it takes."

"Don't say that," he responded. "Not if it means giving up who you are. Don't give up your heart. I fear that would be the death of our world."

I stood and then helped him up. We mounted.

"What now?" my father asked.

"When I signal, we all need to move forward together," I said.

Without waiting for acknowledgement, I closed my eyes and called up the image that Ryan had shared. I sent out wisps of my power and wrapped them around Ryan and my father. I could sense their tension and apprehension, but I didn't let that distract me. I reached a little further and pulled the horses into the bubble. I opened my eyes.

"Now," I said firmly.

Together, we stepped forward onto the field outside of Han.

The city of Han was located at the apex of the Aeran Pass. The pass was the easiest way through the Breton Mountains at the northern end of the range; it was a gap large enough to march an army through. The pass was nearly four miles long and varied from one and a half to two miles wide. It was as if some titan had stomped the mountains flat at that point. The city had been built for one purpose: to prevent the Kelmar from pouring through the pass into Alomar lands. When the Alomar first settled in their new lands, they built a fortress overlooking the pass, a structure large enough to house enough cavalry, infantry, and archers to repel Kelmar forces. Soldiers stationed at Aeran Fort for long periods of time desired to have their families nearby and a town sprang up below the fort and flanking the road. To protect the growing town, the fort's commander, a man named Han, built a gated wall at the eastern end of the pass. After several concerted attacks by the Kelmar breached the gate, another wall was built inside the first to provide a second line of defense. Out of an abundance of caution, a wall was also built across the western end of the pass enclosing the town and part of the Camm River, which was the main source of water. The town eventually became the seat of a new Alomar kingdom with Han as its first king. The people so loved their king that on his death they changed the name of the town—now a small city—to Han in his honor.

The image Ryan had given me brought us into a grassy meadow some quarter of a mile from the western wall with a small copse of trees between us and any watchers on the walls. An echo of thunder rolled back at us from the surrounding mountains.

"That was remarkable," Ryan said, awe and excitement mixed in his voice.

"I didn't feel anything," my father added. "We just rode forward, and we were here."

I just smiled and urged Windsfoal toward the road. A few moments later, we were approaching the western gate of Han. It was open, but as we drew near, four archers stationed atop the towers on either side stepped into view. Their arrows were nocked and pointed at us.

"Stop!" one of them commanded.

We reined in and looked up at the men on the walls.

"Who are you and why have you come here?"

My father urged Steadfast forward a couple of steps.

"I am Dalach, War Duke of the Army of the Federated Kingdoms. With me are two Minstrels of Alomar. We pose no threat."

The man who had spoken lowered his bow and stepped back from the parapet. A moment later, he stepped into view with a woman who leaned over the edge to peer more closely at us. She straightened and said something to the men with her and they lowered their bows.

"Dalach," she called. "It is good to see you again."

My father smiled.

"Aedion," he called back. "I am glad to see that you survived the Kelmar occupation. Will you let us enter or do you plan to have your men shoot us?"

Even from the foot of the wall I could see her smile.

"I'll meet you inside the gate."

We rode slowly through the gate and dismounted in the square inside. Beyond the square, the road crossed the Camm on a stone arch bridge. A moment later, Aedion joined us, leading a horse of her own.

She was of a height with my father and clad in the uniform of Han: a gray tunic and trousers with deep sky blue piping at the cuffs and the lower edge of the tunic. She wore a breastplate of hammered steel adorned with the gray dragon rampant that was the symbol of Han. Her long blonde hair was tied back with a leather tie and framed a long, thin face with a petite nose and sparkling blue eyes. She was smiling broadly. To my surprise, she walked up to my father, threw her arms around him, and kissed him. I had never seen anyone hug my father, much less kiss him. To my even greater surprise, he put his arms around Aedion and kissed her back. After a long moment, they broke the kiss, but remained in each other's arms, speaking too quietly for me to hear what they were saying.

Ryan nudged me.

"You're staring," he said.

I tore my gaze away from my father and Aedion to glance at Ryan.

"What?" I asked. My gaze returned to my father and the warrior from Han.

"You're staring at them."

"I'm just very surprised. No one has ever kissed my father."

Ryan laughed.

"At least one other person has," he said and shook his head.

A moment after he said it, his meaning hit me, and my face flushed. I was saved from having to respond by the approach of my father and Aedion.

"Houl's son Steafán is now king of Han," my father said. "Aedion will take us to see him."

We mounted and Aedion led us into the city. The road we had come in on was the end of Beacon Road, which linked Han with Badon. Inside the city, it ran from the western gate to the eastern gate and was known as Gate Road. It was lined on either side by neatly kept shops and inns. At intervals, smaller streets intersected the road and led to residential areas that extended onto the lower slopes of the mountains on either side of the pass. On the slopes to the north stood the turreted bulk of the old Aeran Fort, now the residence of the kings of Han. Aedion was leading us toward it.

The Fort was built of massive blocks of the dark gray granite native to the Bretons. It had been built to house nearly 700 men along with cavalry horses, livestock, granaries, blacksmiths, and everything else needed to protect the pass. There was no artistry to its design; in shape it was a rectangle with the long side parallel to Gate Road. The structure was four stories high with turrets at each corner. There were four more turrets on each long wall. It was ugly and utilitarian, and it had been Peg's home.

Thoughts of Peg occupied my mind until we rode through the gates in the center of the wall overlooking the pass. We were met in the courtyard within by soldiers in the gray and blue of Han's army. We dismounted and several members of the seneschal's staff took charge of our belongings before grooms led our mounts away to the stables.

"I'll take you to the king," Aedion said.

She led us into the building and down a series of dimly lit, cramped feeling corridors and up two flights of stairs. We turned to the right down a hallway. Halfway down, two guards stood on either side of a door very much like all the other doors. When we reached them, Aedion spoke.

"War Duke Dalach to see the king. With him are his son Lauren and Ryan, both Minstrels of Alomar."

The men nodded. One of them knocked, then opened the door, and stepped inside.

"Your Highness, War Duke Dalach to see you."

"Send him in please."

As we entered the room, I glimpsed a window straight ahead that looked out of the rear of the building toward the mountains. Then my attention was drawn to a blazing fire in a fireplace to my left. Even though it was late in the second moon of *Tymnagena,* much of the day was still cool at the higher elevations in the mountains. There was a pair of chairs drawn up in front of the fire. Steafán was seated in the one closest to us and he rose to greet us as we entered. A woman was seated in the other chair.

Peg.

She froze in the act of rising when she saw me. For a heartbeat that could have been hours we simply drank in each other's face and then we crossed the distance between us and wrapped our arms around each other. She molded her body to mine, and we kissed. She broke the kiss but didn't let go of me. Instead, she laid her head on my shoulder.

"Peg," I said softly, my voice choked with emotion.

Behind me, Steafán said, "Aedion, have the guards bring us some additional chairs."

"Yes, Your Highness."

"Peg," I said again. "How? I thought you died in the attack on Songhaven."

She took a breath to reply but at that moment, the guards and Aedion returned with chairs for all of us. Steafán said, "I suspect that we all have stories to share. Let's get comfortable and then we can share them." He turned to one of the guards. "Malvynn, have the kitchen send us several large pots of tea. Other than that, I do not wish to be disturbed."

"Yes, Your Highness," Malvynn responded. Then he bowed and left the room.

We arranged the chairs in a semicircle near the fire with Peg at one end of the arc and Steafán at the other. I sat next to Peg with Ryan on my right. My father sat to Ryan's right and close to Aedion who sat between him and Steafán.

"Well," Steafán started. "The last reliable news that I received was that the Alomar army had been driven out toward Landfall. The people who told me that also said that there was an army of Elves with them."

He looked directly at me.

"They also said that you were with them and that you were going to save everyone. What happened and what brings the three of you to Han?"

I told them about my flight from Songhaven after the attack and how I'd found the *Eldar* hidden in the southern Breton Mountains. I didn't mention Élan or the trip to *Elsgard*, but I did tell them about finding the sword, my attempts to learn to use my power, my capture by Garth, and my battle with the being that we knew as Mar. I finished with *Saer's* appearance at Point Lookout and my quest to locate the Old Ones.

"I sense that there is far more to the story than that," Steafán said. "We'll get to that later. I think Peg and I should share where we've been and what we've done." He paused and swept his gaze over all of us. "The last time that I saw any of you was when I helped Lauren escape from the dungeon under Badon. Let me tell you what I've done since then.

"I got Lauren out of Badon just after the first Kelmar assault on this city," he said. "I planned to return here to assist with the defense after I met Lauren in Willow Bank. On the road back toward Badon, though, I met a merchant friend who told me that the search for Lauren was widening to include people who might have had ties to him. Someone told them about you two." He gestured toward me and Peg. "I figured that they'd want to talk to me, and I didn't want to talk to them. Everyone knew that I was heading for home, so I decided that home was the last place I should go. I went to Canim instead. I was there when Han fell."

There was a knock at the door. It opened a crack, and a woman said, "Your Highness, it is Maizy. We have your tea."

"Bring it in, please Maizy."

The door opened further, and a young woman entered followed by several other of the kitchen staff. They set up a small table in front of us and placed a couple of large pots of tea and several mugs on it. They had also brought small plates of fruit and cheeses.

"My thanks to you, Maizy," the king said as the girl and her helpers left the room. We all helped ourselves to a mug of tea and then Steafán resumed his story.

"Sooner than I would have expected, a force of Kelmar showed up at Canim. Roth had taken almost his entire army with him to Badon, so the city was undefended. It was probably not a bad place for me to be during the occupation; no one knew me there so the Kelmar didn't know that I was from a ruling family. I actually spent my time working in a stable. Then the Kelmar just vanished." He paused and glanced at me. "When I realized that they were gone, I took one of their horses and headed here as quickly as I could. When I got here, the city was all but deserted. The Kelmar were gone, but so was the majority of the civilian population."

"That was my doing," Peg said. She set down her mug and looked at me. "I wasn't at Songhaven during the attack. My father was worried about what would happen to the people of the city if the Kelmar attacked in earnest. He wrote and asked me to come home to help. I left the day before the attack. I asked Rachel to let you know if you came in while I was gone."

I hung my head.

"She tried," I told Peg. "I found her the morning after the attack. She'd been stabbed by one of the Kelmar soldiers. She died before she could tell me."

"Rachel's dead?"

"Yes."

"We lost so many..." Peg's voice trailed off. She was silent a moment and then said, "What I am about to tell you has never been shared with anyone outside our family."

She looked directly at me.

"I led the civilians out of the city to *Ciel na fal Arth*."

"The Roof of the World," Ryan translated, sounding puzzled.

"Yes," Peg confirmed. "It is a valley deep in the mountains about ten miles north of here. *Wyn* lives there. We were under his protection."

None of us spoke. After a moment, I glanced at Ryan. He looked as shocked as I felt. Steafán broke the silence.

"There is a reason that there's a dragon on our banner," he said.

"When *Wyn* went quiescent," Peg continued, "I wasn't sure what to do. He was our protection. Then a messenger arrived and that worried me even more; it has always been the case that only people led by someone from our family were allowed to reach *Ciel na fal Arth*. The message that the man carried was sealed with Steafán's seal though and the message was that the Kelmar were gone. I led the people back and since then we've been trying to get the city functioning normally again."

She paused and took my hand.

"I can take you there," she said.

Later that afternoon, Peg and I were walking hand in hand on the parapet overlooking the city. She tugged me to a stop and pulled me in for a hug. Then she stepped back at looked up at me.

"You've changed," she said. "You seem much, much older. It's as if something childlike in you has gone."

I reached out and took her hands in mine.

"I'm still me," I said.

"I've heard things. Some people said that you killed Aerman Sorren. Or that you killed Ambrose. Or both. I've even heard that you tried to kill Prince Anders."

I saw her eyes flick to *Endolsar*.

"Lauren..." she asked in a frightened tone.

"I didn't kill the high king," I told her. "I was on the road with Ambrose when Aerman was murdered. I was with Ambrose when he died, but it was a soldier from Meren who killed him. And I saved Anders when Larsen tried to kill him. I've been with the Alomar army. Anders trusts me.

"Peg, it was all Mar. She's the one who killed Aerman. She was at Songhaven. It was her desire that drove the attack. She punished the minstrels simply because I am a minstrel. She sent the Kelmar into the Federated Kingdoms. She tried to seduce me and when she couldn't, she tried to kill me. For now, I've cut her off from the world, but if I can't learn what I need from the *Cogen*, she'll be back."

Her eyes were wide.

"Lauren, what are you?"

"You've heard me called the Lawbreaker?"

"Yes. I thought it was because of the murders."

I told her about *The Book of Kings* and Lorrestian's prophecy. Then I shared what *Ëyn* had told me about the creation of the world.

When I finished, she didn't say anything, but took my hand and we walked toward the western end of the building. We didn't speak again until we reached the back side of the Fort, which faced the mountains.

"The mountains are so much more rugged here than near Songhaven," I said.

"They are," Peg agreed. "It seems like it has been a long time since we were there."

"It does. So much has happened since then."

"I thought of you all the time," she said.

"I thought of you, too."

Something in my tone took the smile from her face and clouded her eyes with doubt. Then, suddenly, the doubt was replaced by sorrow and pain.

"There was someone else."

"Peg, I..."

A tear rolled down her cheek, but she didn't say anything more.

"After Songhaven, I thought you were dead," I explained. "Rachel told me that you'd been teaching at the college, and I watched Garth burn the Masters on stage. I tried to intervene, but my power stopped me; I wasn't ready to face Mar. I woke the next morning and I searched the city for you. When I reached the Grotto, I finally admitted to myself that you were a Master and that you had been onstage.

"Peg, the knowledge that you were dead broke me. I walked out of Songhaven with nothing but my guitar. I headed south into the mountains, and I walked until I couldn't walk anymore. I didn't eat; I barely drank. I walked until I passed out from exhaustion and when I woke again, I walked more. Finally, I sat down under a tree, and I gave up. I thought I was going to die. I felt myself losing consciousness and I didn't think I was ever going to wake up.

"But I did. The *Eldar*–the Elves–found me."

I fell silent and stared out at the mountains. Everything was strangely silent. I could sense Peg beside me, but I couldn't look at her. I couldn't bear to see the hurt I was causing her. Long moments went by and then I continued.

"I didn't know what it was at the time, but I could feel Mar searching for me. I knew that whatever it was had taken you away from me. I didn't want to lose anyone else, and the *Eldar* seemed to know more about what was happening to me than I did. I asked them for help."

"She's one of them?" Peg asked quietly.

"Yes. The king's daughter. We grew close. Not as close as you and me. Even though I thought you were gone, I couldn't..."

My heart was breaking. I hated that I was hurting Peg, but I felt as if I was betraying Élan.

Peg rested her hand on my shoulder for a moment but didn't speak. As she removed it, she said, "I'll see you at the evening meal."

I listened as she walked away. One step, two...

The constant pressure that I felt from *Melcurie-ar* flared into a blinding spear of agony thrust through my head. My knees buckled. I cried out and felt my power react just before my chin hit the edge of the parapet and everything went black.

When I woke, I was lying in a bed. Peg was standing to my left, holding my hand. Ryan and my father were on my right.

"Lauren," my father said. "How are you feeling?"

"Like I got punched by a fort," I answered.

Peg smiled and squeezed my hand. My father looked at Ryan in surprise.

"I've told jokes before," I told him.

"Never in my hearing," he answered.

"And not in mine either," Ryan said. The smile dropped from his face. "Lauren, what happened?"

My head no longer hurt, but my chin felt raw and my teeth ached.

"*Melcurie-ar*," I answered. "She's getting more aggressive. I was distracted and she took advantage. I'm running out of time."

"It's too late to head into the mountains tonight," Peg said. "We can leave first thing tomorrow morning."

"They're serving dinner now," Ryan said. "We should head down to the dining room. Are you well enough to walk?"

"I am, but you and father go ahead. I need a minute with Peg."

My father nodded and they left.

Peg hadn't let go of my hand. I looked up at her. She was wearing a gown of emerald green velvet with a deep round neckline. It was edged at the cuffs and around the neckline with an intricate pattern done in gold. It reminded me of the pattern the *Eldar* used on their doors...

I forced away thoughts of the *Eldar*.

"Peg, I'm sorry," I said.

"Lauren, I understand. You thought I was dead," she replied. She searched my face. "Now that you know that I'm not, what about the Elven girl?"

I sat up and swung my legs over the edge of the bed. I paused to see whether I got dizzy and when I didn't, I stood. I took both of Peg's hands in mine.

"I love you, Peg. I want to spend the rest of my life with you."

She searched my face again.

"But you love her, too," she replied.

I couldn't deny that. She could see that in my face. Tears were welling up in her eyes. She blinked them away and I could see that something had changed.

"I love you, too, Lauren," she said. She pulled me into a hug. "But I know that you have to go. You must visit the rest of the *Cogen* and deal with Mar. We'll figure this out after that."

She kissed me, then, a quick light kiss. Then she pulled me closer and kissed me again with such passion that she took my breath away. She stepped back and smiled up at me.

"Let's go to dinner."

I was standing in the field outside of Songhaven. The residents of the city stood around me in a wide circle. Peg and Élan stood in front of me. Peg was wearing a gown like the one she'd been wearing at dinner, but the colors were reversed: the gown was a rich golden yellow and the trim was emerald green. Élan was dressed similarly, but her gown was a deep midnight blue edged in silver.

Someone behind me nudged me forward and the people of Songhaven said, "We are the Alomar. You must choose."

Then I was standing on a sandy beach at the end of a long thin peninsula. I was reminded of Point Lookout but knew that this was a different place.

A name bubbled up from deep within the knowledge I had gained from *Ëyn*: Land's End. Overhead, black clouds gathered and churned, lit from within by almost constant lightning. All around me, the sea was whipped into a frenzy of massive, white capped waves that pounded the shore as if they intended to tear it to pieces. Then I felt the barrier I had built around *Melcurie-ar* fail and the sky cracked open. In an instant, I was alone in a black, featureless void.

I woke howling my denial of the fate that I'd dreamed. It was still dark outside, but I knew that I'd never get back to sleep. I sat by the window of my room, staring out the window as the growing light of dawn slowly picked the mountains out of the black of night.

I tried not to think, but my thoughts assailed me. As soon as I pushed one away, another took its place. Was my dream prophetic? Was I going to destroy the world, not because of something I did, but because I did nothing? Peg was alive and I wanted to be with her, but I wanted Élan, too. How could I possibly choose between them? It wouldn't matter if I couldn't save the world, but how could I do that?

I was nearly in tears when someone knocked on the door. I wiped my eyes and opened it to find a page–a very young man–clad in the gray and blue of Han standing there.

"I was sent to tell you that the king wishes for you to join him for the morning meal," he said. "Further, the princess wishes to depart as soon as you have eaten and asks that you bring anything you wish to take with you when you go."

I considered taking my guitar but decided against it. Instead, I put my flute into a pouch that I tied to my belt. Then I followed the page to the dining hall.

A little over an hour later, we rode out of the rear gate of Aeran Fort. Peg led the way, with Ryan, my father, me, and five soldiers following. She had hardly spoken to me during our morning meal. We had never been like that with one another before then and the silence between us broke my heart. I spurred Windsfoal forward to pull alongside her. She glanced my way but didn't speak.

"Peg..." I started, but she cut me off.

"Lauren, please. I said that we could deal with things after you do what you need to do."

"But..."

"Lauren, I know that it hasn't been easy for you. You thought you lost me. Now you've lost your Elf girl. But I've lost people, too. My father and one of my brothers were killed by the Kelmar. We haven't been able to find out what happened to my mother or my other brother.

"And you're different. You always seemed to feel like you didn't deserve me because I was a princess, and you were just a farm boy. I never really understood why you felt that way. Now..." She faltered. "You fought the Keepers and killed them. You fought the goddess and banished her. You saved the Federation and probably the whole world. And I'm just a princess."

She paused.

"And you've found someone else."

"Peg, I love you. I want to marry you."

"You say that now. But what if you manage to bring back the Elves? What then?"

She looked at me then and I could see the pain in her eyes.

"I love you, Peg, and I will love you as long as I live."

I dropped back then. The rest of the ride was quiet, with only a few muted conversations between the others in the party. The path wound its way through narrow defiles barely wide enough for a pair of riders to go side-by-side. In places, the rock walls on either side of us were so high that they blocked the sun, and we rode through a midmorning twilight. Several times I thought we were approaching a dead end only to discover an opening hidden from view by an outcropping of rock. Late in the morning I began to sense the tattered remains of *Wyn's* Forbidding. An hour later, the passageway we had been following opened into the south end of a long narrow valley. Peg halted us there.

"It might be best if you wait here," she said to the soldiers. "Ryan and Dalach found the Forbidding especially strong when Lauren woke *Ëyn*. *Wyn* has always allowed those accompanied by one of my family to approach, but he's quiescent now, and we don't know for sure what will happen when he wakes."

It took us half an hour to cross to the north end of the valley. The mountains came back together there and in a cave located at the back of the shallow V formed by the joining we found *Wyn*.

We dismounted at some distance from the opening, tied our horses to a small tree, and entered the cave on foot. It wasn't deep and there was sufficient sunlight entering to show us our way. *Wyn* was in dragon form, curled up at the back of the cave like a cat sleeping before a fire. His body was covered in silver-gray scales, with a line of black scales standing upright over his spine. I pulled my flute out of its pouch.

"What's that for?" Peg asked quietly.

"I use it to play a song called the *Arimë Daelyr*," I answered. "It seems to help me call up my power." Knowledge rose from the depths of my mind. "The title means *The Grief of the Makers*. The song expresses the *Arimë's* sorrow and pain at the emptiness of the Void." I stopped in surprise.

"Lauren, what is it?"

"I didn't know that I knew that," I answered. "It must be part of what I learned from *Ëyn*. Taking in what she taught me was overwhelming and even now I don't have conscious access to most of it."

She simply nodded. I raised the flute to my lips and began. Almost at once, I felt my power stir. I felt my ties to the land, to all the things of the Earth. I looked at Peg. Her eyes were wide with wonder and her lips curved upward in a slight smile. I loved seeing her happy and I wondered if I could do anything to ease her pain. I sent a thread of power toward her, formed a bond between us and then I opened my heart to her, allowed her to see how I felt about her. The tension between us flowed away and, letting the bond between us drop, I turned my attention to *Wyn*. I sent a wisp of power his way and felt a bond form between us. He opened his eyes and lifted his head.

"*Vorath, Endollin*," he said, his voice deep and resonant. "*A ne Wian*."

Peg looked at me with a puzzled frown on her face.

"He welcomed me," I explained. "His name in the Language of Making is *Wian*."

I turned back to the dragon.

"*Vorath, Wian*," I said. "*A ne* Lauren."

He nodded his head to me and then turned toward Peg.

"Welcome, Daughter of Han."

"Greetings to you, *Wyn*."

The dragon turned back to me.

"*Endollin*, you come seeking knowledge of my domain."

"I do."

He held out his paw. Even my experience with *Ëyn* hadn't prepared me for what happened when we touched. My physical being came apart and I found myself flying down the valley. I was racing along the surface of the ground and tracing every bump and recess of its surface and at the same instant, I was far above the valley. I picked up a fallen leaf in Marsden Forge and spun it around in a ragged meander through the still parts of myself. My awareness shifted and I was far out over the ocean, pushing the water's surface into a frenzy of whitecapped waves. I was filling the sails of a sloop rigged racing boat off the coast of Meren. A small bit of my self was trapped in a small pocket in the rock above the surface of an underground river. I was warm and rising above the Mordel River where it flowed down from the Gray Mountains, lifting an eagle above his fishing grounds. I was a small finger probing beneath the heavy fur cloak wrapped around a person in the far north. Everywhere, I felt the subtle wrongness of *Melcurie-ar*. Overwhelmed again, I cried out and my cry was the booming voice of the wind through a narrow pass high in the Gray Mountains...

When I came back to myself, I was lying with my head on Peg's lap, and she was gently stroking my hair back from my forehead.

"Peg," I said. My own voice sounded small and weak to me after speaking with the voice of the wind.

"Lauren, are you well?"

"I am," I answered as I sat up. Something had changed; Peg's expression was warm and open and without even a trace of the hurt that had been there since I arrived in Han. I turned from her to *Wian*.

"My thanks to you, *Wian*."

The dragon nodded in acknowledgement and then said, "I saw some of what *Ëyn* shared with you. That knowledge is true, but somewhat incomplete. Would you hear more?"

"I would, yes."

"I am *Wian*, and all things of the air are under my dominion. *Ëyn* is Earth, and all things of the Earth are hers. But the *Cogen* do not work in isolation; we work together. *Ëyn* creates the form, and I give it breath. She creates a bird, and I hold it aloft. The winds are mine and they scatter the seeds of plants and trees and that makes her earth fruitful. We are separate, but equal, but we are also bound one to the other. You would do well to be mindful of our interactions."

I turned to go, but *Wian* spoke again.

"*Endollin*."

I turned back.

"*Melcurie-ar* warps everything she touches. If she returns, the world will eventually become a dismal place wracked with eternal chaos. The power to make it right resides in you. I beg you: make it right."

I started to reach for the hilt of *Endolsar* but stopped. Instead, I took Peg's hand and brought it to my lips. I kissed it lightly and then looked at them both.

"I swear that if I can make it right, I will."

CHAPTER EIGHT

I stumbled a little as we walked toward the mouth of the cave and Peg took my hand to steady me.

"How long was I out?" I asked.

"Several hours," she answered. "It must be late afternoon by now."

"We missed the midday meal, then. No wonder I'm so hungry."

"With luck, the others will have saved us something."

We rode back down the valley in companionable silence. The others had, in fact, saved us a little fruit and cheese. I wolfed down my portion before we remounted. Peg nibbled on hers as she led the group back into the maze of passageways while I hung back to fill my father and Ryan in on what I had learned from *Wian*. Several times I saw her twist in her saddle to look back at me. I smiled when I caught her eye, and she smiled back.

"Where to next?" my father asked.

"*Tael*, I think," I replied. "Water. According to the decahedron, she must be somewhere near *Gorthin Mear*."

"That makes sense to me," Ryan said. "When I was young, before I went to study at Songhaven, I took a trip intending to camp on the shores of *Gorthin Mear*. I spent the first night on the north shore. The next day I planned to cross the Glaess and work my way down the eastern side of the lake but the further I went, the more uncomfortable I became. Eventually,

I gave up and turned back. I hadn't thought about that in many rounds of the seasons."

"That sounds as if you ran into a Forbidding," I noted. "How well do you remember the north end of the lake?"

"Well enough. Did you want to Read me?"

"If you're willing."

"I am. I assume that we'll leave in the morning?"

"We can't afford to delay," I said.

My father, Ryan, and I dined that evening with Steafán, Peg, and several other leaders of Han. Most of them were relatively young and new to their positions; the Kelmar had executed almost all the Alomar leadership in the city. The meal was somewhat meager as the city's food supplies had been severely depleted by the Kelmar occupiers. After we ate, Ryan, Peg, and I spent an hour or so performing. When we finished, I went to my room. There was a washbasin and a pitcher full of water, so I undressed and washed up. The soap was strongly scented, so much so that it made me sneeze, but it was good to feel clean. After I washed, I climbed into bed and was thinking back on what I had learned from *Wian* when there was a quiet knock at the door.

"Just a moment," I called. "Let me get dressed."

Before I could rise, the door opened, and Peg slipped in. She was barefoot and wore only a short open-front robe made of some thin yellow fabric. She quietly closed the door and turned back to me.

"You're leaving in the morning," she said.

"I am," I replied.

"Then tonight is all we have."

She untied the belt and let the robe slip to the floor. She climbed into the bed on top of me and for a time I forgot everything except the joy of her presence.

Sometime later we were lying together, her head on my left shoulder, her left arm and leg laid across me. I wasn't sure, but I thought she was asleep. I was awake, though, and very aware of her presence, the feel of her skin against mine, the weight of her head on my shoulder, the delicate scent of lilacs. I had seen so many wonders in my life, but of all of them, what I truly treasured were moments like that one: those moments of closeness and intimacy between me and Peg. I tried to look at her without moving. Her brown hair was a little longer than she normally wore it. Her closed eyes were—I knew—brown. I ran my gaze down the length of her naked body. She had a slender build, and the curve of her hips was gentle; Peg could not be called curvaceous. Unbidden, what Garth had said about her came to mind: she was in many ways utterly ordinary. Yet the reality of her, of the person she was, was so much more and I loved her more than anyone.

Except Élan.

I must have made some sound because she raised herself up on her right arm to gaze down at me.

"I love you, Peg," I whispered.

"I know," she said. "And I know that now in a way that I never did before. When we talked yesterday and you told me that you loved me but that you loved Élan, too, I was sure that you just wanted to be with me until you could get her back. Lauren, I love you, but I don't want to be nothing to you but a stand-in for the person you really want. When we were with *Wyn*, though, you showed me that's not how it is."

"Never. I want to be with you forever," I replied. Then something she'd said hit me. "Peg, how do you know Élan's name. I never told you."

She gave a short little laugh and smiled.

"I think maybe you shared more with me than you intended."

I felt my face flush.

"How much do you know?"

"Enough to know that your feelings for her are every bit as real as your feelings for me." She paused and leaned down to kiss me gently on the lips. "I know that you thought I was dead, and I know that you weren't looking for someone to fall in love with. This is still hard for me, though. Lauren if you can bring the Elves back, what will you do?"

I gazed up into her face but all I saw there was concern and caring, with none of the pain and anger that had been there before.

"I don't know, Peg. I honestly do not know. I made promises to both of you, promises that I do not wish to break."

I stopped; cold tendrils of anxiety flowed down my limbs threatening to freeze me into immobility.

"I don't know what to do about Mar–*Melcurie-ar*–or the other thing that is trying to break into our world. I need to find a solution to that problem, or it won't matter what I promised to you or Élan."

I reached up and laid my hand on her cheek.

"Peg, I don't know what to do. I don't know what I can do. If I could find a way to permanently exile *Melcurie-ar*, we would still have the world, but there would be no magic. We'd lose the *Eldar*, the *aynekahrn*, and the *Cogen*."

"*Aynekahrn?*" she asked.

"Animals like horses, but because of *Melcurie-ar's* presence, they were imbued with magic. They are more intelligent, hardier, and more graceful than any horse. They gave rise to the legends of unicorns."

I paused for a moment, remembering the exhilaration of galloping across the Lellarin Plains on *Yrtenstal's* back.

"They're beautiful Peg. I hope you get to see them."

She smiled.

"If I just let *Melcurie-ar* come back," I continued, "she'll eventually warp the whole world. I've talked with my father and Master Ryan. My father quoted a strategist and said that if I can't win, the best I can hope for is to not lose. Ryan just told me to remember who and what I am. Neither of those helps."

She didn't answer for a moment. Then she sat up to sit cross legged beside me on the bed. Her expression was serious and thoughtful.

"I think I'm going to echo Master Ryan," she said slowly as she carefully chose her words. "You need to remember who and what you are. You're a minstrel, Lauren. You became a minstrel because you loved to learn. You wanted to seek out and preserve knowledge of our world. That's an act of love. Whatever you do when you face *Melcurie-ar* again should be based on that love. Don't face off with her in anger or fear. The world would not be the world you love without her."

"You are a very wise woman, Pegara of Han," I said. The lamplight lent a warm golden glow to her naked skin and sparkled in her hair like tiny bits of topaz. My breath caught in my throat; I couldn't believe that a woman like her would be with me. "The world would not be the world I love without you."

She smiled and began leaning toward me. I opened my arms to gather her to me and let go of my worries in the warmth of her love.

One moment I was aware of nothing and the next I was wide awake. Peg was sleeping soundly with her head on my shoulder. Someone was knocking loudly on the door to my room. Before I could react, the door opened, and Ryan stepped in.

"Lauren," he said, a note of urgency in his voice. "The sun is up, and the fort is in an uproar. People went to wake the princess, and she isn't in her..."

His voice trailed off and he stopped halfway to the bed.

"Oh," he said quietly. "I see that you two made up."

Peg shifted and raised her head slightly.

"Good morning, Master Ryan."

"Good morning, Princess. Everyone is looking for you. No one knows where you are."

"At least two people do," she said, and I could feel her shaking as she stifled a laugh.

Ryan pursed his lips and frowned at her response.

"You two may want to consider getting up," he said. "The princess should let her people know where she is so that they can stop searching for her and get back to their regular duties. And, Lauren, you have a journey to make."

"We'll need a moment, Ryan," I responded.

"I'll meet you in the dining hall," he replied and turned to go. As he turned away, I was pretty sure that I saw him smile.

When we were alone, Peg let go the laugh she'd been holding in.

"I really should go," she said.

"So should I," I replied. I hugged her to me just a little tighter. "Peg, come with me."

"Lauren, I don't want to be apart from you again, but I can't go with you."

"Why not?"

"Because I have obligations here now. Unless we find Tarron or until Steafán marries and has a child, I am the crown princess of Han."

We laid there for several more minutes just holding one another. Then she kissed me lightly and slipped out of bed. I watched as she padded across the room to where her robe lay on the floor. Before she could bend over to retrieve it, I said her name. She stopped and looked at me.

"I always want to remember you like this," I told her.

"Naked?"

"That is a treasured memory," I said, smiling, "but not what I was thinking. I was thinking about the closeness we shared last night. And what you said to me helped. I'm still not sure what to do about *Melcurie-ar*, but the part of me that felt like I'd never find an answer has been stilled. My thanks to you."

She simply smiled in response and bent to pick up her robe. She held it at arm's length, examining it with a little frown on her face.

"What's wrong?" I asked.

"I should have put a little more thought into coming here," she said. "Walking through the fort in nothing but this last night when most people were already in bed was one thing. Going back to my room this morning with the whole fort looking for me..." She shrugged, slipped the robe on, and tied the belt. "I guess it doesn't matter. By the time we get down to the morning meal, everyone will know where I was last night."

"Will it embarrass you for people to know that you were with me?"

"Not really. I'm just thinking of Steafán."

"What about him?"

"You'll see."

She slipped out the door and I rose and began dressing. I didn't bother with formal clothing but instead put on my traveling clothes. We'd be leaving as soon as we finished the morning meal. I tied my bright blue minstrel's sash around my waist and slung my guitar in its case over my right shoulder. Then I headed for the dining hall. By chance, Peg and I arrived in the corridor outside the dining hall at the same time. She was wearing a white cotton blouse, with a deep v-shaped neckline and long puffy sleeves over a long deep green skirt. She, too, was wearing her minstrel's sash. Somehow in the little time we'd had, she'd managed to brush out her hair and it was perfectly coifed. She looked beautiful and royal.

"You look beautiful," I told her.

"My thanks to you," she replied. She glanced at the archway opening into the dining hall with a look of resignation on her face. "You know what's going to happen if we walk in together?"

I shook my head and held out my arm.

"Let's face whatever it is together."

She took my arm, and we walked arm-in-arm into the dining hall. Given Peg's comments, I was half expecting everyone to stop talking and stare at us as we entered, but very few people seemed to pay any attention to us. Ryan, my father, and Aedion were sitting with Steafán on the other side of the room. Ryan saw us and waved us over. As we approached the table, Steafán spotted us.

"Well, there they are," he said, a little more loudly than I thought was necessary. People did turn our way then. He turned to my father. "War Duke Dalach, did I mention that I'm the one who broke him out of the dungeons in Badon?"

"Yes, Your Highness, you did. You mentioned it to me the night before last if I'm not mistaken."

Steafán nodded.

"That's what I thought. Had I known then that he was going to debauch my sister under my own roof, I just might have left him there."

"You do have dungeons here," my father observed.

"Steafán, please stop," Peg said. At the same moment, Aedion punched my father's shoulder.

"Dalach, leave them alone," she said. "Unless you'd like to also discuss what we were doing last night."

My father's face flushed red, but he smiled and Steafán and Ryan laughed.

"Sit down," Steafán said. "Break your fast. We all have much to do today."

A little over an hour later, we were all gathered in the field outside the rear gate of the fort. Steafán's people had given us what little they could spare to replenish our food supplies. Four stable hands held the reins to our horses. Ryan and I were seated on the ground facing each other.

"We've done this before," I said. "Relax and call to mind an image of *Gorthin Mear*. Let me know when you're ready."

"I have it," Ryan said quietly.

I placed my left hand on his forehead and concentrated. In an instant, I had an image of the lake.

"My thanks to you, Master," I said to Ryan.

He opened his eyes.

"That's it? That was quick and there was no emotional spillover."

"I'm learning," I replied.

My father offered each of us a hand up. When I gained my feet, I went to Peg. We hugged and kissed and then stepped back from one another still holding hands.

"I love you, Lauren," she said. "Safe travels."

"I love you, too, Peg."

My father was speaking quietly to Aedion. She nodded and they kissed. Then he, Ryan and I mounted, and the stable hand gave my father the lead to the pack horse. He moved to my left and Ryan lined up to my right.

"Safe travels," Steafán said. "Know that our hopes travel with you. Know as well that you always have a home here in Han."

"Our thanks to you, Steafán," I responded. Then I looked to my father and Ryan. "Ready?"

"Aye," they replied together.

I closed my eyes and called up the image Ryan had shared with me. I reached out to the minds of my companions and our mounts.

"Now," I said quietly, and we stepped forward onto the shore of *Gorthin Mear*.

Gorthin Mear is a large lake located just inside the northern end of *Seldenawé*, the valley between the eastern end of the Gray Mountains and the southern end of the Breton Mountains. Its major source of water is the Glaess River, though countless smaller streams from the nearby mountains empty into the lake. The waters of *Gorthin Mear* are unusually placid, even in the most turbulent weather and on calm days, the lake nearly perfectly reflects the mountains on either side.

We stepped onto the shore of *Gorthin Mear* on the eastern side of the Glaess River. I turned to say something to Ryan and a white-hot blaze of pain burned through my mind. I didn't even have time to scream. My vision fragmented and the pieces flared into a blinding argent glare. I felt myself sliding out of my saddle and tried to grab onto something to stop my fall, but my body would not respond. My consciousness was gone before I hit the ground.

I smelled smoke. I was floating in a sea of endless black but knew that I was at Songhaven, and that Peg was onstage. A deeper black was reaching through the void for her. I struggled up out of the darkness, my heart pounding. I was lying on the ground, covered with a light blanket. My father was cooking something over a small fire–the source of the smoke I had smelled. I tried to sit up, but every muscle in my body protested and I groaned. The darkness crowded in at the edges of my vision.

"Ryan," my father said. "He's awake."

I think I heard Ryan reply, but I was already sinking back into unconsciousness.

I woke just before dawn the next morning. Ryan and my father were sleeping on the other side of the fire, each of them wrapped in a blanket. The fire was dying so I added a couple of small logs from the pile lying next to it. Then I walked down to the water.

The lake was still, and the world was silent. Wisps of mist floated over the surface of the lake, their reflections pale ghosts of the world above the lake. The sky was just beginning to brighten and the colors around me were washed out and gray. Somewhere in the distance, a solitary wood thrush gave voice to its haunting, flute-like song, a solo singer before the dawn chorus. I felt light and empty, drained, but at the same time, I could feel that the pressure had increased on the barriers that I had built around the world.

The attack the day before had been different. It had felt more powerful and–somehow–I knew that it had come from a different place than *Melcurie-ar's* previous attempts to breach the barrier. I puzzled over those differences and searched through the things that *Ëyn* and *Wian* had told me. Just as the pieces came together, I heard a faint footstep behind me, and Ryan joined me at the water's edge.

"It's beautiful, isn't it?" he asked quietly.

"It is," I agreed.

"Are you well? What happened yesterday? Was it *Melcurie-ar* again?"

"I'm better," I answered. "And no, it wasn't *Melcurie-ar*. It was that thing from outside the world. Just as we reached here, it hit my barrier with far more force than *Melcurie-ar* has used. The barrier held, obviously, but it hurt. I don't know how much longer I'll be able to hold out against the two of them. Sooner or later *Melcurie-ar* or that thing–or both–will break through. I don't know what will happen then."

"Lauren, do you know what that thing is? Can you give it its name."

I turned to face him. He was watching me patiently, the way he had through countless lessons. I reviewed everything that I had learned...

"I can," I said, suddenly sure. "Ryan, it's the Creator. *Melcurie-ar's* sibling. He's trying to get to her. That's why she was afraid and quit fighting me back at Point Lookout. She doesn't want her brother to reach her."

After a moment's consideration, Ryan nodded. "Well reasoned. Now you're thinking like a minstrel."

"Maybe. But how does a human minstrel stand against two of the *Arimë*?"

He didn't answer and after a moment, we turned to walk back to our camp site. My father was up and had set a pot of water near the fire to boil for tea.

"Lauren, are you well?" he asked as we settled in near the fire.

"I am better," I answered as I rummaged through one of the food packs.

"What happened?"

"The Creator attacked my barrier just as we reached here."

"The Creator? The *Arimë* who made the world?"

I nodded and poured myself a cup of tea. The cups we had were made of thin metal and I had to wrap a piece of cloth around the handle to avoid burning my hand.

"Is it going to happen again?"

I thought for a moment before responding.

"I believe it will. He wants to get to *Melcurie-ar*. She wants to be fully back in this world. Sooner or later one of them will break through."

My father poured a cup of tea and handed it to Ryan and then poured one for himself.

"What can we do?"

"What you did yesterday. Pick me up when I fall. Eventually I'll find an answer." I didn't say it aloud, but in my mind, I added "I hope."

A short time later, we mounted up and turned our horses eastward.

"This is the way I went," Ryan told us. "I'd only ridden a few hours when I felt the urge to turn back. I persisted for perhaps another hour, but then I couldn't ignore the feeling any longer and I turned around."

"With *Tael* quiescent, we'll probably get farther than you did," I said. "Do you remember any significant obstacles in the part that you covered?"

"No. We'll have to ford a couple of small streams, but my memory is that the water didn't even reach my mount's knees."

We rode for several hours in companionable silence. In places, our way took us through wide grassy fields. In other places, the tree line came right down to the water's edge and trees that were old when my grandfather's grandfather was born dipped their roots into the still waters of the lake. The sun was halfway to its zenith when we first sensed the fraying remains of *Tael's* Forbidding. An hour later, my father and Ryan said that they couldn't go on and Windsfoal planted his hooves and would not go even one step further. At that point, sheer rock walls rose to over three times our height to our left. From their base, a silty beach peppered with rocks the size of hail stones sloped down to the water. I dismounted and slipped my guitar off my back. From its pocket on my guitar's case, I retrieved my flute and placed it in a pouch tied to my belt.

"I'll be back as soon as I can," I told them.

My father looked around the rock-strewn beach.

"Not a particularly comfortable place to wait," he said, "but we'll be here."

I walked alone down the shore. The farther I went, the closer the cliff wall came to the edge of the lake. Eventually, I had no choice but to remove my boots and wade into the water. It was cold, but so clear that I could easily see the bottom. I looked up. Trees and bushes peeked over the rim of the cliff and hinted at a lush forest out of sight up there. Here and there on the cliff face, a small sapling clung to a small ledge of weathered gray rock. A quarter mile further on, the top of the cliff began to slope down and faded into the floor of a hollow with a wide stream flowing down its center. I could sense the remains of *Tael's* Forbidding in there, so I waded out of the lake and followed the stream into the hollow. I hadn't gone far before I had to stop and dry my feet with my sleeves and pull my boots back on.

For a quarter of an hour the floor of the hollow was relatively level, and the stream was perhaps knee deep and ran quietly in its course. Then the ground began to climb, and the stream hissed over rocks through shallow falls punctuated with deep pools. After a time, the ground leveled out again and the hollow spread out into a wide, steep-sided bowl. Trees and thickets of rhododendron crowded each other all around and the stream spread out into a deep wide pool that filled the floor of the bowl from side to side. A sheer rock face rose some thirty feet above the far side of the pool and the water spilled over it in a spectacular waterfall. Narrow shafts of sunlight pierced the forest canopy and sparked tiny rainbows in the mist around the fall. Above and beyond the fall, the ground continued to slope up into the side of a mountain with the stream churning and foaming down a twisted rocky bed. The air in the bowl was cool and moist and smelled of damp rock and water-soaked loam.

At the base of the waterfall, its top just barely above the surface of the water, was a large flat stone. A dragon slept there.

Tael's scales were an iridescent blue. Down her back was a line of upright scales that were green, and the blue of her body faded into green on her feet and at the end of her tail. It was almost fifty feet from me to the stone table where she slept. I had no idea how deep the pool was, and I didn't want to wade back into cold water, so I stayed where I was and pulled out my flute.

My power stirred almost as soon as I began to play. I reached out to the sleeping *Cogen* and a bond almost instantly formed between us. It almost seemed as if I was reestablishing an old bond, and I wondered at that. Then *Tael* opened her eyes and raised her head.

"*Vorath, Endollin. A ne Tëlyn.*"

"*Vorath, Tëlyn. A ne* Lauren."

She rose and slipped into the water. As she made her way across the pool toward me her form shifted so that when she reached me, she was in the form of a woman. She was about my height and dressed in a long blue sleeveless gown. The top of the gown was oddly asymmetrical; The left strap was over an inch wide where it crossed over her shoulder and flared out to cover most of her left breast but the right strap was thinner than my little finger and left most of her right breast exposed. The gown was soaking wet and clung to the curves of her body, but I felt none of the overpowering desire that *Ëyn* had elicited. *Tëlyn* had an oval face framed by shoulder length black hair. Her wide eyes, set on either side of a petit nose–were mesmerizing. Their color seemed fluid and changing, one moment the gray of a storm-tossed sea and the next the blue of a lake under a sunny summer sky and the next the green of a placid forest pool.

"You are surprised that we know each other," she said. Her voice sounded like water flowing over stones, but at the same time echoed the power of the surf that pounded on all the shores of the world. "Do you not remember? I called to you all those seasons ago. I was the first you knew."

"I remember," I replied. "You led me to you and to Ryan. You started me on this path."

She shook her head.

"No, I did not. This path was yours from the moment the world was made. You are the Creator's answer to *Melcurie-ar's* incursion. You need to rid the world of her and her influence."

She paused and held out her hand to me.

"Will you accept knowledge of my domain?"

"I will," I answered and reached for her hand.

I had been expecting the sense of expansion that I felt as I absorbed knowledge from *Ëyn* and *Wian*. As our hands met, I drew in a quick gasp of surprise and my eyes widened with wonder. I felt *Tëlyn* inside me; I could sense her presence in every part of my body from the tips of my toes to the very depths of my heart. Then my awareness went deeper. My body was made of smaller things, thousands or millions or millions of millions of them, and she was in each of them. Then my awareness began to expand, and I flowed into the soil under my feet and parts of me pervaded the soil and all of the things crawling in the soil. I soaked into the roots of the plants around me and was converted into food that I carried back to the plant. I was the vastness of the ocean, endlessly lapping at the edges of the land and I was the timeless drip of water that carried minerals out of the earth to create stalactites and stalagmites deep underground. Animals and plants breathed me out where, tiny beyond belief, I drifted on the currents of the air. I sensed myself everywhere in all of the creatures and plants, in crevices in rocks, and I drifted in the air, gathered parts of myself together as clouds, rained upon the land, filled rivers and lakes and streams and puddles...

When I fell back into myself, I was lying on the ground with my head cradled in *Tĕlyn's* lap. The gentle touch of her hand on my cheek brought me back to myself. When I opened my eyes, she smiled.

"And now you know me as I know you," she said. "I know that you must go; I felt *Melcurie-ar's* attempts to reenter the world. I have one more piece of knowledge to share and I wish to give you a gift. Will you have them."

"Yes."

"Then know this," she told me. "*Wian* is correct. The *Cogen* do work together, but there is also tension between us. *Ëyn* yearns for the perfect landscape. Water carves the land, changes the shape of it, and it is no longer perfect for her. And *Ëyn's* unyielding rock alters the path of my streams, and they are not perfect for me. Through all the countless seasons of the world, we have never resolved that tension."

I nodded my understanding.

"And now my gift."

She placed her hand on my forehead and images of a desolate valley flowed into my mind.

"*Söarin's* home," she said. "You will find her there. Now, you must go."

I stood and *Tëlyn* stood with me. I checked to make sure that I still had my flute.

"My thanks to you, *Tëlyn*," I said and turned to go.

"Lauren," she said. There was an odd note in her voice, something I couldn't recognize. I turned back and waited, but she said nothing more. She simply stood watching me as if she was about to lose something precious.

"Be well, *Tëlyn*," I said finally and stepped through the distance to the lakeshore where Ryan and my father waited for me.

Ryan and my father looked up as the thunder of my appearance echoed off the cliff walls and rolled across the lake. They looked thoroughly uncomfortable. I glanced around; the sun was halfway to the horizon. They both rose and went to the horses.

"If we get started now, we might be able to get back to a place where we can camp comfortably and that has decent forage for the horses before nightfall," my father said.

"It shouldn't really take that long," I observed.

My father simply looked at me with a puzzled frown.

"We can go back to where we camped last night," I explained. "I know that place."

Comprehension brought a smile to his face, and he nodded. I reached out to encompass the minds around me, men and horses.

"Now," I said, and we stepped through space to our former campsite. For a moment, I felt a growing sense of pressure deep in my mind, but I had been prepared for an attack and had reinforced the barriers. I did stumble a little, but neither my father nor Ryan noticed. We hobbled the horses, and my father took his bow and headed into the woods to hunt. I headed in a different direction than my father to gather firewood and Ryan took one of our pots to the lake to get water.

An hour or so later, we were sitting around the fire finishing our evening meal.

"Lauren," my father said, "You've said our time is running out. We need to go to Fire Vale next, but it's going to take us a moon to get there and over another to get from there to Shade's Isle. Do we have that much time?"

"It won't take us a moon to reach Fire Vale," I answered. "*Tëlyn* gave me an image of the Vale, so we can translocate there."

"Why did neither of the others do that?" Ryan asked.

I shook my head. "I really can't say, and I don't have time to go back and ask them."

"Do we know anything about this Fire Vale?" my father asked.

"From the image *Tëlyn* gave me, it looks pretty desolate."

"That part of Altiera is a desert," Ryan said. "If we will be there for a significant amount of time, we'll need to take plenty of water."

"Could one of us wait here with the horses?" my father asked?

I closed my eyes and called up the image of Fire Vale. There was nothing that suggested *Saer's* location.

"I'm not sure how far it will be from where we'll enter the valley to where *Saer* is," I said. "I think we'll need the horses."

My father nodded.

"We'll just have to make sure that they're well-watered before we go," he said. "Then we just hope that it won't take too long."

We stepped into a heat more intense than any I had ever experienced. Within seconds, I could feel sweat break out on my face. The sun was bright, and its light reflected from the sandy ground; I had to squint against the glare.

"*Mirdl*," my father swore. "It is even hotter than I expected."

As my eyes adjusted, I was able to look around me at an entirely alien landscape. The jagged, broken-looking sandstone cliffs towering over us were rusty red with large talus slopes at their feet. The floor of the valley was undulating and dotted with boulders. The sandy soil and the rocks were all the same rusty red color. There were some plants there, more than I thought would be in a desert, but they looked dead to my eyes. Some looked like little more than clusters of dried gray-brown branches; others looked like puffs of gray-green.

"Which way?" my father asked.

The southern end of the Vale of Fire opened onto the great desert of Altiera, and the valley wound its way roughly north north-west into the southern foothills of the Gray Mountains. From what I could see, *Tëlyn* had directed us to a place about a mile up the valley from its mouth.

"North," I answered and urged Windsfoal into a walk in that direction. My father and Ryan followed. We kept our horses to a slow walk given the heat and two hours after we started, we felt *Saer's* Forbidding. I dismounted and took one of our waterskins from the pack horse and set out to cover the remaining ground on foot. Half an hour later, my clothes were soaked through with sweat, and I had reached the end of the valley.

Two pitted, craggy cliff walls came together there forming a V that pointed to the north. A large talus pile sloped out from the walls and in the middle of it, *Saer* had dug out a shallow nest and was curled up there, her head resting on the tip of her tail, just as she had been the first time I saw her. I reached for my flute but paused in the act of taking it out. She had said things to me the first time we met. I had questions about those things and wondered whether she would be open to answering them.

I began to play and—as I expected because we had met before—the bond between us formed quickly. She raised her head and regarded me out of yellow eyes.

"*Endollin*," she said. "*A ne Söarin. Vorath.*

"*Vorath, Söarin. A ne* Lauren," I answered.

"You have come for knowledge of fire."

"I have, but I have questions. Would you be willing to answer them?"

She bent her neck slightly, which I took as an affirmative nod.

"When we first met, you said that you were bound in the cave with the sword by your oath."

"I was. I gave my word to Lorrestian that I would stay with the sword until the *Endollin* came to retrieve it."

"But how did you know who I was? We had never met."

She cocked her head at me.

"Even now you do not understand? *Endollin* is not who you are, it is what you are. Anyone with a mind, anyone with eyes can see it."

For a moment, I puzzled over what she'd said.

"So, am I not a person? A human?

"Not exactly."

"Then what am I?"

"The *Endollin*."

I felt as if we were talking in circles. I dropped that line of thought.

"So, when I claimed the sword, you were released from that binding. You said there was another one?"

"Yes."

I waited for her to say more, but she simply stared at me, her yellow eyes unblinking.

"Can you tell me about that binding," I asked finally.

She stood and, in the standing, became a woman robed in red. She stepped lightly down the talus slope, skipping from stone to stone far faster than I would have dared. When she reached the bottom, she sat on a large rock and motioned for me to come closer.

"Uncounted rounds of the seasons ago, long before the *Enwilion Arastalon* came to these lands, we were free to go where we would. When the *Enwilion Arastalon* arrived, we met them, taught them. Before we became aware of her, *Melcurie-ar* had regained enough of herself to appear to them and she craved their worship. She grew concerned that the *Enwilion Arastalon* would learn from us who she really was. To prevent that, she bound our physical forms to our homes; we could no longer go where we wished. After a time, we discovered that we could appear outside our homes as sendings and we continued to meet with the *Enwilion Arastalon*. Then, around a thousand rounds of the seasons ago, *Melcurie-ar* discovered our meetings and she tightened the bindings to prevent even our sendings.

"Your birth weakened those bindings. The first time you exercised your power, that weakened them even further and we began trying to reach out to you. *Tëlyn* succeeded."

I nodded.

"She did."

"*Endollin*, are you ready?"

"I am."

I held out my hand. She took it...

I was alone in the darkness. It was cold around me, but the cold did not touch me. Deep in my core was fuel and I was consuming it. There was water there and it fled at my approach. The rest was mine and I grew larger and hotter as I consumed the dehydrated fuel. Then I realized that my fuel was running out, but then something–someone–moved in the darkness and added more fuel. I realized then that I was a campfire, burning logs to keep people warm. With that realization, I spun away to a blacksmith's forge, to a candle on the table of a minstrel, to a spark as steel met flint. I was... I'm not sure where I was. I was hot, I felt rock and metal flow, and I heard *Söarin's* voice say "core" and then I was again in darkness, surrounded by nothing except a cold beyond any I had ever known, but I was huge and hot–incandescently hot–and I flung the light of my heat into the empty space around me and toward the tiny dot in the distance...

I was myself. I was lying on the hot, rocky ground, my head cradled on *Söarin's* lap. She had my waterskin and held it to my lips.

"Drink, *Endollin*."

I took a mouthful of the water, felt the parched skin in my mouth absorb it, and then drank deeply.

"I was..."

"You were the sun," she said.

I struggled to sit up and she helped. The sun was over halfway to the horizon.

"*Endollin*, you must go. But before you go, hear this. *Tëlyn* told you of the tension among the *Cogen*. My fire melts rock and builds new land to *Ëyn's* design and so the world becomes more perfect for her. But the fire dies, the rock cools, and the world is less perfect for me. Worse than that, though, is what *Melcurie-ar* has done. Even though we *Cogen* have reached an uneasy standoff, she warps all and twists everything away from the Creator's design. You must drive her out. You must make the world what the Creator meant it to be."

I stood.

"You told me to wake the Old Ones. I have almost accomplished that. When I have, what do I do next?"

She smiled sadly.

"It is not my place to tell you what to do. You are the *Endollin*."

My heart sank and I turned to go.

"*Endollin*," she said. I turned back.

"When you have met with all of us, you will know more than any one of us. You will find an answer."

I nodded and set off down the valley. Though the sun was well past the zenith, the heat was still oppressive. It was hard to breathe, and my arms and legs felt far too heavy. Moving was difficult, and it took me far longer to return than it had taken to reach *Söarin*. I ran out of water before I was halfway back, and I was parched and stumbling by the time I reached Ryan and my father.

They made me sit and gave me water–almost an entire skin of it–before they would let me speak. When I did speak, my voice was hoarse. I was overly hot and exhausted, and I wanted nothing more than to lie down, but I knew that I couldn't.

"I need to get us out of here," I told them.

"Can't it wait until the sun goes down?" Ryan asked.

"I don't think so," I said. "I don't know how much more of this heat I can take." I looked to my father. "How are the horses?"

"They would do better someplace cooler," he answered.

I held my hand out to him, and he gave me a hand up. Ryan had gathered the horses and handed the leads for Steadfast and the pack horse to my father. I reached for Windsfoal's reins, but he shook his head.

"I'll take care of him," he said. "You just get us where we're going."

"Landfall," I told them. "We need to go to Shade's Isle."

I closed my eyes and called up an image of the field outside the landside gates of Landfall.

"Now," I said and stepped forward. Cooler air washed over me, and I caught a glimpse of the city wall. Then the pressure inside my head exploded and my world went incandescent. Pain flared inside me; in an instant it became white hot and overwhelmed my senses with argent fire. I was the sun again, but I wasn't *Söarin,* and I was being consumed from within. My being was fraying in the intense light. I felt my power respond just before my consciousness faded into the overwhelming brilliance.

I was alone in my room at Songhaven. The room was dark; there was no fire, and no lamp was lit. There was a faint glow from somewhere, just enough to make out the shapes of my furniture. My heart was pounding, I could feel it in my throat, and I was breathing hard. I was afraid. Someone or something was trying to get in. Suddenly, I was lying face down on the ground with my head near the door. My arms were stretched out in front of me, trying to hold the door shut against the dark thing that was trying to get in. I pushed back as hard as I could, but the angle was wrong, and I felt the door shift slightly.

"No," I shouted, and my own shout woke me to a glimpse of a room and a confusion of voices and then the brilliant agony overwhelmed me again.

I was floating in the darkness of the Void. I had no form, but things were trying to tear me apart. Somehow, with no arms, I pushed back against them, and the tearing ceased. Alone, I faded into the utter stillness...

I woke in a plush bed, washed in the warm sunlight of a spring day. The walls were of stone and were covered with tapestries, all of which were decorated with ships and sea creatures. From that, I guessed that I was in Marwynn's castle in Landfall. I shifted a bit to sit up and found that I was not alone. Ryan was gazing out a window, a bandage wound around his head. My father was asleep in a chair and his left arm was bandaged from wrist to elbow. Another chair was occupied by a dark-haired woman who was reading a book. She wore black trousers and a gray tunic belted at the waist with a wizard's white sash. Leaning against her chair was a silver-shod ash staff.

"Where am I?" I asked.

In an instant, they were all at my bedside.

"How are you," Ryan asked.

I felt drained and ravenously hungry, but I was no longer in pain.

"I am well," I answered. "Where are we?"

"This is Marwynn's castle," Ryan answered. "Lauren, what happened to you?"

"*Melcurie-ar* and the Creator both attacked again. Either they are using more power than they have before, or I was weakened by walking in the heat; I couldn't resist them as well as I have in the past."

"And after that?" the wizard asked. She had a husky, gravelly voice.

"I don't understand," I replied.

"Several times while you were lying unconscious, the jewels on your ring and sword flared with light. I was summoned after the first such occurrence. When it happened again, I could sense power being expended, but I did not understand its type nor what was being done."

"Before I answer," I said, "do I know you?"

"My apologies, *Endollin*," she said. "I am Duna, Wizard of Alomar. I was summoned by the king, who was concerned about whether you were going to inadvertently destroy his castle from within." She smiled wryly. "Though given that the wizards are currently almost without power, I am unsure what I could have done to prevent any damage."

"Duna, I am Lauren, Minstrel of Alomar."

"And the *Endollin*," she noted.

"Yes," I acknowledged. "To answer your question, I am unsure what was happening while I was unconscious. I was dreaming of fighting things I could not see, but my power often responds to threats on its own."

"It is also possible that your dreams were not just dreams," the wizard said.

"True. But I'm awake now."

"Indeed. I do not believe that I am needed here any longer."

Duna sketched a quick bow in my direction, then retrieved her staff and departed. I turned to Ryan and my father.

"You're bandaged," I observed. "What happened?"

"You passed out when we arrived," my father answered. "Ryan and I managed to get you onto my saddle in front of me. Then we rode into the city. You were recognized. Word of your arrival got to a group of religious zealots. At first, they just yelled threats at us as we passed, but some of them were shouting that you murdered their goddess. The next thing we knew, someone threw a rock and things went downhill from there. We ended up in a fight that only ended when some of Marwynn's troops showed up."

My dismay must have been plain on my face because Ryan said, "Lauren, it's not your fault."

"But we ran into the same thing in Amersford, Ryan. Kivyn said that many people there felt the way that he did. Now we find people here willing to kill us in retribution over the loss of their goddess." Grief and anger warred inside my chest and a sob forced its way out of me. "Even if I figure out how to deal with *Melcurie-ar*, I'm never going to have any peace. The people I save from her are going to hate me."

"Lauren..." Ryan started, but I cut him off.

"I'm never enough," I said. "No matter what I do or how much I know, I'm never enough." I turned my attention to my father. "I was never enough for you. You weren't satisfied with me. You demanded that I be something different."

My father didn't respond, but his eyes narrowed, and his mouth tightened to a straight line. He crossed his arms and just held my gaze without speaking, but I quickly turned to Ryan.

"I spent seven rounds of the seasons becoming a minstrel. You taught me more about the world than my friends were taught and even with all of that, I wasn't enough. Ambrose and I couldn't stop what happened to Aerman Sorren and I couldn't save Ambrose. I couldn't stop what happened at Songhaven. I brought the *Eldar* out of hiding..." Grief welled up in my chest and choked off the next words. "They came out of hiding for me and in return, I sent them out of the world."

My father locked eyes with Ryan, nodded, and without speaking they left the room together.

That reaction shocked me into silence. Guilt replaced the grief and anger; they had been injured protecting me and I had treated them poorly in return. I rose from the bed and located my belongings so that I could dress. I had finished dressing and was heading for the door when someone knocked. I opened the door to find the young page whom I had met the last time I was in Landfall standing there.

"Gori," I said. "It's good to see you again."

"My thanks to you, sir," she answered. "The king heard that you were awake and sent me to request that you join him for the midday meal."

"I would be happy to do so," I replied. "Would I have time to find my father and Master Ryan first? I need to speak with them."

"They are also dining with the king," she told me. "Shall I take you there?"

"Yes. Please do."

She led me through the castle to the king's private quarters. When she knocked, Marwynn himself answered the door.

"My thanks to you, Gori," he said. "You may go have something to eat yourself. I won't need you again until later this afternoon."

"My thanks to you, your Highness," she replied. She bowed slightly to me and then quickly headed back the way we had come.

"Lauren, it's good to see you up," Marwynn said. "Join us."

The king stood aside to allow me to enter.

I glanced around quickly as I entered. The room was obviously the king's solar and a door in the far right hand wall most likely led to the king's bedchamber. The solar was quite large and a double door directly across from the entry led to a balcony. To my left were four overstuffed chairs and my father and Ryan were already seated there. The walls behind them were covered with ornate tapestries depicting ships at sea. One of them depicted a ship caught in a storm and the maker had woven silver threads into the images of lightning; they caught the flickering of the firelight and brought the images to life. To my right was a desk, the top of which was covered with a sea of papers and scrolls. A huge sea chart, its corners held down by brass weights shaped like light houses, was spread over a large table. The walls on the right side of the room were lined with bookcases stuffed full of books and what I surmised were sea charts. On one of the shelves was what looked like a miniature of the *Black Marlin*. I wanted to go examine it, but the king directed me toward the chairs. My father and Ryan stood as we approached.

"I owe you both an apology," I told them. "You fought to protect me when people were trying to kill me. I should have extended my thanks to you and instead I yelled at you."

My father simply nodded his acknowledgement and Ryan said, "Apology accepted."

The king took his seat and the rest of us then sat down. At that moment, several of the kitchen staff entered with platters of bread, fruit, cheese, and several fish dishes. We filled our plates and for several minutes no one spoke as we ate. The food was all excellent and I even enjoyed the fish that I tried. Then the king looked around the table at us and said, "When you arrived yesterday, you asked me if there would be anyone willing to take you out to Shade's Isle. I sent several of my people down to the docks this morning to ask around. They arrived back here a short time ago." He paused and took a sip of his wine. "Sailors are a superstitious lot, you know, and they all know that the island is said to be haunted. There wasn't a single captain in port who was willing to even get close to it."

My heart sank and my father and Ryan exchanged worried looks. Marwynn laughed.

"Don't look like that," he said. "I was there at Point Lookout, and I understand what's at stake. I'll take you out on the *Black Marlin*."

"Will your crew be willing?" Ryan asked.

"I've got a good crew on the *Marlin*. They've sailed with me into the ice fields of the far north and into the teeth of the worst gales the sea could throw at us. They will not balk at this. We'll get you to Shade's Isle."

We spent the rest of the afternoon planning the trip. Marwynn and Trefor–the Fleet Captain who was going to serve as Steward in Marwynn's absence–spent an hour or so searching for nautical charts with information on the waters around the island. Other than the island's location, though, none of the charts had any information that would help us locate

Ynes. Eventually, they gave up and Marwynn sent Trefor out to round up the crew of the *Black Marlin.*

"Would it be possible to leave tonight?" I asked after the Fleet Captain had gone. "I'd like to leave as soon as possible. I feel like my time is running out."

"We have to sail with the outgoing tide," Marwynn responded. "There's no way we'll be ready before the turn of the tide this evening. The first time we can go will be midmorning tomorrow."

I sighed and then said, "I understand."

"I'm assuming that you're traveling light," Marwynn said.

"Just us, our horses, and whatever food we can fit into our packs."

Marwynn shook his head.

"What?" I asked.

"The *Marlin* is ostensibly a cargo ship," he answered. "But she was built primarily for the Merchant's Cup competition. The hold was sized to haul nothing bigger than crates of fruit. There's no room below decks for horses."

"You mean we're going to have to explore the island on foot?" Ryan asked.

"I'm afraid so," Marwynn answered. "Unless you can figure out where this *Ynes* is likely to be so I can put you ashore near him. None of my ships that would suit are in port right now. I could locate a ship in the harbor that would be large enough to haul your horses, but I'd have to commandeer it, and I'd rather not do that. It's bad for business if I start taking people's ships."

My father turned to Ryan.

"Ryan, didn't your people once have a settlement on the island," he asked.

Ryan nodded.

"When our ancestors first arrived here from wherever the homeland was, they first landed on the island. They founded a settlement on the western side. In exploring the island, they saw the continent and many of them set out to explore it. When they returned to the island, they found the settlement abandoned. As they searched, a sense of dread gripped them and grew so overwhelming that they fled the island. They renamed it *Ech Numen*, Shade's Isle, and they never returned. If anyone has ever set foot there since then, I've never heard of it."

"The earliest records in the royal library here," Marwynn said, "report three different ships that set out for the island at different times. None of them ever returned. Several captains' logs contain entries about strange occurrences when they got too close to the island, but what those occurrences were was not recorded."

"Back to your question, Dalach," Ryan said, "the *Eldarin* settlement was on the western side of the island. If *Ynes* was there, they would most likely have encountered him. I think we should begin on the eastern side of the island."

"Lauren, how about you?" my father asked. "Did you learn anything from the other *Cogen* that might help us locate *Ynes*?"

"Possibly," I replied. "But I cannot consciously access most of it. It's infuriating. I spend a great deal of time feeling as if what I want to know is right on the tip of my tongue, but I can't get it out."

"I guess there's not much more we can do, then," Marwynn said. "And I must go hold court this afternoon." He stood, prompting us to follow suit. "Tomorrow morning, then?"

"Tomorrow," we all confirmed.

CHAPTER NINE

I woke in the small hours of the morning, my heart racing, my mouth dry, and my hands knotted in the bedclothes. I was confused; I'd been standing in sunlight. I was trying to understand how I'd come to be there, and my gaze darted around the dark room, searching frantically for the threat that had awakened me. A gentle breeze wafted in the open balcony door. I'd been outside and felt a breeze that carried the salt smell of the sea and the world had been coming apart. By the time that my sleep-fogged mind realized that it had only been a dream, the images had faded. It took a moment for me to loosen my grip on the bed and force my breathing back to normal.

Though I could not recall the dream that woke me, each time that I began to drift back into sleep, fear gripped my heart and forced me back to wakefulness. When the sky outside my room began to lighten, I gave up trying to sleep and rose. It took me some time, but I finally found my way to the bathing room on the first floor of the palace where I spent nearly an hour soaking in the tepid water. It wasn't very satisfying, but I had no idea when I'd be able to bathe again. When I got back to my room, my father and Ryan were just exiting theirs and together we went to the dining hall to break our fast. As the city bells were chiming the ninth hour, we left the palace and headed for the docks.

When we reached the *Black Marlin*, Marwynn was already aboard and shouting orders to the crew. He met us at the top of the gangplank.

"Permission to come aboard, Your Highness," my father requested.

"Granted," Marwynn answered. "But on board the *Marlin*, I'm Captain."

"Understood, Captain," my father replied.

As we stepped off the gangplank and onto the deck, Marwynn said, "Welcome aboard. The tide has turned, and we'll cast off soon. We're just waiting for a final few supplies to be brought aboard."

He gestured to someone behind us and Adaryn, the sailor we had met on our previous trip on the *Black Marlin*, joined us.

"Adaryn, show them where to store their belongings."

"Aye, Captain," she replied with a slight bow in Marwynn's direction. "If you all will follow me."

She led us below deck and toward the stern of the boat. We each had a small cabin, my father on the starboard side of the passageway and Ryan and I on the port side.

"We may hit some heavy seas," she told us. Her eyes went to our guitars. "Make sure that anything you don't want thrown around the cabin is secured before you leave."

"Understood," Ryan responded.

"Is there anything else you require, *Endollin*?"

"No. My thanks to you, Adaryn," I replied.

"Then I'll return to my duties. Join us on deck when you're ready."

My cabin was small, barely large enough for a bed that was only an inch or two wider than my shoulders and an inch or two shorter than me. Sleeping would be cramped at best. There was a storage space under the bed with a net to prevent items from sliding out and I carefully packed my guitar in there along with my backpack. I stepped back into the passageway at the same moment as Ryan. My father was waiting for us.

When we reached the deck, a dozen men were working in pairs to roll six casks of what I presumed to be fresh water up the gangplank. They were followed by another four men carrying boxes and bags of food. We found Marwynn near the head of the gangplank speaking with Trefor.

"The problem isn't the Repentant," Marwynn was saying as we approached. "It's the damned Restorationists."

"Restorationists?" I asked. I had never heard of them. "Who are they and why are they a problem?"

"They're the ones who attacked you," Trefor answered.

"The Repentant," Marwynn explained, "have all locked themselves up in their churches trying to reconcile their belief in Mar as a just ruler of the world with her actions. The Restorationists are a radical group who have not given up their worship of Mar. They believe that her attacks on the Alomar were warranted, and that evil has banished her from the world. They want her back and they're willing to do whatever it takes to bring about her return."

"Why are we discussing them now?" my father asked. "Are they likely to try and interfere with this trip?"

"No," Marwynn replied. "We've kept the purpose of this trip quiet. Trefor was expressing concern that they might try another revolt when they learn that I'm away."

Trefor shot a wry glance at the king.

"It's not like they haven't done so before," he said. He put a hand to his neck. "I don't want to end up at the end of a rope."

"But unlike last time, you won't be left with only a couple of companies of soldiers," Marwynn replied. "With the exception of the *Marlin's* crew, I'm leaving you all our sailors who are not currently at sea and all our soldiers. You know the commanders and they know the people in their units. Any stranger who shows up in uniform shouldn't be trusted. Feel free to arrest them and hold them until I return. Treat them gently, but don't allow them to roam the city."

Marwynn glanced around. When he saw no one near, he lowered his voice.

"Keep a watch out for Kendra. If she shows up, see her immediately. I have her infiltrating the Restorationists. If they're planning anything, she'll make sure that you hear about it."

"Aye, Your Highness. May the sea be kind."

With that, Trefor turned and strode off down the gangplank. At a shout from Marwynn, the gangplank was removed, and sailors fore and aft cast off the lines that tied us to the dock. The tide was with us, and we immediately began drifting forward. Marwynn had moved to the helm and taken the wheel from one of his sailors. He shouted again and the orange sails were raised. We had a stiff following wind, so the sails immediately bellied out and the *Black Marlin* leapt forward. A few moments later, we had cleared all the other boats in the harbor and Marwynn set a north-north-west course.

"What do we do now?" Ryan asked.

"We try to stay out of their way," my father answered. "I think I'll go talk to Marwynn. I have some questions about the Restorationists."

"I didn't sleep so well last night," Ryan said. "I think I'll go below and rest."

They looked at me and I shrugged.

"I think I'll just find someplace out of the way and sit. I need to think. Maybe I can dredge up some knowledge about Shade's Isle."

I wandered the deck until I reached the bow of the boat where, for lack of any obvious place for it, I sat on the bowsprit. I half expected the sailors to chase me off, but no one said anything and after a few moments I relaxed and let my mind drift. Despite what I'd told my father and Ryan, I wasn't trying to think. I was tired and I felt drained and empty. An hour later, I spotted land in the distance.

"Point Lookout," Marwynn called to the crew. "Prepare to bring her about."

I looked back and saw sailors scrambling across the deck. The sails boomed as Marwynn turned the *Black Marlin* due west. As we settled in on the new heading, the sailors tied off lines and then went back to other duties.

Unbidden, images of Point Lookout flooded my mind: the haggard faces of the Alomar soldiers, the jeering ranks of the Kelmar, Mar flickering from shape to shape, the iron gray waves crashing in when I realized that Élan and the *Eldar* were gone. Echoes of the previous night's dream brushed the edges of my consciousness. A memory–a single phrase–from *Ëyn* surfaced: Land's End. My blood ran cold. Point Lookout was the battle that Lorrestian foresaw, but not the one that I had been dreaming of all my life.

Point Lookout fell away behind us as we entered the open sea. A pod of whales kept pace with us for a time. One by one they leapt out of the water in front of me; it seemed as if they were greeting me.

I felt nothing. No, that's not quite correct. I felt empty. I simply sat and watched the gray-blue waves slip past. I heard the snap of the sails as the wind gusted. Marwynn's shouted commands and the responses of the crew seemed to come from a great distance. I think I heard someone say something about the evening meal to me, but I was too removed from myself to respond.

The sun painted the western sky in broad streaks of red, gold, and orange as it dropped below the horizon. That signaled fair weather the next day, but the thought was abstract and meant nothing to me. I was lost and was just beginning to realize it.

After a time, I realized that it had grown so dark that I could no longer see the water. Overhead, the stars burned bright, a vast, wheeling map that could keep the *Marlin* on course, but that had no guidance for me. I had been sitting facing the port side of the boat–toward the south–and I turned then to the starboard and the north. The north star hung there, halfway between the horizon and the zenith. Its violet light seemed to pulse, almost like a heartbeat and I thought I saw hints of red and blue there. Then a pair of shadows interposed themselves between me and the light.

"Lauren, are you well?"

I recognized the man's voice but could not recall what he was called. Names rolled through my mind, names of people, animals, trees, rocks, specks of dust, all the endless knowledge of the *Arimë*. My mind flitted from one to the next, but I couldn't find the one that belonged to that voice. Despair began to fill my chest.

"Lauren?" the voice repeated, and the concern in its tone somehow pulled his name out of the confusion of knowledge raging in my mind.

"Ryan," I said and in naming him, I came back to myself.

"Lauren, are you well?" he repeated.

"You haven't moved in hours," my father added.

"Ryan," I started, but my voice was hoarse and my throat dry and I faltered. "Master? What happens when we die?"

"Lauren, what's troubling you?" my father asked. "Are you afraid to go to Shade's Isle?"

I didn't answer and Ryan finally responded to my question.

"When we die, our note in the Song of the Seasons ends," he said.

"And that's it," I asked. "Is there nothing of us left? We're just gone?"

"I believe so."

"I'd hoped to see Élan again," I said quietly. "I just found Peg. I wanted to marry, maybe have children. I wish…" I fought down a sob.

"Lauren, what's happened?" my father asked.

I looked in his direction, but I couldn't see his face in the dark.

"I'm going to have to face *Melcurie-ar*," I explained. "I'm going to have to face the Creator at the same time. I've barely been able to hold out against their attacks on the barriers I put up." I paused; I didn't want to say the next part, but I forced myself to. "I'm going to die. There are so many things that I still want to do and I'm going to die."

No one said anything for several moments.

"Lauren, you can't let yourself think like that," my father said quietly. "A soldier who believes that he's going to die will most likely find a way for it to happen."

He paused a moment before continuing.

"I'm a soldier. I've known from the time that I first picked up a sword that I would be risking death on a regular basis. I decided then, though, that what I would be fighting for was worth that risk. I also decided that I would never just give up and die. Someone might kill me, but I would be damned to the outer darkness if I would just give up and die. If…" His voice faltered and I heard him swallow nervously. Then he continued hesitantly. "If you could Read me and take that determination…"

I knew what that offer cost him. I didn't know whether he just didn't want anyone to Read him or whether his reticence was specific to me, but I knew he wasn't comfortable with being Read. I stood and stepped over the bowsprit to stand next to him.

"You would do that for me?"

"I would," he answered. "You're my son. I came to help you."

"You just did," I told him. "My thanks to you."

"Lauren," Ryan said quietly after a moment. "I've given this a great deal of thought. At Point Lookout, *Melcurie-ar* tried to kill you and could not. You have the power of the *Arimë* and the *Arimë* cannot die. Every time your life has been threatened, your power has acted to prevent your death. Moreover, it has even prevented serious harm to you. I'm not sure that your power will even let you age. I think you may be immortal."

"Ryan, I..." I started to say but stopped to consider what he'd said. "That is consistent with something *Söarin* said to me," I said. "I asked her whether I was a human and she said, 'Not exactly.'"

We stood without speaking for several minutes. The night was quiet; the *Black Marlin* was well-built and aside from an occasional soft creak of the masts and the slap of the waves against the hull there were no sounds.

"I'm hungry and tired," I said finally. "I think I'll try to find a little something to eat and then go to bed."

"You're feeling better, then?" Ryan asked.

"I'm still afraid," I admitted. "I'm not sure that I can't be killed." I reached out and put my hand on my father's shoulder. "But I'll be damned to the outer darkness if I'll just lay down and die."

I turned to head aft when my father asked, "Ryan, do your people not believe in an afterlife?"

"We haven't ruled it out, but we have no way of knowing for sure. No one has ever come back to confirm that there is. We have no belief in nor stories of ghosts."

"What of the tale Lauren told me of Shade's Isle? That sounds as if your people may have been seeing ghosts."

"That story is an anomaly," Ryan answered. "There is nothing else like it in our history. What about you, Dalach? You mentioned the outer darkness earlier. Do you believe in an afterlife?"

"I think I do," my father said, slowly and thoughtfully. "I'm not sure why, though, or what I think it would be like. The thought that I might just cease to exist is unsettling. But even before we found out what Mar really was, I never truly believed the stories taught by the Repentant. The idea that we dwell with Mar after death? Is *Surmasifa* populated with shades of the departed? I don't think so."

"What about you, Lauren?" Ryan asked.

I thought for a moment but came up with no answer. Like my father, it was upsetting to me to think that I would just not exist anymore, but I had no idea what an afterlife would be, and no answers surfaced from what I had learned from the *Cogen*.

"I believe that I'm hungry," I dodged and turned to seek out the galley.

I woke the next morning after a dreamless sleep of exhaustion. My cabin was filled with a wan gray light admitted by the small porthole above my bed. I could hear the waves breaking on a shoreline in the distance and could tell from the gentle rocking of the boat that we were no longer underway.

My muscles protested as I sat up. I'd spent the night curled in a fetal position because the bed wasn't long enough for me to stretch out and my back and neck were stiff and sore. I stood and stretched as well as I could and then headed for the deck.

When I reached the deck, I was facing the bow of the boat. In the east, the sky was just beginning to lighten. The *Marlin* was tugging gently on her anchor chain and before us all I could see was the open sea. The sails were furled, and the masts stood bare and empty like trees in winter.

I turned toward the stern and caught my first sight of Shade's Isle. We were anchored perhaps three hundred yards from the shore. A wide stretch of sandy beach, pocked with dark humps of rock, ran up to the edge of a dense forest. Towering above the forest was a moderately steep, flat-topped mountain. I heard someone coming up from below and I moved aside. It was my father. A moment later, Ryan joined us.

"I've never seen a mountain like that before," my father said softly.

Knowledge from *Ëyn* bubbled up in my mind. "It's called a volcano," I said.

"A volcano?"

"A crack in the earth's crust allows molten rock to flow up from below the surface. As it cools, it forms a mountain like that."

I paused and then looked at the summit, suddenly aware of something else.

"*Ynes* is up there."

"You're sure?" Ryan asked.

"I am."

I heard soft footsteps on the deck behind us and Marwynn joined us.

"We reached here a little after the third bell this morning," he told us. "We've been keeping watch. We heard nothing while it was still dark. Since it's gotten lighter, we've seen a couple of gulls and what looked like an osprey, but there have been no other signs of life."

He looked at me with a skeptical expression on his face.

"You sure you want to go over there?"

"I have to," I replied. "I need to see *Ynes* and he's up there." I pointed to the top of the volcano.

"Then the three of you should go below and have something to eat. We're readying a boat. It will just be the four of us so you're all going to have to row. I'm not going to ask any of my crew to go ashore. We haven't seen anything unchancy, but I won't ask them to take the risk."

The morning meal was porridge. It had been made with milk and the cook had mixed in blueberries and bits of sausage. It didn't take us long to finish and then we went to our cabins to retrieve our packs. I had planned to leave my guitar on the boat, but as I settled my pack on my back, I reconsidered and slipped my guitar on as well. I was the first one back on deck, but Ryan and my father were not far behind. Marwynn eyed the guitar on my back.

"You sure you want to take that?" he asked.

"Something tells me that I might need it," I said.

"Should I bring mine?" Ryan asked.

I shrugged.

"Only if you want," I answered. "I just feel like I might need mine."

Moments later, we were seated in the captain's gig. I shared a bench with Ryan and my father was seated with Marwynn.

"Take your boots off," Marwynn told us. "We're going to have to get out to beach the boat and you're not going to want to hike up that mountain in wet boots."

We did as Marwynn instructed. Sailors on board the *Marlin* then cast off the lines and we each took hold of an oar. Marwynn began calling out a rhythm. I dipped my oar into the water and tried to pull but I hadn't gone deep enough, and I ended up just splashing and nearly fell off the bench. Apparently, I wasn't the only one who had a problem because Marwynn stopped his chant and said, "You all have obviously never rowed before. Turn around and watch me for a moment."

Ryan and I twisted in our seats to look toward Marwynn.

"Lift the oar and lean forward," he instructed. "Bring the oar down into the water–make sure that you're deep enough to dig in–and then pull back. Then lift the oar out of the water and feather it–turn it sideways like this–and repeat. I'll count the rhythm; we all want to work together."

It took another few minutes for us to get into the rhythm, but then we made rapid progress toward the shore. It took us less than ten minutes to reach the beach. I have no doubt that Marwynn's sailors could have done it in much less time. As we drew near to the shore, Marwynn shouted, "Ship the oars."

As soon as all the oars were aboard, Marwynn slipped overside carrying a line that was tied to the bow. He pulled us the last bit to the beach and then the rest of us stepped out and helped carry the boat up above the high tide mark. Then we leaned against the gunwales and looked around.

For all the island's fearsome reputation, there was nothing particularly frightening or threatening about what we could see. The beach was covered in a dark yellowish-gray sand that had flecks of some darker stuff mixed in. The rocks dotting the beach were formed of dark gray–almost black–basalt and were mostly likely the source of the dark specks in the sand. A ragged line of dried out brown seaweed marked the high tide line. Other than us, there were no living things in sight.

The beach was edged by a forest that appeared to be an impenetrable wall of dense vegetation. The major trees appeared to be oak, but I thought that I could see some birch trees mixed in. Below them, black gum and holly trees shared space with maples and packed around their bases were thick stands of rhododendron and laurel.

"If we're going up there," my father said, gazing up at the peak of the volcano, "we should get started. It's going to take us the better part of the day to get there."

No one answered, but we all stood and retrieved our footwear from the boat and pulled it on. While we were pulling on our boots, a flock of gulls appeared from the south, wheeling in an intricate dance around one another as they scanned the beach and the shallows for food. Their appearance relaxed a tension that I hadn't even been aware I was feeling; the lack of obvious signs of life had been weighing on my mind. As the gulls disappeared to the north, we shouldered our packs, I grabbed my guitar, and we headed up the beach toward the tree line.

The underbrush was so thickly intertwined that we couldn't find an opening into the forest, and we couldn't force our way through. After several minutes of searching unsuccessfully for a path through, my father and I drew our swords and began cutting our way into the forest. It took us a quarter of an hour to progress about thirty feet, but then the underbrush was shaded out by the dense canopy overhead and we were able to sheathe our swords and walk unimpeded. The sounds of the surf quickly faded behind us. The forest was not unlike forests on the mainland; birds called in the distance and squirrels scampered up tree trucks and leapt from branch to branch overhead. We also saw an occasional paw print or pile of scat, evidence of other, larger animals. Despite the appearance of normality, though, something felt off. My companions said nothing, but their wary glances into the forest told me that they felt it, too.

We'd been walking for about half an hour when I heard Ryan gasp. He and my father were walking in front of me, and they stopped suddenly. I had just begun a step forward when they froze. In the middle of my step, the world changed. The air was bitter cold, the trees were bare, and the snow was covered in a thick blanket of snow. As I completed my step, the world returned to normal. Behind me, Marwynn muttered something that sounded like a curse.

"Did you see that?" my father asked.

"A glimpse of winter?" I asked in reply.

"Yes."

"I did. Do any of you have any idea what that was?"

"No," they said simultaneously.

"I wonder," Ryan said. "Was that some kind of Forbidding?"

"I didn't feel a compulsion to turn back," my father replied.

"Neither did I," Marwynn said.

"There was no feeling of power associated with whatever that was," I told them.

Ryan turned to me.

"Lauren, what should we do?"

"I don't know whether that was dangerous, and I don't know whether it will happen again, but I have to speak with *Ynes*," I answered. "I have to go on."

I looked around at them.

"I have to go on," I repeated, "but none of you do. I won't risk you. You should head back to the beach."

"Son, you're not going up there without us," my father answered. "We should go."

"Aye, we should," Marwynn agreed.

Ryan said nothing, but stood aside to let me pass.

Twice more that morning, the world changed around us. We were still on relatively flat ground with the forest all around us the first time. For an instant, it was fall. A patchy fog drifted through the trees, which were cloaked in shades of gold and scarlet and orange. I thought I saw a hunting party in the distance, but before I could be sure, the world returned to normal.

The second time occurred shortly after we began our climb up the volcano. The forest had thinned out and the trees were somewhat smaller.

Wide swaths of the ground were covered in a blanket of ferns. In other spots, the dark volcanic rock–pocked with pale green lichen–poked through the leaf-covered soil. Then, for one terrifying instant the ground all around us was bare and a waist-high wall of molten lava was flowing down toward us.

Almost immediately the world changed back.

"Mar's sweet tits," Marwynn swore.

We were all shaken and we each gratefully accepted a swig of wine from a skin that the king passed around.

"I think I know what's going on," I said after we'd had a moment to collect ourselves.

"And what would that be?" Ryan asked.

"I think what we've been seeing are glimpses of the past," I said. "That has to be it; the volcano hasn't been active for hundreds of thousands of rounds of the seasons."

"The world is that old?" Marwynn asked incredulously.

"Older," I told him.

There was a pause as they all considered that.

"Are those glimpses something that *Ynes* is doing?" Ryan asked.

"I don't think so," I answered. "Like the other *Cogen*, he's quiescent. I think they're remnants of things that he did, the same way that we experienced fading remains of the others' Forbiddings."

Several hours later, in the early afternoon, we encountered the first barely perceptible remains of *Ynes*' Forbidding. The trail continued upward toward the summit. The trees were mostly evergreens and they were short and twisted by unforgiving wind and harsh conditions near the top of the volcano. The final hundred yards to the top were nearly vertical and we had to use our hands as well as our feet to pick our way carefully up the steep incline. Then we reached the crest and crossed over the rim into the crater.

Inside the crater, the ground sloped fairly steeply down to a huge azure lake. The trees were all conifers. Near the rim, they were stunted like the ones outside, but down inside the crater, protected by the wind, the pine and spruce trees grew straight and true. The deep blue water in the lake was still. The air was crisp and clear, with just a faint hint of pine.

"I've never seen anything like this before," Ryan said.

"Neither have I," my father replied. "It is beautiful."

"I still prefer the open sea," Marwynn told us. "But I could get used to this."

"Where to, Lauren?" my father asked.

Perhaps a third of the way down toward the water, the ground below us dropped off suddenly, but it was clear that there was a patch of reasonably level ground below the drop off.

"There," I said, pointing.

We detoured to our left to find an easier way down and then worked our way back to our original path. There we found a broad clearing in front of a cave mouth.

"*Ynes* must be inside," Ryan said quietly.

"I think so," I agreed, just as quietly. "I don't want to go in there. The others urged me to be cautious around *Ynes*."

"Why?" my father asked, his right hand straying toward the hilt of his sword.

"I don't know. But I'd rather be out here when I meet him."

I slipped my guitar off my shoulder and retrieved my flute from its pocket. My power stirred as I lifted the flute to my lips. As the first notes of the *Arimë Daelyr* sounded, the world around us fell silent. I felt a connection form and then a few moments later, there was a deep rumbling within the cave and *Ynes* emerged.

He was larger than any of the others—at least ten feet longer—and at least three hands taller at his shoulders. At first, he appeared to be white, but as he walked slowly toward me, flares of color rippled along his length. His scales were iridescent, reflecting all the colors of the rainbow as he moved. The upright scales down his back were silver, as were the talons at the end of his feet. Even more striking were his eyes. They were completely black, as if they were windows that opened on the vastness of eternity. All the *Cogen* had two forms, one of them human. *Ynes* had a human form; I had seen it at least once. Unlike the others, however, who seemed equally at ease as dragon or human, this was who he was. He was the dragon.

"*Vorath, Endollin. A ne Ùyne.*"

His voice was deep and rumbling and seemed to echo, though there was no overt echo.

"*Vorath, Ùyne,*" I replied. "*A ne* Lauren."

"So," he said, switching to the Alomar tongue. "You are here at last." He paused, his black gaze firmly on me. "You are the first to come in a long count of the seasons."

"The last to come were the *Eldar*?" I asked.

"Indeed."

I couldn't contain my curiosity.

"Do you know where they went?" I asked.

"It is not so much where they went as it is when." He paused a moment. "In my presence, time often behaves in ways that you would find strange. Sometimes, a window will open on another time. Sometimes the window shows the past. Other times it shows a future."

"A future?" I asked.

"The future is not yet written. It is a realm of infinite possibilities."

"And what of the *Eldar* who lived here?"

"Sometimes what opens is not a window to another time, but a door."

"So, they went through that door to the past?"

"That is not possible. The past has been written. It is immutable. They went to a future."

"We will catch up to them, then?"

"If that future is the one that comes to be. It may not." He paused again, staring intently at me. "Little one, is this truly what you were seeking when you came here?"

"No," I answered. "I came to acquire knowledge of your domain. Before we get to that, though, *Ëyn* urged me to be cautious around you. Why?"

He snorted. It might have been a laugh.

"The others find me strange. They–most especially *Ëyn*–are the essence of structure and stability. Their conception of perfection is static, un-changing. I am the very essence of change. Such a notion is antithetical to them."

I touched the knowledge given to me by the other *Cogen*. For once, I was able to easily access what I wanted. What *Ùyne* said was consistent with what I had learned from them.

"I understand," I replied. "Will you share knowledge of your domain with me?"

He cocked his head and focused one pitch black eye on me.

"Little one, you were born a mortal. You have already experienced growth and change. You have seen aging. You have witnessed death. You understand that each note in the Great Song sounds for only a limited time. You already know my domain more intimately than any of the *Cogen* save me."

His answer surprised me. I glanced at my companions.

"Little one, is there nothing else you would have from me?"

I thought for a moment before responding.

"*Ùyne*, I tore the world in two. I locked *Melcurie-ar* away so that she could do no harm, and I sealed the world against the Creator. But now magic is gone from the world and with it the *Eldar*, and the *aynekahrn*. I can feel the Unmaker and her brother fighting me. The barriers I put up are slipping. I'm not sure that I can hold out against them much longer."

Ùyne nodded. "So, what would you know from me?"

"Is there anything I can do?"

The dragon snorted again. This one sounded even more like a laugh.

"You are the *Endollin*. You can do anything." He put special emphasis on the word "do."

"Then what should I do?"

Ùyne stared at me, his gaze intent. His jet-black eyes made it difficult to read his expression, but it looked as if he were furiously considering what to tell me.

"You are a Maker of songs?" he asked finally.

"I play and sing, yes."

"No. That is not what I asked. You are a Maker of songs?"

"I have written some songs."

"And do you still sing those songs exactly the way you made them?"

"No. Some I changed when I found something that wasn't quite..."

The import of what he was suggesting hit me and I stopped, my eyes wide in surprise.

"You're saying that I should rewrite the world? To take out the parts that are wrong? Can I do that?"

"You are the *Endollin*," the dragon repeated. "You can do anything."

"But how should it be?"

"That is not mine to decide. For good or for ill, the power for change was granted to you."

"But my power came from the Creator. He intended that I destroy the world. I don't want to do that."

"Then don't."

I didn't know how to respond to that. Before I could figure that out, *Ùyne* spoke again.

"Know this, *Endollin*. You are being watched. What you do here could reverberate across the Void and affect countless other worlds."

The dragon rose and turned toward the cave mouth. He paused and looked back at me over his shoulder.

"Little one, this conversation begins to bore me," he said. "Go now and do what you must."

"Where do you go to remake the world?" my father muttered.

"Go?" I called after *Ùyne*. "Go where?"

"Very well," he responded though he continued to walk away. "Remake the world on my doorstep if you must. At least have the courtesy to sweep up when you finish."

I turned to my companions. They looked as surprised as I felt.

"Were they all like that?" my father asked.

"No," I replied. "I can see why the others find him strange."

Marwynn was gazing across the lake toward the west. The sun was almost touching the western rim.

"It looks as if it gets dark early up here," he said. "I don't think that there's a better place than this to camp, at least not one that we could reach before the light is gone. I don't relish the idea of trying to scramble down the side of this mountain in the dark." He glanced toward the cave mouth. "Will he mind if we stay here? He won't eat us, will he?"

I searched my borrowed memories briefly. "I don't think they eat," I answered.

"That's not as comforting as it could have been," Marwynn said dryly. "You know that, right?"

I just grinned at him, "I'll go down to the lake and get some water."

The next several hours passed quickly. My father started a small fire, and we had hot tea and toasted bread with our meal of cheese and fruit. After the meal the others talked about inconsequential things. Marwynn told us about the building of the *Black Marlin* and the first race in which he'd sailed her. Ryan shared a description of the ships that the *Eldar* had sailed from their long-lost homeland. Later, my father told us about how he'd met Aedion during the siege of Han. I listened, but didn't join in. Long after dark, we banked the fire and laid down on our blankets.

I stared up at the night sky and watched the familiar constellations as they moved slowly along their nightly paths. My mind would not quiet, and I couldn't relax. I'd now awakened the five major *Cogen* and gained their knowledge of how the Creator had intended the world to be. I wasn't, however, any closer to a decision about what to do than I had been when I began my journey. I knew how the Creator intended the world to be, and I knew that the *Cogen* wanted me to remake the world consistent with that vision. That world, though, had no magic. I didn't want that world. After a time, I gave up trying to sleep and–as quietly as I could–I picked up my guitar and headed down toward the lake.

There was only the thinnest crescent of a new moon in the sky, so I picked my way carefully down the slope. When I reached the lake shore, I stopped and spent several minutes just staring at the view. With no appreciable light, the lake appeared to be a gaping black hole in the world. A shiver of fear ran down my spine; it reminded me of the visions of the

Void I'd had in my dreams. A whip-poor-will called from a nearby tree and the utter normalcy of its song pulled me back from the Void.

I found a fallen tree, sat down, and slipped my guitar out of its case. My hands found their places and soft, meditative chords drifted into the darkness. Tears welled up in my eyes and my heart ached. I wanted the world the way I had known it. I wanted the *Eldar* and the *aynekahrn* back. To get them back, I had to allow *Melcurie-ar* to return. But if I did that, she would eventually subjugate all the people of the world. Whether or not I allowed her to return, the Creator would eventually destroy the world to get at her. I wanted to spend the rest of my life with Peg. I wanted to spend the rest of my life with Élan.

To get magic back, I would have to allow *Melcurie-ar* to return. She would attempt to exact retribution for having been banished. She would also resume her attempts to rule the world. I could oppose her, but she was one of the *Arimë* and immortal while I was mortal. Eventually, I would die, and she would take over the world. Ryan thought that I might be immortal, as well, that my power would not let me die, but even if that was true, did I want to spend eternity locked in a struggle with *Melcurie-ar*? Then it occurred to me that she would strike first at the people I loved. Peg would never be safe. Élan would never be safe. The thought of that dark, bleak future tore a quiet sob out of me.

Ùyne had suggested that I rewrite the world. *Melcurie-ar's* presence had altered the world and everything in it. To get the world I wanted, I would have to replace that influence. I searched the knowledge of the *Cogen*, but nothing there suggested how to create anything like the power of the *Arimë*. For a moment, I set that aside and considered how I would alter the structure of the world. Even the simplest object—a pebble—was made of smaller particles that were each made of even smaller particles, and I would have to reach into each one and replace *Melcurie-ar's* influence with the new one. The sheer scope of it exceeded me; I could not hold it all in my mind. I had the power of the *Arimë* but the mind of a human. And even if I could work out how to change the world, the Creator was there in the Void, waiting for a moment of vulnerability to tear the world asunder to strike at his sister.

Off to my left, I caught a hint of motion out of the corner of my eye. I turned my head in that direction. I thought I saw a tall figure dressed in white standing among the trees. I blinked the tears out of my eyes, and it was gone, but I was certain that *Ùyne* had been watching me.

I turned my attention back to my guitar. The sixth string–the octave of the G–had gone a bit flat. I reached for the peg to tune it and paused in mid-motion as an answer rose in my mind. I adjusted the tuning on my guitar and then slipped it back into its case. Then I returned to our camp, wrapped myself in my blanket, and dropped into a deep, dreamless sleep.

I awoke early the next morning. There was just enough light to see by. I sat up and retrieved my flute from its pocket on my guitar case. Then I stood and looked around our camp. My gaze rested for a moment on my father and then on Ryan. Marwynn was up and stirring up the fire. He looked up as I approached. I squatted down beside him.

"Tea?" he asked quietly.

"My thanks to you, but no," I replied, just as quietly. "But I do need you to do something for me."

"Name it. If it is in my power, it will be done."

"I know now what I must do, but I must do it alone." I gestured toward my father and Ryan. "I need you to get them safely back to the mainland."

He nodded.

"I will."

"Give them my thanks," I said as I stood. "Tell them that I appreciate everything that they did for me."

"I will do that, as well." He stood and put his hand on my shoulder. "Lauren, will you be coming back?"

"I hope so," I said. Then I turned, reinforced the barriers, and stepped across the miles to Land's End.

Land's End was a low-lying peninsula on the south side of the long, narrow estuary formed where the Mordel River flowed into the sea. It was little more than a massive sandbar that was barely above sea level and *Ëyn's* memories told me that it was often submerged during the worst storms. I arrived at the very end of the peninsula with the sea on three sides of me. The tan-colored sand was flecked with small shells, broken bits of shells, and the bones of small fish stranded by the receding tide. Scraggly patches of beach grass poked up from the middle of the peninsula, above the typical tide levels. A crab scuttled sideways away from me, startled by my sudden appearance.

A stiff breeze was blowing from the south driving scraps of gray clouds ahead of it. A few scattered drops of rain hit my face. The dawn wasn't far off, and the sea was iron gray in the early morning light. The nearest people were hundreds of miles away. I had never been so alone.

I pulled out my flute but then paused and reconsidered what I was about to do. Tuning my guitar the night before had reminded me that even the finest instrument had to be adjusted from time to time. The tension of the strings strained against the bracing in the neck. Tension and rigidity. The *Cogen* had taught me that the world faced the same conflict: the rigidity of *Ëyn* strained against the change of *Ùyne*. *Melcurie-ar* was unbridled change, she was chaos. What the *Cogen* had asked me for, though–to exile her from the world–that was not the answer.

What I had realized was that I was the *Endollin*. The Lawbreaker. The Lawgiver. But I didn't have to choose to be one or the other. I could be both.

I needed *Melcurie-ar* in the world. Her power gave the world magic. I needed a counter, though, a check on her whims.

It couldn't be me. I was human. I had the power of the *Arimë,* but I was not one of the *Arimë*. I might be able to stand against her for a time, but eventually I would slip, and she would prevail. I needed someone who could match her move for move for eternity.

She was the Unmaker. I needed a Maker. I needed the Creator.

I needed to integrate the Creator into the world in the same way that *Melcurie-ar* had been integrated into the world, but I wasn't sure how to accomplish that. I had the knowledge that I had received from the *Cogen*, but the sheer volume of that information overwhelmed my human mind. There was no one in the world who could help me. I lifted my flute to my lips and poured all my sorrow and desire into the *Arimë Daelyr*. Around me, everything went still and quiet. The wind died away. Even the sea seemed to pause its relentless caress of the shore. From the heart of that stillness, I flung a thought–a single word–into the Void. *Celeadh*. Help.

A moment later, I felt a presence in my mind. There were no words, just a sense of curiosity and surprise.

In response, I allowed my desire to save the world to rise to the top of my mind.

The alien consciousness responded. There were no words in its communication, yet I understood.

You endeavor to preserve this Making?

"I do," I thought in return.

We respect that desire.

I allowed my half-formed thoughts about the Creator to surface. I sensed surprise from the *Arimë* again. Several heartbeats passed.

It can be done.

Several more heartbeats passed.

Our Law has been violated. He sought to Unmake your world. Only your actions and ours prevented that end. This fate suits. Here is how it may be done.

It was barely perceptible, but I felt knowledge begin to flow into my mind.

You must act quickly. Your mind cannot long retain this volume of knowledge.

In that instant, my flute song–the *Arimë Daelyr*–was transformed from grief to joy. Lyrics in the Language of Making flooded my mind and I lowered my flute and began to sing the *Arimë Drymwir*, the great Song of Creation. The world trembled as I began to sing, and the forces of Creation were unleashed. I took command of those forces and reinforced the structure of the world.

I dropped the barriers that had held back *Melcurie-ar* and the Creator. Magic surged back into the world. I felt the *Eldar* return to *Evendim. Melcurie-ar* appeared before me. Above me, the sky shrieked, and a brilliant argent crack opened as the Creator attempted to enter the world. They both flung multiple massive white-hot bolts of raw power at me. The song protected me, however, and their attacks were deflected and struck the nearby ground. Patches of sand all around me were fused into glowing orange pools of molten glass.

My power, guided by the Song, snared *Melcurie-ar* and froze her where she was. In the sky, a form was thrust through that crack from the Void beyond. With a thought, I grabbed the physical form of the Creator and wrapped the forces of Creation tightly around him. Within that bubble, he cried out in agony as those forces–as they had done to his sister at the beginning of time–shredded his physical form, freeing his power from his will.

I allowed that power to leak out from the protective bubble around his remains and began to bind it into the world. Without the aid of the *Arimë*, I would never have been able to even begin the task; I could never have conceived of the number of bindings to be made. A tiny bright wisp of the Creator's power was linked into every one of the countless tiny particles of the world, following the dark gossamer threads of *Melcurie-ar's* power. Stronger threads formed and reached out for the *Eldar* and the *aynekahrn* and in the sea, the dolphins.

When the last binding had been made–it might have taken hours or days or even years–I turned my attention back to the Creator. I accelerated time within the bubble so that thousands of rounds of the seasons passed in just moments, and I watched as the Creator's will exerted its influence and began pulling his form together. I paused the progression just as he regained a shadowy ghost of a form. Then I focused on *Melcurie-ar*. She struggled as I lifted her from the ground and stripped away the shell of her physical form. For an instant, I caught sight of the brown-haired woman I had seen at Point Lookout, but the power of the Song brooked no delay, and that form vanished, leaving a dark shadow that echoed that of the Creator. She ceased struggling as I moved her toward the bubble and her brother. The instant that I forced her into the bubble, the two of them leapt at one another and the world trembled again as they struggled against one another. Within moments, however, they were locked in an eternal stalemate and the world quieted. As the Song reached its crescendo, I bound them into the core of the world.

The full knowledge of the True Speech that I had been gifted was fading rapidly. I acted before it was completely gone. I maybe shouldn't have, but the world would not be the world I loved without Peg. With a final phrase of my own, I made sure that it never would be without her. Then I allowed the Song to die away.

As the last notes of the *Arimë Drymwir* faded in my mind, I came back to myself. The breach from the Void had been closed by the *Arimë*. I was no longer alone. All the *Cogen* were there. The five greatest–*Ëyn*, *Wian*, *Söarin*, *Tëlyn*, and *Ùyne*–stood before me in their human forms, but I felt the presence of all the others crowded around us. *Ëyn* stepped forward. Her expression was grave.

"*Endollin*, your actions were unexpected."

Then she smiled.

"The world is healed. All our thanks and gratitude are yours."

I tried to respond, but exhaustion overwhelmed me, my knees gave way, and I crumbled to the sand.

I woke on a bed of soft moss in the clearing where *Ëyn* made her home. I wasn't sure what time it was. I glanced around the clearing and noted that the sun was still low in the eastern sky. I must have slept the rest of the previous day and the entire night. The *Cogen* were there, still in their human forms, seated on rocks scattered around the clearing and watching me. When I sat up, they stood and came to stand before me. *Ùyne* offered me a hand up.

"Little one," he said, "you found your own way."

"You surprised us," *Ëyn* said. "We asked for absolutes, and you gave us balance. You have taught us a new definition of perfection."

Wian nodded and added, "You have also returned to us our freedom. We are no longer bound. We can move freely about the world again."

For just a moment, no one spoke. Then *Tëlyn* said, "We have visited the *Enwilion Arastalon*. They suggested that you might be hungry when you woke, so we obtained food while we were there. Would you like some?"

"Yes, my thanks to you," I replied. I was glad to hear that the *Cogen* had already renewed their ties to the *Eldar*. Then I remembered what I had done to Élan and her people. "They must hate me."

"They do not," *Ùyne* said. "They desire that you visit them as soon as possible. The princess especially yearns to see you."

Tëlyn handed me a plate heaped with slices of apple, cheese, and ham.

They watched in silence as I ate. When I had finished, *Ëyn* asked, "*Endollin*, what will you do now?"

My thoughts turned immediately to Peg and Élan.

"I need to..." I started but faltered, unsure whether either of them would want to speak to me. "There are some people I need to talk to."

I fell silent and closed my eyes, fighting back tears. It had been more than twenty rounds of the seasons, but time hadn't eased the pain or the weariness. I reached out to take a sip of wine, but my goblet was empty. Our pitcher, it turned out, was empty as well. The girl who had been serving us was nowhere in sight.

"I decided to rebuild the cabin just north of Songhaven," I said. My throat was dry, making my voice rough and raspy. "It was in an out of the way place and after everything I'd been through, I desperately wanted peace."

My companion gave me a confused frown.

"Surely with Melcurie-ar *gone..." she started, but I cut her off.*

"It's true that many people in the Federation understood what had happened and were grateful. A great many others, though, were not. Rumors that I had murdered Aerman Sorren persisted, and some people insisted that I was the one who had started the war. Both of those ideas were common amongst the Restorationists, and they preached them anywhere they could find someone who would listen. Eventually, the more radical among them joined up with groups inside the Kelmar Empire looking for a way to bring back Mar. I had sent Mar away and they came to believe that killing me would allow her to return. They and their followers sent groups of would-be assassins in search of me, and I had to put a Forbidding around the cabin to protect the people I love."

She had been shaking her head slightly in disbelief as I spoke, but that last phrase elicited a hint of a smile.

"I'll make sure that the real story gets told," she said. "I'll see to it that it's recorded in the library at Songhaven and that copies go to libraries across the Federated Kingdoms. The minstrels will begin telling the tale in its true form. That should help."

She drained the last dregs from her goblet.

"What have you been doing since then?" she asked.

Thinking about what I had been doing made me aware of the profound sense of exhaustion and sorrow that was my constant companion. The weight of all we had lost, all the people whose notes in the Song of the Seasons had been stilled, all of that was lodged deep in the marrow of my bones. I ran my finger around the rim of my empty goblet as I considered how much to tell her.

"I still cannot consistently access all that I learned from the Cogen," I told her, trying to evade answering. "When something does come to mind, I write it down so that it can be shared."

"*I know that,*" *she replied.* "*I've read most of the books you've sent to Songhaven.*"

She looked intently at me.

"*There's more, isn't there?*"

I looked back at her with the same intensity. It was clear that she wasn't going to be put off.

"*I watch,*" *was all I said.*

Something in my tone dimmed the enthusiasm that had been lighting her face.

"*Watch what?*" *she asked hesitantly.*

"*I bound two of the Arimë into the structure of the world,*" *I explained quietly.* "*They are at odds with one another, and the balance of their energies balances the world. If they were to put their animosity toward one another aside...*"

Her eyes grew wide, and I could see the beginning of fear there.

"*I watch,*" *I repeated.*

"*But what will happen when you're gone?*"

"*It turns out that Ryan was right,*" *I answered, and she wrinkled her face in a puzzled frown.* "*I sensed it at Land's End. My power will not let me die. If* Melcurie-ar *and the Creator ever do attack the world, I'll be here.*"

I could hear the weariness in my voice. She could, too. I could see a faint echo of my pain in her face and for a moment it seemed as if she was going to ask me something more. Instead, she pushed back from the table and stood.

"*I'll be right back,*" *she said.*

A few moments later, she returned carrying our guitars and packs. I wasn't sure how she'd gotten into my room to get mine, but it didn't seem the time to ask.

"*What about Peg and Élan?*" *she asked quietly.* "*You didn't say.*"

I didn't reply for a long moment; I couldn't find enough breath to speak, and tears stung my eyes.

"I think you know the answer to that," I said finally, my voice strained.

"I guess I do," she said as she handed me my guitar. She reached out and took my hand. "Let's go home now, Father."

Cast of Characters

Adaryn (ah-DARE-uhn) – a sailor from Landfall.

Aedion (EYE-dee-on) – a warrior in Han.

Alyn (al-UHN) – a stable hand for King Marc. Brother of Joff.

Bredwyr (BREAD-wuhr) – Torlen's son.

Crom (crahm) – a wizard. Formerly Master of the House in Amersford (deceased).

Dalach (day-LOCH)– Son of Egan and Lauren's father.

Duna (do-NA) – a wizard.

Egan (EE-gan) – Dalach's father and Lauren's grandfather.

Goriwyn (GORE-ih-wuhn) – a page in Landfall.

Jaret (rhymes with "parrot") – Duke of Kerith and Chamberlain of Amersford.

Jelor (jeh-LORE) – a member of the High King's Guard.

Joff (jahf) – a stable hand for King Marc. Brother of Alyn.

Kaitrin (kay-TRIN) – an innkeeper in Amersford. Owner of the Minstrel's Haven.

Keilin (kie-LIN) – a warrior from Amersford.

Kendra (KEN-dra) – a spy for Landfall's king.

Kivyn (KIH-vuhn) – Kaitrin's nephew.

Maizy (MAY-zee) – one of the staff at the Aeran Fort.

Malvynn (MAL-vuhn) – a warrior in Han.

Olen (oh-LEN) – a wizard. Master of the House in Amersford.

Oscon (AHS-cahn) – the General in charge of Amersford's army.

Phelan (rhymes with "felon") – a long-ago smith who made the gates of the Twin Cities or a "magician" in Amersford.

Rolf (rahlf) – a messenger in the service of the high king.

Sloanne (SLOW-ann) – a strategist. Author of a series of books on strategy and warfare.

Torlen (TOR-len) – the Steward of Landfall.

Trahern (TRA-hurn) – a high-ranking member of the high king's army.

Trefor (TREH-for) – Fleet Captain of Landfall's fleet.

Trost (trahst) – an Alomar scout.

Minstrels

Ambrose (AM-broz) – a Minstrel of Alomar. Master of the College of Minstrels and a prophet.

Pegara (pe-GAHR-a) – one of Lauren's fellow students. Daughter of Houl of Han. Usually called Peg.

Rachel – one of Lauren's fellow students at Songhaven.

The Kings of the Alomar

Alwyn (al-WUHN) – past high king (deceased).

Anders Sorren (an-DERS SOAR-in) – High King of the Federated King-doms of Alomar.

Aran Sorren (AIR-an SOAR-in) – past high king (deceased).

Artos Sorren (AR-tos SOAR-in) – past high king (deceased).

Houl (rhymes with "cool") – petty king of Han.

Farnir (far-NIHR) – past petty king of Meren.

Jorlith (jor-LITH) – a past petty king of Landfall.

Larsen (LAR-sen) – petty king of Meren.

Marc–petty king of Amersford.

Marwynn (mar-WUHN) – petty king of Landfall

Moireach (MOY-rick) – petty queen of Marsden Forge.

Reigin (RYE-gihn) – past petty king of Marsden Forge (deceased).

Roth – petty king of Canim. Also the name of a past high king (deceased).

Steafán (stef-ON) – petty king of Han after Houl's death. Peg's older brother.

Eldar

Alain (AL-ane) – King of the Eldar. Son of Lorrestian

Élan (AY-lahn) – daughter of Alain and Réalta.

Iseabail (IHZ-eh-bale) – one of the *Cadwynir*

Jorith (jor-LITH) – one of the *Cadwynir*

Konne – a general.

Lorrestian (LORE-es-tee-an) – a king of the Eldar and a prophet (de-ceased).

Pyrett (PUH-ret) – First Captain of the *Cadwynir*

Rolugh (ROW-loo) – a general.

Ryan / Rhion (RIGH-uhn / RIH-on) – an Eldarin minstrel. Lauren's
Master at Songhaven.

Kelmar

Arkath (ahr-KATH) – a Kelmar soldier.

Bragin (BRAG-in) – a Hand of Mar.

Malash (MAH-lish) – a Kelmar scout.

Valir (VAH-leer) – a Hand of Mar.

The Keepers

???? – The Destroyer. The patron of warriors. Wears a black robe trimmed
in red. The most powerful of the Keepers.

Cimone (sih-MOAN) – The patron of builders and crafters. He wears a
gray robe.

Garth (GAHR-th) – The patron of the minstrels and protector of travelers. He wears a blue robe. Garth is second only to the Destroyer in Mar's
favor.

Gorfin (GORE-fihn) – The patron of the smiths. He wears a burnt orange
robe.

Mancier (MAN-see-er) – The patron of the wizards. He wears a white robe.

Nordel (NOR-del) – The patron of the priests. He is a strong telepath and is often called the Dream Giver. He wears a gold robe.

Thorne – The patron of the Healers. He wears a dull green robe.

The Old Ones

Aenn / Ëyn (eyenn / EE-yuhn)–one of the major Old Ones. The embodiment of earth.

Saer / Söarin (sire / sue-AIR-in) – one of the major Old Ones. The embodiment of fire.

Tael / Tëlyn (tile / tay-LUHN) – one of the major Old Ones. The embodiment of water.

Tyth (tuhth)–One of the minor Old Ones. Associated with journeys. Watches over travelers.

Wyn / Wian (wuhn / WEE-an) – one of the major Old Ones. The embodiment of air.

Ynes / *Ùyne* (uh-NESS / oo-UHN-eh) – one of the major Old Ones. The embodiment of time.

A Note on Languages

The Andol tongue spoken by the Alomar was originally shared amongst all the people of what is now the Kelmar Empire. Its current form came about when the Alomar crossed into the lands west of the Breton Mountains. There they encountered the Eldar and the Altierans and an entirely new environment: the ocean. All three shaped the language spoken by the exiled Alomar.

Though Andol was once a single tongue, thousands of rounds of antagonism and isolation resulted in shifts in pronunciation and idiom in both the Alomar Kingdoms and the Kelmar Empire. Further, the Alomar freely borrowed words from the Eldar and the Altierans and invented some of their own to describe their new world. Thus, though the Alomar and Kelmar could understand one another, the speech of one sounded odd to the other.

Throughout the books, Andol is rendered as English. Words from other tongues are printed in italics, including a small number of words from the unknown old Andol tongue.

Old Andol

The origin of some words in the Andol tongue have been lost to time. Amongst those are the names of the seasons. Minstrels, noting the similarities in the initial syllables, suggest that the names may once have been phrases rather than single words, phrases that–perhaps–began with "season of..." of "time of..." What the original language may have been, however, is unclear as those initial syllables are not cognates of words in any known language.

Tymnagena–spring.

Tymnacynn–summer.

Tymnahaef–fall.

Tymnahunoch–winter.

The Eldarin Tongue

The Eldar revered the stars and words and imagery concerning stars permeated Eldarin culture. In the Eldarin language, this is seen in the fact that in compound words, star (el) was always the first word in the compound. Thus, Elsgard is literally StarCity, but is more properly translated as City of Stars.

Like English, the Eldarin tongue signals the function of a word in a sentence by its location in the sentence and like English, the preferred order is Subject-Verb-Object (SVO).

Some notes on pronunciation:

a is pronounced as in "at" (IPA /æ/), except when preceding an "r" or an "l" sound, then it is pronounced as in "father" (IPA /a:/)

ae is pronounced as a long "i" sound as in "my". So *Aenn* is pronounced like the English "eye" with the extended n sound on the end.

c is always pronounced as a hard "k" sound as in "cat." The one exception is the word "ciel"–a word borrowed from the True Speech–in which the "c" has a soft "s" sound.

ch is pronounced as a combination of the hard "k" and softer "tch" sounds, somewhere between the ch sounds in "character" and "church."

dd is pronounced "th" as in "though."

e is the short /e/ sound as in "head."

The acute accent (é) is used over the letter e to indicate that the vowel should be pronounced as ay as in "hay."

ea is pronounced as a long e as in "see"

i is pronounced as in "kit" or "hit."

ie is pronounced as a long e, as in "brief".

A doubled nn at the end of a word is slightly longer and receives just a little more emphasis than a single n. The difference is similar to the difference in the English but and butt.

o is pronounced as in "horse" (IPA /ɔː/)

u is pronounced as in "blue" (IPA /uː/)

ü is pronounced like the long umlauted u in German, roughly like the "ew" sound you make when you smell something bad.

y is the unstressed schwa sound (roughly uh).

Eldarin Dictionary

aduné (ah-doo-NAY)–sir

Aeldar Singu (aisle-DAR sin-goo)–Old Ones

aenn (eyenn)–earth

Aenn (eyenn)–one of the major Old Ones; a major river named for the Old One

Aennsrhyd (eyenns-RUHD)–crossing of the river Aenn

alhynn (AL-huhnn)–river

an (rhymes with the English "can")–of

arrint (sounds very similar to the English word aren't with the stress on the
    first syllable)– assist

Arth (areth; sounds like the English "are" with a th on the end) - world

astolé (as-toe-LAY)–greetings

awl (sounds like the English owl)–full

calyth (cah-LUTH)–haven

cali (cah-LIH)–have

ciel (see-EL)–roof (borrowed from the True Speech)

condi (con-DIH)–would

Creagalt (cree-GALT)–round top

dar (rhymes with the English "car")–people

dolgin - shared

dor (rhymes with the English "for")–the

ech (similar to the English "etch")–shade's

el–star

elmaen (el-MINE)–master, as in an expert in some field

Eldar–(from el–star and dar–people)–People of the Stars.

elested (el-LES-ted)–brightened

elmar (EL-mar)–king (pl. elmaren)

elmyr (EL-muhr)–queen (pl. elmyren)

elnir (EL-nir)–light

elnar (EL-nar)–prince

elnyr (EL-nuhr)–princess (pl. elnyren)

Elsgard–City of Stars (from el–star and gard city)

en (pronounced the same as the letter "n." IPA /ˈen/)–am, is

er (rhymes with the English "her")–be

erven (er-VENN)–earth

Ervenschal–literally, earth-fall. The Eldar name for Landfall.

Evendim (EH-ven-dim)–twilight

gard (rhymes with the English "hard")–city

gorthin (GORE-thin)–gathering

gwenfed (gwen-FED)–joy

grat/gratyn/gratyl (grat/grat-UHN/grat-UHL)–deep/deeper/deepest

hyda (HUH-dah) - with

il (similar to the English "ill", but the "L" sound is shorter)–are

kahill (KAH-hill)–a capo

kalyn (CALL-uhn)–cute

kareth (CAR-eth)–book

Lellarin (lehl-LAR-in)

manana (MAH-nah-nah)–honored

masyl (MAHS-uhl)–her

mear (meer)–lake

Mordel–(MORE-del)

morosin (MORE-oh-sin)–lost

mun (rhymes with the English "moon")–do

myl (muhl)–this

na (nah)–as

nal (rhymes with the English "wall")–and

navoram (nah-VOOR-um)–presence

nul (nool)–our

numen (NEW-men)–isle

ol (pronounced ole like the English "old" without the d sound)–my

olin (ole-IN)–mine

orismë (or-is-MAY)–journey's end

orron (OR-ron)–how

pürdonnen (pure-DON-nen)–anything

rhyd (ruhd)–crossing

saer (sire)–fire

Saer (sire)–one of the major Old Ones

saft (pronounced like the English "aft" with an s on the beginning)–next

schal (rhymes with the English word "all")–fall

scrifail (SKRI-fail)–ruin

se (seh)–I

sel (rhymes with the English "sell")–you

selé (SELL-ay)–we

seli (SELL-ih)–your

Seldenawé (sell-DEN-a-way)–Valley of Thrushes

sely (SELL-uh)–yours

selyn (SELL-uhn)–thanks

sharit (SHAR-it)–love

shynsen (shun-SEN)–a personal practice hall, dojo

stal (pronounced like the English word "stall", but with a shortened L
  sound)–foal

sym (some)–day

tael (tile)–water

Tael (tile)–one of the major Old Ones

tel (sounds like the English word "tell" but the l sound is shortened)–may

tiom (tih-ohm)–me

tol (sounds like the English word "toll" but the l sound is shortened)–for

tul (tool)–by

tybith (TUH-bith)–restaurant

weal (wheel)–serve

wealtyr (wheel-TUHR)–service

wydd (wuhth)–round, cycle (as in round of the seasons)

yn (uhn)–to

ynes (uh-NES)–time

Ynes (uh-NES)–one of the major Old Ones

yrten (uhr-TEN)–wind

wyn (wuhn)–air

Wyn (wuhn)–one of the major Old Ones

Acknowledgements

Well, here we are. We've reached the end of Lauren's story or, at least, this chapter of Lauren's story. Getting here has been quite a journey for me and it's unclear whether this is the destination or simply a rest stop. In any case, this is a good time to look around and thank the people who helped me get here. At the top of that list is Sandi Sheehan. She had already been dealing with the travails of living with a crazy psychology professor, but then I announced that I was writing a fantasy trilogy. She didn't laugh and she didn't run away. She just gave me tons of love and support and that's meant more than I can express with mere words. My son Benjamin also listened to me ramble on about what must at times have seemed to be a vaporware trilogy and he never once even hinted that he didn't think that I could finish it. Many thanks are due again to Stephanie Slocum-Schaffer, the first person to read a draft of all three books. I really appreciated the conversations, the feedback, and the support. And I especially appreciated that, after reading the original ending for this book, she cared enough for me and for Lauren to tell me that she hated it. The book is far better because she did.

I am also indebted to all the teachers who taught me to express myself via the written word. I have forgotten many of their names, but three stand out: Marion McLean, Daphne Doward Hogstrom, and C. Alan Boneau.

Ms. McLean was the most influential of my high school English teachers. My life and career path would have been very different had I not been in her classes. Daphne was my mentor and guided me through the mail-order writing course at the Institute of Children's Literature, my solitary credential as a creative writer. Alan was my mentor as a psychologist. He taught me to dare to succeed and made me aware of what he called my "idiosyncratic comma usage." I've tried very hard to do the former and to avoid the latter.

The wizards at Damonza have once again turned out an amazing cover. They are an absolute joy to work with and there are not enough superlatives in all the languages of the world to describe them. Finally, as I did in the other books, I want to thank all the people who have worked in the Shenandoah National Park and who have labored over the decades to preserve Virginia's beautiful Blue Ridge Mountains, the place I love best and the inspiration for my Breton Mountains.

About the author

Larry Daily was born in Covington, Kentucky and currently resides with his girlfriend Sandi Sheehan in the eastern panhandle of West Virginia. He holds a Ph.D. in Psychology and teaches psychology classes at Shepherd University. The Chronicles of the Lawbreaker is the result of a decades long love of fantasy inspired by J. R. R. Tolkien, Ursula K. Le Guin, Patricia McKillip, and Mary Stewart. In his spare time Larry builds HO scale model trains, plays folk music on six- and twelve-string guitars, and devours fantasy novels.

Connect online at http://www.larryzdaily.net/